A FLORA FARRINGTON MYSTERY

FLORA'S FRENCH MURDER MYSTERY

Published in the UK in 2025 by The Cotswold Writer Press

Paperback ISBN: 978-1-7394217-6-2
eBook ISBN: 978-1-7394217-7-9

Cover design by Viktoriya Avramova/SpiffingCovers
Typeset by Spiffing Covers

A FLORA FARRINGTON MYSTERY

FLORA'S FRENCH MURDER MYSTERY

ANNA A. ARMSTRONG

For Clara and Elodie

CAST OF CHARACTERS

The Honourable Flora Farrington – war widow and mother of Tony and Debo – in her thirties. She lives in Farrington Hall in the Cotswolds.

Inspector Busby – early thirties (Flora suspects he's a few years younger than her).

Dorothy – Flora's dachshund.

Nanny – Flora's childhood nanny.

Anne – Flora's young and beautiful lady's maid, with violet eyes and a love of literature.

Uncle Cyril or Sir Cyril Forsythe – something high up in the Foreign Office.

The Stans

Before you reach for your atlas and get rather confused, let me explain; think C.S. Lewis rather than geographical fact. I was inspired by the historical reality that if you happened to be a country blessed (or cursed) to have a trade route (a precious mountain pass) you were in political trouble, especially if it was in the Hindu Kush. From the early 1800s, those countries found themselves embroiled with the world's most powerful nations' political agendas. The Khyber Pass has long been politically sensitive and in the 1920s (and beyond) Russia was heavily involved with Kazakhstan. Britain has always been keen to encourage key political persons to receive an education in Britain, be it at school, university, or the military college of Sandhurst. Princess Firuza – eighteen-year-old orphaned heir to a throne in the Stans (Abbastan) and Flora's goddaughter.

Crown Prince Dimash – heir to the neighbouring kingdom of KabuStan. He has grey eyes, is tall and slim with a vivid scar across his face. The scar is the legacy from when he was a baby and a relative tried to kill him. He has a degree from Oxford and has just finished at Sandhurst.

Prince Parviz – younger brother, passionate and energetic. He is about to start studying at Oxford.

The Venerable Uncle – Dimash and Parviz' uncle, advisor, and chaperone. With a portly figure and piggy eyes, he manages to cut an impressive figure by sporting an impressive moustache and wearing magnificent traditional dress.

At the Château

The château itself is loosely based on Chateau de Dampierre. You can follow the château's restoration on YouTube and Instagram. The oubliette I modelled on a couple of different châteaux.

Count Christoff – dashing and suave, he is (as Flora could testify) a rather attractive older widower.

Sister Claire – Count Christoff's austere sister. A fearsomely religious nun who, along with Father Luke, is briefly staying at the château.

Amelie – Count Christoff's younger (in her forties), flamboyant sister. She lives permanently at the château. Exceptionally tall and with flaming red hair, she is an artist with her studio in the garden.

Father Luke – an older man, painfully thin and with poor eyesight, he speaks little and is far from a striking figure.

Roberts – small, compact, and full of vitality. He is an extremely efficient British butler.

Minor Characters

Jean le Coeur – the dead footman.

Susan – Debo's school frenemy.

Miss Crawford – the poor lady who has the misfortune to be the headmistress at Debo's boarding school.

Mr Bert – Flora's elderly gardener.

Mrs Wilkes – housekeeper-cum-cook.

Mavis and Gladys – maids.

If you would like to learn more head over to my webpage for a free mini book.

CHAPTER ONE

A RAMBLING CHÂTEAU JUST OUTSIDE PARIS
SPRING 1924

France in the spring was everything Flora had hoped it would be: pink cherry blossom, chic dresses and pastries.

The dead body on the floor of her room in the château had definitely not featured in her dreams.

'Well, you've got yourself a problem there, my girl, and no mistake,' stated Nanny with just a hint of Irish mist about her brogue. As she spoke, she shook her head sadly, causing a cascade of hairpins to fall from her unruly grey bun, bounce off her ample black bosom, and land on the rug next to her lisle stockings and sturdy shoes.

'When I was a child, I always assumed that by the time I was in my thirties I would be immune to your comments, Nanny, but judging by my rising annoyance this is not the case. May I just say that you are definitely not helping?' muttered Flora while scrutinising the dead young man. He was slim with bony wrists showing beyond his slightly frayed cuffs. A shock of blonde hair added to his youthful appearance; he was perhaps seventeen or eighteen with fuzz on his upper lip where a moustache should have been. His huddled position made it difficult to judge his actual height – perhaps six feet, give or take an inch either way. 'I don't recognise him, do you?'

Nanny bent stiffly forward, clutching her carpetbag with its protruding knitting needles in front of her abundant stomach. 'No! But then he's in a footman's uniform and no one really looks at footmen or maids when away from home. Do you think he was after the diamonds or the princess?'

Flora wrinkled her forehead and sighed. 'Who knows? Perhaps both? I suppose I need to tell Inspector Busby right away. So inconvenient as I believe we are having beef bourguignon for dinner tonight and there is nothing like a stiff to ruin one's digestion.'

Nanny straightened up, causing her bones and old-fashioned corset to creak. 'Tell you what, my girl, you nip along the passageway and tell that nice inspector everything and I'll check the princess is all right.'

As ever, the mention of 'that nice inspector' – otherwise known as Busby – caused Flora to feel a little warm. 'Right oh!' she agreed, trying to avoid Nanny's scrutiny.

Nanny's black eyes twinkled like an inquisitive hedgehog. 'What's with the blush?'

'What blush?' Flora hoped she didn't look as flustered as she felt.

'You resemble a ripe strawberry – just remember you are a respectable widow and a matronly mother of two.'

'Really, Nanny, you get worse with age.' Flora left the room with a swish of her scarlet silk dress and what dignity she could muster while muttering, 'Matronly? Hardly, I'm only thirty-three and a half – the woman needs her eyes testing.'

Flora hurried down the passageway with its high ceiling. It was lit by the sunshine pouring in from the majestic window at the end. Like all of the château, it was cool and softly scented with lilies, a masterpiece of style – if one didn't look too closely at the peeling paint or the cobwebs. Busby was in the other wing of the château; it was far enough away for Flora to realise her new kitten-heel shoes were lamentably uncomfortable.

Outside Busby's door she paused for a second to regain her composure before knocking. She smoothed down her evening dress; it was demurely cut in a colour that rather suited her warm complexion.

It was just as well she had, as the sight of Busby, with his good looks and his rusty hair boyishly dishevelled, was enough to destroy the composure of even the most austere matron. He was considerably taller than Flora but then, as she was only just five foot two, most people were. His mangled tie and perplexed expression suggested he was wrestling with the mysteries of putting on a black tie. *He is normally so capable, it's rather adorable that he can't do such a simple thing.*

Flora swallowed. 'Oh, I say,' she stammered.

He regarded her for a moment, with gratifying admiration in his brown russet eyes, before enquiring, 'Mrs Farrington?'

'Yes?' she answered eagerly.

'Is there some reason you knocked? I can see that you are ready for dinner, but I thought we had at least an hour before the gong will sound.'

Recalled to the reason for her knocking on Busby's door, she said, 'Yes, well about that.' He raised one quizzical eyebrow and Flora continued, 'We have a spot of trouble.'

His brow furrowed and he tilted his head on one side. 'A spot of trouble?'

Flora nodded. 'Yes. To be exact, there is a man in my bedroom.'

Busby's russet brown eyes widened. 'A man?'

Flora felt a hot burning of embarrassment flood her. 'Oh, it's quite alright – he's dead.'

Busby swallowed, a frown on his lightly freckled face. He appeared to be having some difficulty following Flora's reasoning. Slowly he clarified, 'Let me see if I've got this right. You knocked because there is a dead man on your bedroom floor?'

Flora smiled. 'Yes.'

Busby wasn't smiling as he pushed past her and walked briskly all the way to Flora's room. She followed, a little breathlessly, in his wake. By the time they arrived back at her room, Flora was limping and silently vowed to never wear the shoes again, regardless of how much they cost.

Entering her room, they found the bed with its white linen and the ornate Louis XVI furniture topped with arrangements of stately delphiniums, but there was no body.

Busby scanned the magnificent room, with its ornate parquet

flooring, six windows and generous fireplace, before turning to Flora. 'Where?'

'He was there,' declared Flora, pointing to the immaculate Aubusson rug. Agitated, she ran her hand through her short brown curls.

At that moment Nanny wheezed in, knees creaking and dated black crinolines crackling. Seeing Flora and Busby, she announced dramatically, 'She's gone!'

Busby was nonplussed. Calmly he commented, 'If you mean the princess, did you try the tennis courts?'

Nanny did not try to hide her annoyance at having her moment quashed. Sounding more Irish than usual, she said, 'No I didn't go traipsing all over the place, not with my knees!'

Blandly, Busby stated, 'She'll be there – there's no way any real harm can have come to her. This château is as good as a fortress. With Inspector Le Brun's men guarding every entrance, no one can get in or out – that's why we chose it.'

'Do nuns plays tennis?' Flora wondered out loud.

Busby raised a quizzical eyebrow; he seemed to be finding the evening trying in the extreme. 'What have nuns got to do with anything?'

'Oh, nothing really – it's just that the princess has been talking a lot about wanting to be a nun. Of course, it's probably just a phase, I seem to remember thinking I'd look rather good in a veil at her age. Eighteen is such an impressionable time in a girl's life.' Nanny snorted and Flora ignored her, continuing, 'If she did embrace convent living, it would cause a major diplomatic incident. After all, the girl is more or less betrothed.' A sigh from Busby recalled Flora's thoughts from princesses and nuns back to the present and a rather annoyed British policeman. 'But you are quite right, Inspector – back to the matter in hand: the dead body!'

'There is no dead body,' said Busby coldly.

Flora felt a surge of annoyance. 'No, not now, but there was, right there! Wasn't there, Nanny?'

Nanny nodded as she eased herself down to sit on the bed, still a little puffed from her unaccustomed exertion. 'There was!'

Busby looked from Nanny to Flora. 'Are you sure he was dead?'

Defensively Flora snapped, 'Well he certainly looked dead. And really, Inspector, is it likely that some random footman would decide to take an impromptu nap on my rug?'

Busby pressed his lips together. 'About as likely as him turning up dead on your floor.'

Flora drew herself up to her full height and, turning an imperious eye on Busby, coolly stated, 'Inspector, I do not care for your tone.'

Nanny, from the comfort of Flora's bed interrupted, 'Children, don't squabble! Let's keep focused!'

Flora glowered at Nanny which didn't seem to bother Nanny in the least.

Busby took a calming breath and in an overly patient voice enquired, 'Are you sure the man was actually dead?'

Flora threw him a frosty glance. 'I do apologise, I didn't have my stethoscope with me, but he certainly looked pretty jolly lifeless. I suppose it would have been more convenient if he had had a dagger in his chest and had left a large bloodstain on the mat.'

Nanny nodded and concurred, 'We probably should have examined him – we might have been able to see if he'd been strangled by any bruising on his neck or if he'd been poisoned from signs of frothing at the mouth.'

'Or if he was actually dead,' said Busby dryly.

Nanny sat up outraged and Flora found comfort in having an ally. Nanny was just about to let forth a string of Irish expletives when Flora gasped and ran across the room. She yanked at the ornate gold handle of the top drawer of a Louis XVI cabinet. In a flurry of anxiety, she rifled through the contents. As she searched, her movements and muttering became increasingly desperate. Soon silk, lace-trimmed camisoles, cami-knickers and brassieres in cream, oyster and pink, fluttered from her hands to the floor.

Busby watched, his forehead crinkled.

Flora swung around and with her dark brown eyes wide, she

exclaimed, 'It's gone! The diamond necklace – it's not here!'

With exasperation writ large on every feature and a voice full of incredulity, he queried, 'You kept the priceless Abbastani diamonds with your smalls?'

Flora glanced at the pool of silk and lace at her feet. 'It was a sort of double bluff – I thought it was such an obvious place that no one would think of looking there.'

Busby regarded her and her delicates before commenting, 'Looks like you were wrong.'

Flora and Busby exchanged a dangerous look. To Nanny's eyes they made quite a pair: him, tall with a chiselled jaw and fiery russet eyes; her, petite, angry and dressed in red.

Nanny cleared her throat, and they redirected their attention from each other to where she sat enthroned amid the duck-feather pillows. She wore an air of complacency bordering on smugness. 'Tis a blessing for you that you have a wise and loving Nanny. From the moment I heard that your Uncle Cyril from the Foreign Office had entrusted you with the jewels as well as the princess, I knew I would need to take a hand.'

She delved into her carpetbag and took out her knitting needles and a ball of pink wool. Then, with a flourish, she produced a red leather-and-gold box.

'Voilà!' she declared as she opened it.

Yet again, Flora gasped at the sight of the magnificent necklace twinkling in the light.

Nanny smiled. 'Safe as houses.'

'Well, that's a mercy,' remarked Busby. He glanced around the room before adding, 'Where's the mutt? And come to think of it, why isn't Anne here?'

Curtly, Flora informed him, 'I will have you know, that 'mutt' is a pedigree dachshund, and her name is Dorothy. Her forebears are littered with Crufts prize winners. It just so happens that Anne is taking her for an evening stroll.'

Busby nodded but queried, 'I thought a lady's maid's duties were more in the line of sorting dresses than dog walking?'

Flora looked at him coolly and replied, 'Anne is a treasure.'

Nanny made a guttural sound from her pillowy throne and declared, 'That she is, but back to more important affairs. As there is nothing you can do right now about investigating this mystery, I suggest it would be wise not to alert anyone here at the château that we have a problem. As the château is guarded, whoever committed the murder must still be here and we don't know who we can trust. Why don't you just check on our Wimbledon-ready princess and then the pair of you can go down to dinner? Just to give the impression that it's business as usual.'

Busby and Flora did as Nanny suggested, but their evening meal was frosty and far removed from the delightful event Flora had anticipated.

CHAPTER TWO

'Busby really is the limit. The man is so condescending! Really if you'd heard him last night, Dorothy, my dear, you would have been outraged,' Flora explained to her dachshund as she dressed the next morning.

'*I doubt it, how could I ever be outraged by anything that Busby said? Let's face it – the man is gorgeous*,' thought Dorothy. With Flora distracted, Dorothy quietly stole one of her mistress's new shoes. She had been eyeing them up ever since Flora bought them; the Louis heels looked delicious. '*I'll just take this under the bed, where I can give it a good old gnaw,*' concluded the faithful hound.

Flora was so absorbed in admiring her own reflection in the mirror that she remained blissfully oblivious to the damage Dorothy was causing.

When she was finally ready, Flora was extremely gratified by what she saw in the fly-blown gilded mirror. Out loud she said, 'Matronly indeed! Ridiculous – I am positively girlish.' She swirled backwards and forwards in her new frock. It was red, one of Chanel's best, in easy to wear jersey material and cut like a sailor suit. Being petite and slim, she certainly did have a youthful air. No one would guess that she was a widowed mother of two. Thinking of her widowed state, her eyes flicked over to the photo she kept by her bedside of an ever-youthful man in flying togs.

So sad that neither of the children can remember Roger. He would have been a wonderful father. What a ridiculous way to die, flying a plane that was as useless as a paper kite – and what was it for? The war was over a few days later. She sighed. *Tony was only four, so his memories of him are hazy – hard to believe he's a strapping lad of fourteen now. Little Debo was a baby when she lost her father.* Flora gave herself a mental shake. *Still, Debo is fine – a happy-go-lucky ten-year-old.*

She ran her hands through her hair – even the shortest of bobs couldn't tame its unfashionably brown curls. Her complexion was darker than most. Flora felt Nanny terming her swarthy was a little unjust. She had particularly fine legs and often wished that social class did not prevent her from entering the 'lovely ankles' competitions that seemed all the rage. The neat little heels she was wearing did not do them justice and Flora sought her favourite Louis heels. *Perhaps I kicked them under the bed.*

She lay down on the none-too-clean floor and peered beneath the bed. Seeing her pet with her shoe, she blinked in disbelief. Dorothy blinked back, annoyed at having been disturbed. Fortunately for Dorothy, before Flora's surprise could change to wrath, her lady's maid, Anne, arrived.

Smiling demurely and making no comment on Flora being sprawled on the floor, Anne said, 'Good morning, Ma'am. I'll just be taking Dorothy out for her morning walk.'

Flora sprung to feet. Frantically smoothing down her crumpled dress, she stammered, 'Oh yes! Rather, very good! Carry on.'

Anne was a dear, but Flora often felt rather inferior in her presence. For a start, she was so tall and willowy, and then her long blonde hair and striking violet eyes confirmed her as a beauty. But what so often threw Flora was the way Anne, though not yet twenty, had an air of quiet calm dignity that Flora could only dream of.

Anne clipped on Dorothy's lead and left.

Flora was still lamenting the demise of her shoe as she capered down the spectacular stone staircase. Quite wide enough for ten men to pass by abreast and not even touch shoulders, it reminded Flora of the staircase at the Paris Opera House, although here the count's crest was much in evidence as it was carved on heraldic shields with unnecessary frequency. The two floors that the stairs spanned were well lit by a double row of tall windows.

They must be quite a job to keep clean, thought Flora, but a second glance showed that they were thick with grime. The vast walls were punctuated with extremely old-looking tapestries and one or two family portraits. All the count's forebears seemed to have been blessed with exceptional good looks. Flora noticed that there were one or two gaps on the walls where the white stone was a shade paler.

Was it last month or the month before that when I saw that Sotheby's had that sale of fine French tapestries?

She skipped into the dining room, lured by the smell of coffee and bacon. The room was a marvel of magnificence. Flora paused on the threshold to admire its high-ceilinged proportions. Thanks to Anne having read up on the architecture of the château and having been gracious enough to tell Flora all about it, Flora was able to think *Old Louis Le Vau was on top form when he designed this, but then I suppose he'd had a good warm-up with Versailles.* An ornate sun was beautifully marked out in a wooden mosaic on the floor. Tall windows allowed sunshine to flood in. The most notable feature in Flora's opinion was the vast fireplace. All carved in stone, it dwarfed Flora, with the mantlepiece resting high above her head. The width was a fair expanse too. *But then it would need to be generously sized as I am sure it would take half a forest burning away to take the winter chill off this enormous room.*

Flora glanced at Busby who was already seated and enjoying a fine breakfast of coffee and pastries. As ever, he was infuriatingly attractive. His curls had been momentarily tamed by their morning brushing. He looked rather smart in his light tweed suit. *Not at all like a policeman.*

He smiled up at her. Flora almost smiled back but caught herself just in time. *The cheek of the man! Pretending he doesn't know that I'm still cross with him. I'll show him that I am not the sort of lady you can lightly accuse of imagining that there is a dead footman in her room!* She gave him a haughty glance and jutted her chin in the air. To her added annoyance, this only made him smile more.

Flora was blessed with a healthy appetite and quickly forgot about everything but food.

A splendid breakfast of fresh fruit, pastries, and coffee was on offer. As a concession to the English guests, there were silver salvers containing bacon and eggs. The sunshine, as it flooded in through the multiple floor-to-ceiling windows, was reflected in the gold trim decorations and the abundance of mirrors.

Fate had sat Flora and Busby together but in Flora's mind this didn't mean she needed to make conversation with him. Much to her annoyance, she had to admit to herself, *Busby's proximity is a little unnerving. It's all that needlessly muscled masculinity!* She sighed silently, feeling powerless. *All that, combined with his thick thatch of cinnamon curls and the whole man-boy thing he has going on with his freckles.* She was further exasperated when he silently passed her the butter. *Blast the man! Even his hands are attractive – in a broad, strong sort of way.*

As Flora toyed with her coffee, she regarded the other guests. At the head of the table sat their host, Count Christoff. Widowed and in his fifties, he was tall, dark, well-dressed and utterly charming. Even before having been fortified with his coffee, he greeted Flora with a dazzling smile, a bow and a lingering kiss of her hand.

Flora glanced down, stammered, and wondered, *Oh, my sainted aunts! Does that look mean he's recalling our kiss at the embassy ball? I don't know what came over me.* She was lying to herself. She knew full well that the kiss was the result of more than one too many glasses of champagne.

'May I say, Flora, you look quite delightful in that frock.'

His hooded, pale eyes seemed to be lingering more on her bust than her outfit but still Flora felt gratified by the comment. *I had to hand an enormous number of guineas to Madame Chanel.* Flora was not sure whether she was relieved or offended that the count's admiration for her was forgotten when he spotted the coffee pot.

Next to the count was the Princess Firuza, her striking green eyes set in a heart-shaped face. Her long hair was plaited and fell to her waist. Young and vibrant, she seemed totally uninterested in her betrothed, Crown Prince Dimash. The crown prince shared Firuza's dark complexion, but his eyes were blue-grey not green.

He had fine features with a straight nose and short wavy black hair. Long limbed and slim, he had beautiful hands, and his movements were elegant and graceful. *He has the fingers of a pianist,* mused Flora. *I wonder if the piano is a popular instrument in the Stans or if the altitude plays havoc with the tuning?* The only thing that marred his perfection was the fine slash of a scar across his face.

Princess Firuza was paying Prince Dimash scant attention.

Flora regarded them both critically before concluding, *I must say I am baffled by her lack of interest. After all, he is a remarkably good-looking young man, positively dreamy! Perhaps she doesn't like the crown prince's scar.* She regarded the fine line that ran from just above his right eyebrow diagonally across his noble features. *Personally, I think it adds a certain distinction, especially the romantic way he got it. Although I suppose that in reality agitators bursting into the Palace and attempting an assassination on a child is really rather grim, with no hint of romance.*

Courteously Crown Prince Dimash enquired in a soft, lyrical voice, 'Can I help you to some scrambled eggs, Firuza? Perhaps with a little salmon?'

'No, thank you.' Her reply was curt and her expression unfriendly.

Crown Prince Dimash's younger brother, Prince Parviz, strode over to them. He was a shade shorter than Prince Dimash and, while still slim, he was a little heavier. His movements were quick and agile; without a word he picked up a bread roll and tossed it at the princess. Acting on her reflexes, she caught it, and her face lit up in a broad smile. Laughing, she said something in a foreign tongue which Flora took to be Abbastani.

Next to them by the sideboard was the skeleton of an elderly gentleman, otherwise known as Father Luke. His pale colouring added to his ghost-like appearance. With his watery grey eyes, he peered at the world through thick round glasses. His scooped-out features and thin grey hair with its receding widow's peak did little to add to his attractiveness.

With a bony hand, he handed Princess Firuza a dish of lustrous purple grapes. Her eyebrows shot up in surprise. She accepted them, thanked him politely and, still looking puzzled, came to sit down next to Flora on the other side from Busby.

Flora lent over and enquired, 'Why are you looking so surprised, Firuza?'

The princess darted her a glance and yet again Flora was taken aback by the vivid green of the girl's eyes. In a whisper she murmured, 'I think Father Luke must have second sight. I told Parviz in Abbastani that I'd rather have fruit than the roll he'd just chucked at me and the next thing I knew, Father Luke was offering me these grapes.' She indicated the fruit in front of her. She smiled. 'The man must be clairvoyant.'

Flora laughed. 'I'm not sure being clairvoyant is compatible with being in holy orders. It was probably just a lucky guess.'

Firuza shrugged and dived into her breakfast with gusto.

Flora turned her attention to the prince's great uncle, wondering if he had witnessed the encounter. He certainly seemed to be eyeing Father Luke. Flora thought his title 'Venerable Uncle' rather odd. He had similar colouring to Firuza and the boys, but he was round in stature rather than willowy, and his eyes were distinctly piggy. His one notable feature was his magnificent moustache which was large enough to make Uncle Cyril turn an undiplomatic shade of green with envy.

The Venerable Uncle leaned back in his chair and stared at Father Luke. Throatily, he barked, 'Have we met before?'

Goodness, he may be royalty, but he sounds exactly how I would imagine a walrus would if it could speak.

Father Luke looked vacantly back at him and said nothing but blinked quite a bit.

The austere Sister Claire pinned the Venerable Uncle with an icy stare; clearly, she was far too holy to be impressed by his worldly rank. Dismissively, she stated, 'Impossible!' before resuming her miserly breakfast of a crust of bread without the luxury of jam.

Between sips of coffee, Flora examined the count's two sisters. His relatives were less exotic but possibly more eccentric.

All three siblings shared the same hooded, pale eyes, but beyond that Flora could discern no sibling similarities. His older sister was the austere Sister Claire who Flora knew to be the Mother Superior of a select order of nuns based in the south of France. Stiff as her wimple, Flora had yet to see her smile.

The younger sister, Amelie, looked every inch the flamboyant artist. Sporting oil paint and floaty clothes, she had more wild red curls than were seemly in a middle-aged woman. Her flat-faced Pekingese dog, Venus, snuffled on her velvet cushion by her side. Flora eyed the dog with apprehension; Dorothy and Venus did not get on. There had been one or two near misses when the dogs had crossed paths…

Flora's eyes narrowed. *Amelie is one of those besotted owners who is oblivious to the faults of her pet – when anyone can see it's Venus who is totally at fault and Dorothy only wants to defend herself.*

Myopic Anglican Father Luke sat between the two sisters.

He appears to be slightly bemused by whatever arty Amelie is chatting about, but at least he has the solace of Sister Claire keeping his toast supplied with marmalade. She scrutinised him. *I can't quite see why Nanny has taken a dislike to the fellow; he seems rather insipid to me. Perhaps she is just being a religious snob – she does disapprove so of his adoration of icons, rather too orthodox for her papal tastes.*

'More coffee, Ma'am?' enquired the count's butler, Roberts.

'Thank you, Roberts,' Flora replied coolly. Roberts was extremely English and disturbingly observant. His high forehead flowed into a beak of a nose. Those all-seeing eyes were small and crested by winged, snow-white eyebrows. He was small and compact, not that much taller than Flora. *I am not at all sure about how I feel about Roberts – is he slightly too much 'the perfect English butler'?*

She sighed inwardly as she surveyed the assembled group. *It had all been so simple when Uncle Cyril invited me to tea at the Foreign Office.* She inhaled the rich aroma of the coffee. As she took her first sip, she closed her eyes. *This must be a little taste of heaven – perhaps I should ask the venerable Father? Or is that far too theologically controversial for polite society? Uncle Cyril would know – he tends to know all sorts of things.*

Her mind naturally flowed back to that fateful afternoon at her uncle's office. *Although then we had Earl Grey, not coffee.*

CHAPTER THREE

Uncle Cyril's office was as grand and imposing as the man himself. It was up an impressive staircase and at the end of a long corridor. The walls of both the corridor and staircase were covered with oil paintings of distinguished colonial types.

When Flora had eventually arrived at the office, she found her uncle sitting behind a majestic desk.

Over their teacups Uncle Cyril had cleared his throat, twitched his walrus moustache, and announced, 'There's a spot of bother in the Stans.'

She looked up. 'Abbastan?' She visualised the region on the world map – a bit left of the Himalayas, above India.

He nodded.

Mention of the Stans naturally brought to mind her now-deceased old school friend and her friend's daughter, Princess Firuza, who was very much alive. As the child's godmother, Flora took a keen interest in the girl and made frequent visits to see her at her boarding school.

Uncle Cyril continued, 'I think you might be able to help.'

'Oh, you know me, always happy to help,' replied Flora brightly, then wondered whether she should exhibit less enthusiasm and more poise.

Uncle Cyril nodded. 'As you no doubt are aware, Abbastan is vital for British interests in the region. There has been a lot of upheaval in the area with the changes brought about by the dismantling of the old Imperial Turkistan and the new Soviet quasi-governments.'

Flora wasn't aware of any of this, but she hoped her countenance didn't betray her ignorance.

Uncle Cyril raised one bushy eyebrow and added, 'Those

communists are rather too powerful.'

Flora nodded, hoping she appeared wise.

'Stability is the thing and, fortunately, a rather advantageous marriage has been arranged between Princess Firuza and Crown Prince Dimash.' He smiled. 'The liaison will secure British interests and be a blow for those pesky Russians.'

Flora spluttered through her Earl Grey. She had seen Firuza a few days before and there had been no mention of a marriage, arranged or otherwise. 'Firuza? Engaged? An advantageous marriage? Advantageous for whom? It certainly won't be for dear little Firuza; she's only a child.'

Uncle Cyril's moustache twitched with displeasure. 'The princess is eighteen. In her culture that practically means she's an old maid.'

Flora flapped her hand to emphasise her point, which only led to her spilling some tea as she expostulated, 'But she's brainy! The last time I saw her she spoke of studying at Oxford, not having an arranged marriage.'

'Out of the question.' Uncle Cyril was emphatic.

Flora's lips twitched as she frantically tried to think what she could say to help poor little Firuza. 'A Swiss finishing school, then? I can recommend one.'

Uncle Cyril was losing patience. 'Flora, this is a matter for politicians not for…'

She feared he was about to say 'housewives'.

He cleared his throat again and continued. 'You are known to be acquainted with the family.'

Flora sat back in her chair and nodded. 'Well, yes – I was at school with her mother – briefly. She was whisked off for marriage at fourteen, but we wrote regularly right up until her death. So sad for Firuza to lose both her parents in that plane crash. Naturally, after that I saw a lot of Firuza, what with her being at my old school and my being her godmother.'

Uncle Cyril was not interested in Flora's childhood reminiscing and cut across her. 'It's because of this relationship, your being known in Court circles as the princess's godmother, that you are our obvious choice. It helps that you are a mother of two and a widow to boot – it gives you a suitable air of respectably for the task in hand.'

Flora gave a mental sigh. *Respectability? Is that code for dull?*

Uncle Cyril was in full flow. 'The plan is brilliant in its simplicity. The child needs to meet Crown Prince Dimash before the marriage.'

'So, you have given 'the child' some thought,' remarked Flora sourly.

Uncle Cyril snorted and continued, 'Fortunately, we have the perfect location. My associate, Count Christoff, has a very secluded château just outside Paris.'

'Count Christoff?' queried Flora flushing.

'You know him?' Uncle Cyril raised one shaggy eyebrow.

Hmm, probably better not to mention kissing him in the orangery after a couple of glasses of champagne at the Diplomatic Ball.

'Slightly,' mumbled Flora.

Uncle Cyril nodded. 'He is very well connected. Good chap, known him for years. Such a tragedy about his wife dying so young.'

Flora sat up a bit straighter, curious. 'I knew he was a widower, but I don't know the details.'

'No reason why you should, my dear! All happened years ago, and it was all hushed up at the time.'

'Hushed up?' Flora was now on the edge of her seat.

Uncle Cyril lowered his voice. 'Rumour had it she killed herself, desperate to have children and all that but couldn't. Like I said, tragic. Still, I should think he found the money useful – she was the only child of a Bordeaux shipping magnet.'

Flora would have liked to ask more questions, but Uncle Cyril had already moved on. Briskly, he announced, 'You'll have to take the Stan diamonds with you; they are part of the betrothal contract.'

Flora felt quite dizzy with all these new snippets of information coming at her in rapid succession. Actually, *snippets* was too mild a word to describe her feelings towards all these revelations – perhaps *bombshells* would be more apt. When she could gain her breath, she managed to blurt out, 'The diamonds? But they are priceless! Surely, that's a little rash.'

'Not at all – discretion is the name of the game. No one will suspect you of being charged with the jewels; besides which, Busby is going with you.'

'Busby?' Flora grew rather warm and went pink as memories surfaced of the previous December when she had masqueraded as Busby's wife while they searched for diplomatic papers and evaded a would-be murderer.

Flora realised that Uncle Cyril was staring at her. She had been about to say, 'Oh, whizzo!' however she managed to change it to, 'But he's a policeman.'

'Flora, you make him sound like the village bobby. He's a highly respected police officer and I've found him quite useful for a one or two sticky jobs. Besides which, he speaks fluent French.'

Flora nodded. 'His mother was French.'

Uncle Cyril continued with his explanation. 'Discretion is vital. Not everyone will be thrilled by the alliance. The château is ideal; high-walled and gated. It even has a moat. No one can get in or out unnoticed. An Inspector Le Brun, from the French police force, will be in charge of organising guards. It will be a small party: Crown Prince Dimash will be accompanied by his younger brother, Prince Parviz, and his uncle.'

'Their uncle? What, no title? Surely, he should be an Earl at least?'

Flora's own uncle could not refrain from rolling his eyes beneath his impressively bushy eyebrows. 'Flora, we are talking about the Stans not the Home Counties. Before the boys were born, as next in line after their father he was termed a prince, but after the crown prince's birth, he became 'the Venerable Uncle'.'

Flora's brow creased. 'But surely the Stans are miles away – won't it take months for them to arrive?'

Uncle Cyril eyed her, obviously not pleased by her intruding on his monologue. With impatience he said, 'The princes are both in England. The crown prince has just completed his studies at Oxford and Sandhurst, and Prince Parviz starts at Oxford soon.'

He paused for breath and was about to resume his monologue when Flora interjected, 'But didn't you say you chose the count's château for secrecy's sake?'

He nodded and glanced at his watch.

Flora tilted her head on one side, 'I know he's a widower, but doesn't his sister live with him? Eloise? Or is it Amelie? She does those frightful portraits. Are you sure she can be trusted?'

Uncle Cyril let out a sigh of frustration and his moustache twitched. 'Her name is Amelie and those portraits you term 'frightful' are rather celebrated. Of course, she's trustworthy, she went to Roedean. Actually, when you are there the count's elder sister will also be there.'

Flora was surprised. 'Gosh, I didn't know he had another sister; she must live very quietly.'

He smiled. 'Extremely. She's the Mother Superior of an Anglican nunnery in the South of France. She goes by the name of Sister Claire.'

Flora wrinkled her forehead, 'Isn't that rather a houseful?'

Uncle Cyril tutted again, 'I think a nun – and a Mother Superior, at that – is totally above reproach.'

Flora sighed inwardly. *There speaks a man who didn't have a convent education.*

Unaware of Flora's cynical thoughts, Uncle Cyril continued speaking. 'If anything, having both sisters present will provide an extra level of propriety should word of the crown prince's visit leak out. It will give the impression of a family house party rather than an important diplomatic mission. Now really, Flora, I mustn't keep you any longer.' He glanced at his watch again and began to rise.

'One more thing,' interjected Flora. 'The staff? I mean the count's staff. Surely there will be a few loose lips there.'

Uncle Cyril was evidently extremely keen to get rid of Flora and was already holding the door open for her.

'The count will be running the château with a skeleton staff, all carefully vetted. Now, my dear, it's been lovely to see you and do send my regards to your children.'

That had concluded the meeting, so that here she was now at the château with the princess and that useful chap, Busby.

She glanced across at 'the useful chap' who seemed to be enjoying a selection of cold meats and cheeses.

Let's see just how useful he is. I am still annoyed with him but what's a girl to do when there is sleuthing to be done?

'Psst! Busby, I need a word,' Flora whispered and was immediately irritated by his audible sigh.

She deliberately nudged his crusty bread roll onto the floor. Before any helpful staff members could leap into action, Busby automatically bent down to retrieve it and was surprised to find Flora's breathless face only inches away from his. He blinked, a faint line appearing on his freckled brow, and regarded her with sharp eyes.

'Do you realise that whoever did for that man in my room last night must be sitting around this table? You said yourself that the château is totally secure.'

'The alleged man,' stated Busby, picking up the bread.

'Don't be difficult, Busby. We can't talk here. Meet me in the summerhouse in ten minutes,' hissed Flora, just as Roberts' calm tones enquired, 'Can I assist, Ma'am?'

Flora sat up to find all eyes were upon her. 'No, quite alright, thank you. Just a spot of bother with the bread.'

CHAPTER FOUR

Breakfast finished, Flora excused herself. She had fetched Dorothy. *What could be more inconspicuous than walking my dog? Besides which, she needs an outing.*

The garden was a delight in all its spring glory with blossom trees alive with birds and an abundance of sunshine. The sun sparkled on the fountain at the garden's centre. Its relaxing tinkling sound added a pleasing backdrop to the birdsong. The garden itself was laid out in classical geometric shapes delineated by neat box hedging and punctuated by topiary bay trees.

As she was admiring the flowers, Flora spotted a movement over at the far end of the shrubbery. Glancing over, she was surprised to see that it wasn't Busby, but Firuza's betrothed, Crown Prince Dimash, and her own lady's maid, Anne. Naturally, Anne looked far from being a humble lady's maid. *She would be better suited to be a Pre-Raphaelite princess, depicted wearing a simple medieval robe and with her lustrous blonde hair free from its bun, cascading down her shoulders and sprinkled with flowers.* Flora sighed; for a moment, the romantic in her revelled in Anne's elegant beauty before her common sense kicked in.

Oh cripes, that's going to complicate things! I may not have had Uncle Cyril's diplomatic training but I'm fairly certain that a liaison between my lady's maid and the prince is not going to do much for tensions in the Stans, however accomplished she is with a needle and thread.

The prince, dark and dashing, was handing what looked like a book to the blushing Anne.

Of course, he might just be toying with her – but then we'll have endless tears, and I'll have to face her mother when we get home.

Flora contemplated the two scenarios.

I'm not sure which is worse.

The lovebirds disappeared behind a laurel. Flora saw movement and stared in that direction. *Is that the butler, Roberts? What would he be doing in the garden? Is he eavesdropping?*

Perplexed, she walked around the corner towards the picturesque summerhouse. She was about to slip into it and await Busby, when a whiff of cologne made her realise the count was at her side. He took her elbow. Dorothy gave a low growl.

'Flora, my dear, I'm so glad to find you alone.'

His voice was husky and Flora wondered if he was being seductive or just had a cold coming on. *Either way, I wish he wouldn't stand so close.*

'I've been so wanting to show you around my little domain.'

Flora regarded him and interpreted his downcast eyes as a feeble attempt at modesty. She was happy to play along. 'It's hardly small.'

Dorothy rolled her eyes and looked hopefully at the house, trying to see Busby.

The count rewarded Flora with a smile and, firmly wrapping her hand around his arm, began walking by the moat which encircled the little château and the separate newer, grander château. 'Let us start with the little château.'

Flora glanced over at the moat. A few strides more and they passed the junction of the moat and the river that fed it. A conspicuous man was stationed at the riverbank, ostensibly fishing but Flora suspected he was one of Inspector Le Brun's men standing guard.

'Doesn't look like he's having much luck,' commented Flora.

'What? Oh, yes,' said the count, not really paying him much attention. With a flourish he directed Flora to the medieval four-towered castle. 'Quite something, isn't it?'

It was indeed a small but perfect fairy-tale castle. Straight out of a medieval illustration, the elegant round towers were topped by ornate spires. The soft white stone was carved into gothic scrolls and shields with the count's coat of arms. Once it would have been the centrepiece of local and courtly life; now it was the grandest possible gateway to the main château, with its bridge over the moat and its central archway.

'Oh rather, quite something,' said Flora genuinely enthralled. 'Sort of thriftiness nobility style – refurbishing the old rather than pulling it down.'

The count chose to ignore her comment and pressed on.

'It was built in the fourteenth century by my great – I forget how many generations it is – but a forebear.' A faraway, wistful look came into the count's hooded eyes as he gazed at his Gothic showpiece.

'My, that is a long time! I adore my home in the Cotswolds, Farrington Hall, but it's Georgian – only been in the family for a few generations. Not quite as romantic but the plumbing is probably better.'

The count did not appear interested in Flora's plumbing and he continued speaking earnestly. 'My father always emphasised to me that my life's work – like all of those who have gone before me – is to pass this on to the next generation.'

Before Flora could stop herself, she blurted out, 'But there isn't another generation! You don't have any children.'

He swung round, his eyes no longer wistful but full of anger as they glared at her.

Surprised, Flora took a step back and muttered, 'A handy cousin perhaps?'

He grabbed her and pulled her towards him, his eyes softening as he murmured, 'Let me assure you I am still more than capable of fathering many sons.'

Flustered, she disentangled herself from his grip, and when there was enough space between them said, 'Oh yes, rather, quite sure you are, frightfully fit and all that, in your prime…' Her voice petered out. She realised she was scarlet in the face and that Dorothy was regarding her with disgust. In a desperate attempt to redirect the conversation she gushed, 'Do please show me around those towers, they must have the most wonderful spiral staircases.'

Dismissively, he muttered, 'Impossible – I have renovations

going on.' He was still regarding her rather more intently than she cared for. 'And you, Flora? With your two at school, doesn't your maternal heart yearn for something small to cuddle, the pitter patter of tiny feet?'

Baffled Flora blinked, 'What another dachshund?' She glanced down at her faithful hound and added, 'I'm not sure Dorothy would like that.'

The count showed a hint of exasperation, 'Not a dog! A child! A son!'

All Flora could think to say was, 'Oh!'

She could see the count was moving in. *I dread to think what for!* She brightly made another suggestion, 'The oubliette, then?'

'What?'

Happily, Flora explained, 'The oubliette – all these medieval castles have them along with a dungeon and, if you are lucky, a dinky little torture chamber. I've often thought that those medieval chaps were onto a good thing with their oubliettes. After all, what could be more convenient than having a deep hole in the ground where one could chuck unwanted guests and forget all about them?'

She knew she was babbling but couldn't stop. She didn't care for the gleam in the count's eye, so she pressed on, speaking increasingly fast and becoming less coherent with each syllable. Her heart was beating even faster than the words tumbling out of her mouth and the count appeared to be inching closer, getting ready to pounce.

'Nanny has a bit of a thing for oubliettes.'

'A bit of a thing?' queried the count huskily. It was evidently a new expression to him.

'A fascination – she just loves them. Whenever we visit a medieval castle it's the first thing on her sightseeing list.'

The count wasn't to be distracted by Nanny's macabre interests. In a skilled and practised manner, he encircled Flora's waist and pulled her towards him. Flora leant away, trying to avoid his hot garlicky breath on her face.

Passionately he declared, 'Let's not talk about such grim

topics. Let's talk about love and new life.'

Flora wriggled free. 'Well yes we could talk about that…' She glanced around for a safer topic and her eyes alighted on the magnificent main château. It was a model of proportion and symmetry. A sea of windows and a distinctive dome roof marked it out as the work of the great architect, Le Vau. Flora rather liked its impressive balustrade high above the gravel forecourt. The imposing tricolour flag was waving majestically from its lofty perch, a billowing beacon of red, white, and blue. *I bet there is an amazing view from up there but if I mention it this pesky count will whisk me off to admire it! Help! I need to distract him with a neutral topic of conversation. But what?*

Inspiration struck Flora and triumphantly she declared, 'Or we could talk about architecture!'

The count blinked, reminding Flora of a baffled hunting hawk.

Flora smiled and dredging up a useful fact her well-read maid, Anne, had told her. She said, 'I believe the architect your ancestor used to build the main château was the same chap who built Versailles, Louis Le Vau?'

The count smiled, gratified that she had taken enough interest in his ancestral home to do some research. His happiness was short-lived as she thoughtlessly added, 'What a lot of upkeep it must take! I shudder to think of the cost.'

The count gave a start, and Flora perceived another flash of anger which was quickly suppressed. He wrapped her hand once more in his and patted it. 'But for you, Flora my dear, money is no object. You are known to be one of the richest ladies in England.'

Flora hated the mention of money; her hearty bank account was certainly not a topic for conversation. Using the pretence of Dorothy needing her lead adjusting, she retrieved her hand and bent down to her pet. 'Yes, I suppose it is jolly useful.'

As she stood up, she was overjoyed to see Inspector Le Brun and a couple of his uniformed men approaching. Both Inspector Le Brun and the count were surprised by the rapturous greeting she gave the newcomer.

With aplomb she added, 'Now I really mustn't keep the pair

of you, I'm sure you have lots of important things to discuss.'

Ignoring all their protestations and denials she marched Dorothy firmly towards the other side of the house and the sanctuary of the summerhouse.

Once within the confine of the ornate summerhouse, Flora did not have long to dwell on her disturbing morning. *What with an errant prince and my lady's maid, Roberts – the suspicious butler – and an over-amorous count, I really am having a rather trying time, but at least here comes Busby.*

Dorothy greeted the inspector rapturously which Flora thought was a little disloyal. *After all, I am the one who lavishes attention on her while he refers to her as 'the mutt'.* But Dorothy was looking up at Busby with adoration, her tail wagging as hard as was physically possible, and in doggy-speak was saying, '*He can call me a mutt anytime he likes.*'

Flora regarded the boyish twinkle in his tawny eyes and the way his russet curls were ruffled. *Perhaps Dorothy has a point.*

She cleared her throat and mentally gave herself a shake before saying in an efficient tone, 'Good, you are here. Now we may not have much time before we are interrupted so let's get straight down to business.' She took out a neat little silver notebook with a pleasing matching propelling lead pencil attached by a fine chain. 'I've written the list of suspects; perhaps we could go through them.'

Busby frowned and enquired, 'Suspects for what?'

Flora flashed him a glare. 'You really can be most trying, Busby.'

He grinned, which was adorable but equally annoying.

She tutted. 'You don't seem to appreciate the gravity of the situation. The missing body is proof that someone is onto us and not supportive. It can't be just coincidence that the chap was in my room; he must have been looking for the diamonds. It doesn't take Uncle Cyril to appreciate that any disruption to the betrothal could cause problems for British interests in the Stans.'

Flora made a mental note, I must ask Firuza exactly what

those interests are and what her getting married has to do with it.

She fixed her eyes on Busby and delivered her most compelling argument. 'More immediately, if someone is happy to kill a chap, they won't hesitate to murder a princess.'

Busby nodded, finally taking her seriously. 'Have you asked Nanny to enquire in the servants' quarters about any absent footmen?'

'Yes, but no joy. I rather got the impression she's caused a bit of bad feeling below stairs with her demands for pots of tea.'

Busby grinned. Obviously, he could imagine Nanny causing havoc in a well-run French kitchen with complaints about her 'brew'. 'Anne could ask,' he said. 'It would mean letting her in on what is going on but she's a sensible girl and totally trustworthy.'

Flora thought of Anne gazing up into the crown prince's intense blue-grey eyes and made a noncommittal murmur. *I am not sure Anne would maintain her sleuthing impartiality when it comes to anything regarding Crown Prince Dimash.*

She bit her lip thoughtfully before saying, 'I think it would be far better if I went straight to the count – who better to know if one of his footmen has gone missing?'

Busby wrinkled his forehead. 'Also, who better to know all the details of the betrothal and who better to disrupt and to snaffle the diamonds?'

'Oh.' Flora could see the logic.

'And speaking of the diamonds, I don't suppose you could persuade Nanny to hand them over to me? I have tried but she seems to think her carpetbag is the ultimate in security.'

Flora laughed. 'Busby, do you really think I can persuade Nanny to do anything?'

'Probably not,' he agreed, then, as he watched Flora frantically scribbling in her notebook, asked, 'What are you doing?'

'I'm adding the count to the list of suspects. As far as I can see the motivation must either be financial or political. Financially, those diamonds are worth a pretty penny. I am putting the count top of my list of 'suspects who could be motivated by money'. The count has just been indicating that he needs some dosh.'

Busby was regarding her quizzically, 'So, when you were so keen just now to ditch the count onto Le Brun and me, it was because you were discussing finances?'

'Sort of,' replied Flora briskly, not meeting his gaze. 'Then under my list of 'suspects motivated by politics', I reckon the Venerable Uncle is top – after all, he doesn't approve of Firuza as a consort for Dimash.'

'You've discounted the two younger princes under the political motivation heading?'

'No, they are on the list, but I don't think it can be them – they are both so…' Flora gazed heavenward as she searched for the right word.

Busby observed Flora shrewdly before suggesting, 'Good looking?'

She flushed. 'Well, yes.'

'They may be young but presumably they have the most to win or lose according to what happens with the princess. Are you aware of how Crown Prince Dimash got his scar?'

Flora confidently answered, 'Agitators broke into the palace and tried to assassinate the heir.'

Busby looked serous, 'That's not the whole story. It was the crown prince's own uncle, our esteemed Venerable Uncle's younger brother.'

'Gosh, that must make Christmas at the Palace a tad awkward,' declared Flora, wide-eyed.

'It was the Venerable Uncle who saved young Dimash by running his own brother through with a sword, so don't discount the princes.'

Flora nodded and reluctantly jotted down their two names, after which she explained, 'Then we have people who might want the diamonds – or rather the money they're worth. Amelie is bound to need some money – you know the old cliché of the struggling artist – but she seems rather too fey to go around killing people. While Sister Claire is obviously more than capable of killing anyone, I can't see why she would want money. After all, she will have taken a vow of poverty.'

Busby was looking over her shoulder, clearly not particularly interested in the conversation but going through the motions to humour her.

Flora tried to inject a bit of enthusiasm into their dialogue. 'But perhaps she has a crumbling convent? That would provide a motive for the priest, too. Funds for the abbey?'

Busby shook his head. 'He's so short-sighted, I don't think he'd be capable of finding the diamonds.'

Flora was emphatic. 'He might be feigning that. And what about the staff? That butler is a bit too all-seeing for my liking.'

Busby tilted his head and queried, 'But isn't that a butler's job? To be ever-vigilant to serve?'

Flora would have told him about spotting Roberts acting suspiciously near the crown prince and Anne, but she was distracted by Dorothy. The dachshund was growing increasingly restless.

Had Flora been gifted in dog-speak, she would have known Dorothy was actually saying, '*Will you get a whiff of that! It's that perfumed puff-ball excuse for a dog, Venus.*'

And Venus was lisping, '*Ah! There you are, you short-legged excuse for a hound, hiding in the summerhouse!*'

Dorothy let forth an outraged whimper, '*Who are you calling a short-legged excuse for a hound? You oriental powder puff! Call yourself a dog? You perfumed mop!*'

'Do you hear that?' whispered Flora, pausing and listening intently.

'What?' asked Busby.

'Shhh!' she hissed. She brushed a stray curl out of her eyes and glowered at him.

'Someone is at the door, listening to us,' she mouthed as she tiptoed towards the door.

She pressed her ear against it while Busby watched bemused.

Silently, she placed her hand on the doorknob and then yanked the door open hard.

CHAPTER FIVE

In less than a heartbeat, mayhem broke forth. Dorothy commenced a cacophony of high-pitched yaps and Amelie's Pekingese, Venus, rushed in, a flowing fury of long silky hair. She dashed between Flora's legs, sending her sprawling backwards and making her drop Dorothy's lead.

Flora had that unpleasant sensation of falling and would have landed on the floor had Busby not stepped in and caught her.

His arms wrapped around her; his body felt warm and strong.

It had been a long time since Flora had had the pleasure of being in a man's arms and, instinctively, she leant into him. She heard a small intake of breath on his part and noticed him tightening his hold on her. Her pulse quickened.

But the spirit of romance was not with Flora. Dorothy, with her ruff up and tail erect was facing off with Venus. The Pekingese erupted in snuffling outraged barks.

The noise was deafening.

Flora struggled to her feet and, above the noise, commanded, 'Dorothy, leave it!'

Dorothy took this as an exhortation to attack. She lunged at Venus and bit her neatly on the ear. The Pekingese squealed, turned tail, and ran from the summerhouse with Dorothy in hot pursuit, closely followed by Flora. Flora added to the noise with her futile screams for Dorothy to stop. These cries were occasionally paused while Flora lunged at the trailing lead only to have it repeatedly slip through her fingers.

In doggy tongue, Venus, between breathless wheezes, was yapping, '*You ignoble sausage! All bark and no bite, that's what you are!*'

Dorothy retorted, '*I'll show you my bite if you just stop running and fight like a dog rather than an overgrown mop. Who are you calling German? I may look German, but my soul is French!'*

They lapped the garden before Venus wisely decided to take refuge in Amelie's studio. The pampered Peke burst into the chaotic room with its easels, canvases and smell of oil paint, while Dorothy hesitated on the threshold, allowing Flora to finally grasp the end of her lead.

As Flora straightened up, she was confronted by Amelie.

The artist was a good seven inches taller than Flora and considerably wider. She now deployed all of her inches to intimidate Flora.

'Er, good morning – or perhaps I should say 'bonjour',' stammered Flora, aware her feeble smile was inappropriate.

Standing erect, with her lip curled and her eyebrows drawn together, Amelie observed Dorothy and Flora with equal disdain. Her wild red curls took on a Medusa-like aura. She raised her improbably long cigarette holder to her garishly red smudged lips and slowly inhaled. The end glowed red before she blew out a cloud of acrid smoke.

Dorothy, recognising a superior force, fell silent and slunk behind Flora's ankles. She was brave enough to peer around them and glowered at the triumphant Venus while muttering in low growls, '*I think I'll let you handle this one, Flora.*'

Venus, safe in her mistress's arms, regarded Dorothy with smug satisfaction.

'And what is the meaning of this, Mrs Farrington?' Amelie's voice was cold.

Flora felt the question was unnecessary but politely replied, 'Madame, I am most frightfully sorry – I can assure you I won't let it happen again.'

Amelie's hooded eyes were fixed on Flora. 'I should think so! Poor little Venus is a very sensitive soul, and I cannot permit her to be distressed.'

Venus made a self-satisfied snuffling sound.

Flora nodded. 'Quite, quite, I can't apologise enough.'

'No, you can't,' affirmed the artist, coldly.

Squirming with embarrassment, Flora tentatively asked, 'Is there anything I can do to make amends?'

A gleam came into Amelie's pale eyes. 'Well, there is a little favour you could do.'

Relieved, Flora gushed, 'Anything!'

'Your maid.'

Flora blinked. 'Yes? Anne?'

Amelie nodded. 'Remarkable looking girl; those cheekbones, that fine nose, those violet eyes and her lips,' she sighed before adding, 'bee-stung.'

Flora shifted uneasily. 'Can't say I've ever noticed.'

Amelie's eyes flashed as she declared, 'Ask her to sit for me. I'd like to paint her.'

Flora blinked again, thinking fast. *I'm not sure I like the glint in her eyes, but it would solve the prince problem. After all, she could hardly get into much mischief in this studio. It would be far preferable to have her here than meeting errant princes in shrubberies.*

Flora beamed. 'Delighted.'

That morning was peppered with encounters with the count's sisters.

The distant sound of a tennis ball alerted Flora to the possibility that 'the young' – namely two princes and a princess – were on the tennis court. *Perfect. Between rallies I can ask them all about the political situation in the Stans. If I can understand the politics, I might be able to see who would have a diplomatic reason to interfere.*

With Dorothy's lead firmly looped over her wrist, Flora set off.

At least I've made contact with Amelie even if this encounter was not the time to ask pertinent questions like, 'I say Amelie, old bean, any chance you biffed a footman over the head while trying to steal the priceless Abbastani diamonds?' Still, I am sure Anne sitting for her will provide many opportunities for me to pose Amelie a whole variety of helpful questions. And now to ask

Firuza and the boys to fill me in on the whole 'spot of bother in the Stans' business.

The tennis court was sheltered by a trim hedge. White scrolled chairs gathered around a table, providing a good spot from which to watch the sporting action. A pink blossomed cherry gave some picturesque shade. Sister Claire was sitting stiffly on one of these hard seats and Firuza was gazing at her with something that looked akin to veneration. Father Luke was propped up on a chair to one side of them, with a small book on his knee, but his battered Panama hat was tilted over his eyes, and he appeared to be snoozing.

The two princes were having a good-natured knock-up on the court.

Flora thought *They do look very athletic with those opened-necked shirts and those loose trousers – I believe the young call them 'bags'.*

Meanwhile, Dorothy tugged at the lead, thinking, '*Stupid game, if you ask me. If only Flora would let me off this dratted lead, I'd show them the correct treatment of a tennis ball.*'

Flora came up to the court in time to hear Sister Claire say, 'Oh, yes, we play quite a bit of tennis at our Mother House near Aix-en-Provence.'

Flora's heart sank. *These young people are very trying; not only must I quash Anne and Crown Prince Dimash's amorous inclinations but now it seems I need to steer Firuza away from the convent. I really can't see her being happy spending the rest of her life in a wimple.*

Sister Claire's firm voice carried over the sound of a tennis ball being adroitly hit over the net. 'The cloistered life is far removed from what you might expect. If you are a truly modern woman, it is a rare arena where a woman may live a life independent of the shackles of men. Think of it, Princess, total independence of the mind! What a privilege to pursue one's life's work without the inconvenience of a family.'

Flora observed Sister Claire's steely calm and Firuza's evident admiration. *Interesting, she is bright enough to know exactly what would appeal to Firuza. Clearly, Sister Claire is one to watch. I need to break up this little tryst before she whisks my charge off to her abbey.*

Flora sat herself firmly between Sister Claire and Firuza. Smiling, she declared, 'Goodness, Sister Claire, you make your abbey sound like a positive female Utopia.'

Sister Claire regarded Flora and Dorothy with much the same disdain that her artistic sister Amelie had just a few minutes before. *Oh, gosh, I seem to have fallen foul of both the count's sisters. Given that they both have the same eyes, I wonder if beneath Sister Claire's austere wimple there is a riot of red curls like Madame Amelie's?*

Sister Claire spoke calmly, 'Yes, Mrs Farrington, I can offer a young, curious woman a life of empowerment and intellectual satisfaction.'

The princes paused in their knock-up.

'Come on, Firuza, stop loafing and come and join us,' called Prince Parviz, sending Firuza an appealing smile.

The princess excused herself and was soon expertly wielding her racquet with as much skill as either of the boys.

Flora, Dorothy, and Sister Claire watched the rally, turning their heads in unison, left then right then left again, as they tracked the ball flying back and forth over the net.

Sister Claire broke the hypnotising rhythm. Without taking her eyes away from the court, and in a tone of false casualness, she enquired, 'I understand that the princess's dowry is quite priceless.'

With a note of equal disinterest Flora replied, 'I believe so.'

She gave the nun a sideways look. *Is that a smile playing about the Sister's lips?*

'The abbey needs a new roof,' murmured Sister Claire.

Flora was instantly alert. From her own experience of leaks at Farrington Hall she knew that roofs were jolly expensive. Suddenly Firuza's dowry took on a whole new importance. 'What? Roof?'

Sister Claire smiled in a way that didn't reach her eyes. 'So sorry, I was thinking out loud – just some boring domestic details.

Nothing to worry about. The Lord will provide. Now you must excuse me; it's time for the good Father's medicine and he is likely to forget if I don't remind him.' She glanced over at Father Luke's peaceful form and gave what passed for an indulgent smile in Sister Claire's barren world. 'He is bound to have left it in his room, so I will just fetch it.'

She stood up with a rustle of her habit and departed, leaving Flora thinking, *So much for female independence and freedom from men.*

The Sister's chair was soon occupied by the venerable Uncle. *He certainly looks very magnificent in his cultural garb. All that rich coloured silk is magnificent. They certainly lend him an air of dignity and importance. I suspect that in Western clothes his portly figure and piggy eyes would make him appear more comic than imposing.*

He greeted Flora, and Dorothy gave a low growl. Ignoring the dachshund's disapproval, he began watching the tennis.

After a particularly energetic rally, which had Firuza sending an unstoppable volley past Parviz, the Venerable Uncle tutted. 'I am not at all sure that such vigorous exercise is good for girls.'

Flora would have liked to query this, but the butler, Roberts, arrived at that moment with a silver tray holding a cut-glass jug of lemonade. Ice tinkled and condensation ran down the outside. He set the tray down on the table and commenced pouring it out.

He proffered the first glass to Flora. She thanked him while wondering, *Isn't serving a touch menial for a butler? Surely, it's a role far more suited to, say, a footman?*

Her first sip was heavenly, deliciously cool with just the right hint of tart and sweet.

Seeing that refreshments had arrived, the young left the court and, laughing over some private joke, joined Flora and the Venerable Uncle at the table. Roberts obligingly poured drinks for them. Flora noticed his beady eyes scanning and assessing everyone and everything.

Prince Parviz playfully slapped Firuza's shoulder. 'You well and truly had me running around. I can see I need more practice.'

Firuza's laughter was cut short by the Venerable Uncle's voice. 'The princess will have to give up such undignified hobbies when she marries.' His face was placid, his features settled in calm certainty, the folds of his cheeks and neck resting on the folds of his crimson-and-saffron robes. He relaxed his ringed fingers on his impressive stomach. His moustache was freshly waxed and his eyes sharp.

Firuza heard him. Her smile transformed to a scowl, her laughter died, and her slender hands curled into fists.

Crown Prince Dimash courteously pulled a chair out for her to sit next to Flora. He gave his uncle a gentle smile and when he spoke his voice was quiet, non-confrontational, yet firm. 'But Uncle, we have tennis courts at both the summer and winter palace – it would be a shame for them not to be used.'

Their eyes locked. The Uncle was the first to look away, but he did so with ill grace. 'I've doubted about the wisdom of any girl from the Royal household receiving an education. It makes them ill fitted for their role.'

Firuza took a deep breath in and would have spoken but Flora placed a restraining hand on her arm.

Prince Parviz had no such curb, and he seemed to lack his older brother's self-control. He had a flush about his complexion that Flora thought had little to do with his recent exercise. His sapphire-blue eyes flashed and he breathed heavily. 'I, for one, want an equal partner in my wife. Surely it is vital for anyone in a position of authority to be as educated as possible so that they can lead wisely. You yourself insisted that Prince Dimash and I had extensive tutoring from the greatest scholars at home, followed by Oxford and Sandhurst. Firuza is every bit as bright as us – I think she should be free to pursue her studies at Oxford.'

While Prince Parviz spoke, his uncle unclamped his podgy hands and leant forward. Beads of sweat formed on his forehead. With an edge of barely suppressed anger, he retorted, 'It is well for you and your brother that I am here to advise you. Personally, I feel that my wife's niece would make a far more fitting Queen Consort for Crown Prince Dimash.' He curled his lip and flung a contemptuous glance at Firuza. 'She is a young lady with exquisite manners and embodies all those feminine qualities which our nation so admires.'

Firuza threw off Flora's guarding hand, and snapped, 'But she lacks two vital things – command over the Northern pass and the Abbastani diamonds.'

The uncle stood up abruptly and manners demanded the two younger men also rose to their feet. Stiffly he said, 'If you will excuse me, I have some important correspondence to attend to.'

With a lumbering gait he walked back towards the château.

The boys waited until he was out of sight before resuming their seats.

Prince Parviz laughed, 'I say, Firuza, you certainly told him.'

Firuza was still pale with anger. 'Maybe, but it's rather humiliating to have one's worth defined by a strategic mountain pass and some jewels.'

Prince Parviz laughed again 'You missed out having a killer forehand at tennis.'

Firuza looked at him and her features softened to a smile.

Crown Prince Dimash wasn't smiling. There were deep creases of concern between his eyes as he said, 'It isn't a laughing matter. The pair of you need to learn diplomacy. Uncle wields a lot of power, and you shouldn't directly challenge him; it could be dangerous.'

Flora thought of the body in her room and perked up. Hopefully, she enquired, 'Dangerous? In what way? I mean you don't think he's the sort of chap who might think it's alright to help himself to the diamonds or perhaps even commit a spot of murder if it fitted in with his political goals?'

The two princes and Firuza all looked at her, their wide eyes denoting their surprise.

Crown Prince Dimash tilted his head; from this angle his scar was not visible. 'That is an interesting question, Mrs Farrington.'

'Oh, really?' Flora toyed with the dog lead and nonchalantly replied, 'Just curious.'

Prince Parviz said seriously, 'I wouldn't put anything past

him. He has never really got over being born second in the line of succession to our father. He has spent his life trying to get the power he feels he was cheated of at birth.'

Stay calm, Flora, don't whip out your notebook and put him at the top of your list of suspects. Let's just hope I remember to do it later.

She nodded and put her next question, 'Presumably, he's here to keep an eye on you two boys?'

Firuza said, 'Not exactly – I think he's here to examine me. I've been away at school for rather a long time, and he won't want a troublemaker marrying into the KabuStan royal house.'

'Especially to the future Emperor,' added Prince Parviz with a frown.

Flora shifted uncomfortably in her seat. 'Please forgive me if this is an indelicate question but why are the Brits so keen on Firuza and Prince Dimash getting married?'

Firuza grimaced. 'Geography – between our two kingdoms we control a vital pass through the mountains. Ways to travel through obstacles have always been useful for trade and warfare. And the British are masters of putting pressure on weaker countries to achieve their aims.'

Is this where I apologise on behalf of my nation? wondered Flora.

Firuza continued, a frown line between her eyes and her mouth a grim line. 'The whole area is little more than a political chess board for Britain and Russia. Imperial Russia and now the Soviets dominate Central Asia – Stalin as the People's Commissar of Nationalities is doing a fine job carving up the region.'

Parviz idly tossed a tennis ball back onto the court and added, 'Bit of a joke as they have flooded the whole place with loyal Soviet citizens.'

Now Flora felt on safer, patriotic ground. 'Oh, yes, rather – dastardly communists!'

Father Luke's prayer book dropped from his knee; they glanced over, but seeing him still sleeping resumed their conversation, forgetting he was there.

Firuza said something in Abbastani that Flora didn't quite catch but, judging from the tone, Flora suspected it wasn't any too complimentary.

Parviz smirked while Dimash in a very calm, patronising voice, explained, 'Mrs Farrington, we as independent people would like our own autonomy.'

Flora blinked and he expanded, 'In the same way you wouldn't like the United States to dictate Britain's policies, we would like to be free of outside political interference, regardless of the country.'

Flora was flabbergasted. *Not sure what dear old Uncle Cyril would make of this!* she thought.

Such was her mental turmoil that she was almost pleased when they were interrupted by Count Christoff. A whiff of reassuringly expensive cologne heralded his arrival. He was smiling and as ever exquisitely dressed. He greeted them all but gave Flora a special smile. She found it both gratifying and slightly disconcerting.

He was about to sit down next to her, but a discreet cough alerted them to the presence of Roberts, the butler.

Goodness, how unnerving, Roberts must have been here all the time, listening to everything. Talk about blending into the background. What with the silent Father Luke and the stealthy Roberts I am being to feel as if this château is haunted by ghosts.

'If I may have a word, sir?' His tone was deferential.

The count frowned and excused himself. Roberts and the count conferred a few feet away. After their little conflab, Roberts gave a slight bow and retired in the direction of the house. The count was still frowning when he returned.

'Problem?' asked Flora brightly.

He smiled at her. 'Not at all, Mrs Farrington, just a boring domestic matter. It appears that one of our footmen is missing, which is causing a certain degree of difficulty below stairs as we are running on a skeleton staff for the sake of discretion.'

Flora dropped her glass in delight. Luckily, it didn't break but it did make rather a mess. Dorothy yapped in surprise while 'the young' fussed around, mopping up the lemonade, and Flora thought, *Why is Busby never around when I want to declare, 'I told you so!'?*

Order restored, the count resumed his address. 'Now, on a far more interesting topic, I would like to propose a little adventure to Paris.'

Firuza brightened. 'The Louvre?'

Prince Dimash added, 'What an excellent idea.'

The count looked momentarily embarrassed. 'Well, er yes that would be splendid but unfortunately, due to the necessity of discretion regarding your, er, liaison, our little outing will have to be limited to the princess and Mrs Farrington.'

Crown Prince Dimash looked nonplussed as did Firuza.

Presumably, that pout is at being reminded she is here for a diplomatic purpose rather than art. I'd better say something tactful before she says something unwise.

Flora turned her warmest smile on the count who evidently appreciated it. 'How delightful. This afternoon?'

Arrangements were made and the count excused himself, murmuring vaguely that perhaps it would be better not to mention the outing to the artist, Amelie, as she would insist on joining the party and her artistic passions could be a shade wearing, especially in the Louvre.

CHAPTER SIX

Even after the count had left, Firuza's pout remained in place. Flora noted that it in no way marred her beauty but rather added a layer of intrigue to her young features. Her fingers curled and uncurled around her tennis racket as she contemplated her situation.

Prince Parviz was watching her, his Mediterranean blue-eyes intent, his body leaning towards her. 'Are you alright, Firuza?'

She shrugged. 'It's so humiliating to be reduced to a strategic pass and a handful of diamonds.'

Crown Prince Dimash's voice gave no hint of emotion as he calmly stated, 'It's the fate of older royal offspring across the nations and throughout history – there's no point in taking it personally or fighting against it.'

His words were pragmatic, but Flora thought she detected a certain wistfulness behind his eyes. *Still no time to dwell on Prince Dimash's inner soul. I need to get to the bottom of the politics of this 'spot of bother in the Stans'.*

'A pass? Is that why Uncle Cyril, er, I mean, the British Government are so keen on the pair of you…' She flushed and looked from Crown Prince Dimash's impassive features to Firuza's more expressive pout. The delicacy of the situation struck her with renewed force. *I do see Firuza's point, it's a bit like breeding racehorses. Hardly romantic.'*

Coldly, Firuza explained, 'The Pass is the best route from India through the Himalayas so it's of vital trade and military significance.'

Crown Prince Dimash expanded the explanation. 'The pass is similar to the Kyber Pass.'

Flora was keen to show her knowledge. 'Yes, I remember it well from all those dreary geography lessons with Miss Wilson –

part of the Hindu Kush.'

Father Luke snored on an exhale giving Flora a start. *One does tend to forget he's here. The man has clearly drifted off, book on knee.*

Flora recalled her attention from snoring clerics to strategic passes. 'And, as with the Kyber Pass, do you have lots of trouble with those pesky Russians?'

Firuza's face was impassioned. With her fist clenched she replied, 'That is what we want to avoid.'

Flora felt she was really getting to grips with all this diplomatic malarky. 'Oh, rather, absolutely – I mean who wants Russians all over the place?'

Firuza snorted and muttered something in Abbastani. Judging by Prince Dimash's shocked expression and Parviz's smirk, whatever it was wasn't very complimentary. Adding to the moment, Father Luke gave an explosive snore which dislodged his book from his lap, and it fell to the ground.

In English, Firuza said, 'That comment was typical coming from a daughter of the Empire.'

Even in English Flora didn't quite understand Firuza's comment but she knew from the tone that the Princess had insulted her.

Parviz was grinning but Crown Prince Dimash threw Firuza a look of disapproval before gently saying, 'In today's world it is difficult for small countries to maintain their independence. From our perspective, the British are as much a threat as the Russians.'

Flora sat up extremely rigid and pressed her lips together. *I say, it's one thing for me to be insulted, but Britain? Never!*

Before she could summon up a patriotic retort, Parviz leant forward and enquired in an impassioned tone, 'Mrs Farrington, would you want Britain to be no more than a bone to be squabbled over by two giants of power like Russia and America?'

Taken aback, Flora muttered, 'Er, well, no.'

Firuza's face was flushed as she said, 'Only in our world, 'squabbles' result in bloodshed and lives lost.' She pushed back her chair and stood up, waking Dorothy in the process.

Dorothy eyed her, disapproving of the dramatic disturbing of her snooze.

'I need to breathe,' stated Firuza.

She would have marched off, but Prince Parviz stopped her. 'Where are you going?'

'The balustrade at the top of the château. At least from there I can see Paris and mile after mile of countryside, even if I'm more or less a prisoner.'

Prince Parviz's brow furrowed. Distress filled his eyes as he scanned her face. His hand was still resting on her rigid arm as he insisted, 'I'll go with you.'

'No! I need to be alone!'

She pulled away from him and his shoulders drooped as he watched her angry departure.

He turned back to his brother and Flora. 'I suppose it's just as well, as I really have a ton of correspondence I should be attending to.' He glanced at Prince Dimash, his lips set in a grim line. 'Half of the letters are ones you should be attending to – you are the crown prince, after all, but all you seem to be interested is your sketchbook.'

He gave Flora a courteous bow and strode back towards the château, passing Nanny, all in black and creaking along the path. Her carpetbag was firmly clamped on her arm and there was a determined look in her eye.

'My, what a lot of comings and goings there seem to be this morning,' sighed Flora to no one in particular.

'Speaking of which, please excuse me. I really must go and find my book,' said the crown prince, rising.

Flora's mind flashed to the small volume she had seen him hand to Anne in the shrubbery. Her agitation was not helped by Nanny.

As the prince passed her, she flashed him a shrewd glance, her black eyes twinkling.

Her mane of silver hair was barely contained, despite many grips and pins, and as she spoke there was a shower of pins onto the path. 'Anne's in the laundry, washing Flora's smalls – if you hurry you should catch her alone.'

Flora contained her indignation until the crown prince was out of earshot and Nanny had levered herself into the seat next to her. Dorothy wagged her tail; she approved of Nanny.

'Well, really, Nanny, you are hardly helping the political situation in the Stans. I'll have you know, Britain's trade and military interests rest on the crown prince and Firuza forming a matrimonial alliance. What would Uncle Cyril say if he knew you were encouraging an entirely ill advised, er, friendship? And more to the point, what about Anne's mother when this all ends in tears?' A new thought struck Flora. 'How did you know about it? I only spotted them in the shrubbery this morning.'

'Well, that's because you are as blind as a bat when it comes to love, my girl. Why, anyone with eyes in their head could see the moment that young man laid eyes on her he was smitten. And don't be such old fusspot – political interest be damned. Is there no sense of romance in that matronly heart of yours?'

Once again, the term 'matronly' struck a nerve for Flora. She found herself pulling her tummy in, sitting a shade straighter, and wondering if she could ditch Firuza and the count in the Louvre and go in search of a new lipstick.

'Lemonade?' she enquired, hoping to change the matronly mood.

Nanny nodded, sending a further cascade of hairpins from her wild curly bun to tinkle onto the stone flags at her well shod feet. 'That would be grand,' she wheezed, taking her knitting out of her bag.

Flora fleetingly gave a thought to the priceless Abbastani diamonds nestling in that battered carpetbag. *Perhaps Nanny is right – what villain would ever think to look in there for the jewels?*

Her thoughts strayed back to Anne. *For all her beauty she will never get to wear diamonds.* She sighed loudly and Nanny looked up.

'I was just wondering about Anne,' said Flora.

'What about her?'

'Oh, I don't know,' replied Flora incoherently.

'Well, if it's about what a fine empress consort she would make to young Dimash, I totally agree! Not only is she beautiful – always handy in a monarch – but she is kind, thoughtful, and poised. She has an inherent dignity and is as bright as a button. I wonder where she would go if only she had had the chance of a proper education.' Nanny let out her own sigh before returning to her knitting.

Flora's head was in a whirl. *Anne? A head of state? Has Nanny gone quite potty? How ridiculous!* She observed the older woman and decided to remain silent on the matter.

Nanny was content to knit while Dorothy found a patch of sunshine and luxuriated in its warmth, lying flat out on the grass.

Flora glanced from Nanny – a black beetle of a woman totally absorbed in her task –to Dorothy, a sausage-shaped picture of happiness.

Time to embrace the frightfully French art of simply being! To listen to the bird song, to look at the blossom, to feel the gentle breeze on my face.

She sighed and closed her eyes. Her mind was instantly filled with worrying images: of Firuza's pained expression; of her own young daughter, Debo, who was just transitioning from a gangly child to a young lady; of the two princes, young men with so much crushing responsibility; and of her son, Tony, with his life in front of him. In the turmoil of her mind there wasn't so much as the hint of a songbird, French or otherwise.

She opened her eyes hurriedly, hoping to escape the distress of relaxation.

'Nanny, do you ever worry about the future? Doubt your own ability to steer yourself and your loved ones through the dangers of life?'

Nanny didn't look up from her knitting, she just muttered a curt, 'No!'

Flora was too far down her own mental rabbit hole of despair to notice. 'I can't help thinking of Firuza's dear mother. What would she advise the child to do if she was still alive? Would she be able to find happiness playing tennis in a wimple or would her duty lie in the Stans? How would Debo fare if she had to make up her mind to marry a man she didn't love, rather than fretting over which film to watch at the flicks?'

Flora looked at Nanny hoping for some sage wisdom from the mature woman. *After all, she's simply decades old. She must have gleaned some knowledge of life.*

Obligingly, Nanny glanced up, leaving the swirl of yellow wool on her knee. 'Have you been eating your prunes, love?'

Flora blinked. 'Prunes?'

'Yes, prunes, they're wonderful things for keeping you regular. I could ask that stuck-up butler, Roberts, to make sure you have some by your breakfast plate of a morning.'

Flora glowered at Nanny. 'Really, Nanny, I don't see what prunes have to do with anything.'

Nanny shrugged and placidly resumed her knitting. 'Suit yourself, it's just you seem a little out of sorts. When you were a child and didn't seem quite yourself, I always found prunes worked wonders.'

'That's as maybe, Nanny,' declared Flora mustering what dignity she could as she rose to her feet. 'Dorothy and I are going back to the château to have a bit of a chat with Firuza, and it certainly won't involve prunes.'

Without showing much interest, Nanny murmured, 'If I were you, I'd leave the child be.'

'Well, you are not me,' proclaimed Flora in a tone that was petulant at its best and teetered on the brink of sounding downright sulky. Purposefully, she marched back towards the château, past pink tulips contained behind immaculate box hedging and a fading, softly scented, magnolia tree.

Amelie's studio door was open to let in the morning sun and artistic inspiration. Flora gripped Dorothy's lead more securely. *One never knows where that pampered Peke, Venus, may be lurking.*

Voices drifted out from the studio, indistinct in their actual words but unmissable in their tone. Amelie was asking a question and Anne was answering.

Well at least I can congratulate myself on having solved the problem of Anne, the prince, and the politics of the Pass! Evidently, despite Nanny's best attempts to spoil things, Amelie rescued Anne from washing my smalls and the perils of meeting the crown prince. What harm can come to her safely cloistered in the studio?

But, as she passed the open door, she happened to glance inside and was horrified to see Anne, beautifully posed in a pool of sunlight with Venus on her knee, being drawn not only by Amelie, with her wild red curls ablaze and sweeping pencil strokes, but also by Crown Prince Dimash. Thoughtfully he sat, slowly absorbing every graceful line of Anne's serene face and elegant figure.

Flora stared. *Oh! I fear the Stans are in danger of experiencing more than a 'spot of bother'. But what can I do? I can hardly march in there and confront the crown prince. I mean what would one say? 'Unhand that pencil, Sire!'?*

Just when Flora felt her troubles could hardly get any worse, they did.

'Mrs Farrington!' Surprised, she sprung around to be confronted by the Venerable Uncle, his magnificent silk robes and equally spectacular moustache gleaming in the sunshine.

'Venerable Uncle,' she stammered, thinking, not for the first time, what a stupid title it was and wondering if a little nod of the head would be courteous or over the top.

Keeping her eyes fixed on his portly presence, mentally she reviewed the touching scene she had just witnessed: the princely heir apparent rapturously studying beautiful maid with dog. She shuddered. Keen to prevent a diplomatic incident in the studio, if not the Stans, she took a few strides towards the safety of the château and away from the dangers of the studio. Obligingly, he followed.

His piggy eyes beneath his flyaway eyebrows were anything but friendly when he spoke. 'Mrs Farrington, as you probably know I was totally against your playing the role of the princess's guardian on this important trip.'

Honesty compelled Flora to blurt out, 'Well no!'

Flora felt Dorothy shift uncomfortably, evidently embarrassed at her mistress' gaucheness.

'As you have probably gathered, I have my doubts about the suitability of the match. The princess is so headstrong, I cannot see her making a suitable consort for the crown prince. At the very least the young princess should be guided by someone who is more…' There was a painful pause while he surveyed her and searched for a fitting adjective. Flora could have helped him by coming up with many derogatory descriptive words which she thought summed her up rather well, but he didn't give her the chance, adding simply, '…educated in the sensitivities of the Stans.'

He tilted his head on one side and the sun glinted on the jewels around his neck and the silk of his robe. He appeared to want Flora to comment but she couldn't think of anything to say. She was surreptitiously watching Dorothy sniffing his left foot in its curl-toed shoe and half hoping the faithful hound would decide to bite it.

Dorothy failed to oblige, and the Venerable Uncle continued, his tone menacing, 'It would be most unfortunate if anything were to happen to your ward. You must be vigilant.'

A frisson of fear stabbed at her spine and Dorothy growled. *Gosh! In a second or two, and with a few well-chosen words, the Venerable Uncle has transformed from a vaguely comical figure to a menacing force.*

A discreet cough broke the mood. Roberts, the butler, was beside them, his suit pressed and his manner deferential.

'Sire,' he bowed to the minor royal before turning to Flora. 'Madam, I believe you left these in the dining room. I thought you might need them.'

In his hand he held out a pair of Flora's white summer gloves. Flora stared at them before she gushed with no trace of dignity, 'Oh, rather! I do have a frightful habit of leaving my gloves strewn about in odd places but fortunately, Anne, my lady's maid, seems to have an endless supply of fresh ones.'

She finished with a weak grin and registered the Venerable Uncle gawking at her in amazement and Roberts regarding her with fatherly indulgence.

With an effort, she took a breath and regained what little dignity she could muster. 'Thank you, Roberts,' she smiled at him, hoping to convey to him how grateful she was for the interruption. She took the proffered gloves.

Roberts addressed the Venerable Uncle; he was rather more regal than the rounded royal as he stated, 'Sire, may I accompany you back to the château where I believe Prince Parviz is looking for you?'

With ill grace the Venerable Uncle departed, escorted by Roberts, leaving Flora to wonder, *Is Roberts simply the most efficient butler in Paris, finding the time to personally deliver errant gloves to careless guests or is there more to his actions than that? Is he less of a butler and more of a knight in shining armour?*

She paused on the path pondering which way to go. Dorothy tugged on her lead, keen to follow a delicious scent into the flowerbed.

Flora glanced back in the direction of the studio. *I don't think there is a lot I can do there; I don't want to risk another dog fight between the Pekingese Venus and Dorothy, besides which I'm not sure what I could do to disrupt the budding romance with Amelie present.*

Out loud she said, 'Come on, Dorothy, let's go and find Firuza in the château. I have been meaning to take in the view from the balustrade, I've heard it's quite magnificent. One can see Paris and its surrounding forest.'

CHAPTER SEVEN

For Anne it was a new and not totally unpleasant experience to have an extremely good-looking young man studying her. His dark fine features could have stepped straight out of Hollywood and as for those grey eyes flecked with blue, well, she had never seen anything like them. To her mind, the fine line of his scar only emphasised his chiselled-featured good looks. However, she could have done without the wheezing Pekingese on her knee, and she would have preferred not to have the dotty artist in the room. Anne wasn't sure if her eccentricity was because she was French, aristocratic, or simply a by-product of being an artist. Her murmurs of, 'Those exquisite lips, such cheekbones…' while she sketched were a little off-putting but, as Anne's mother would say, 'You can't have everything in this life.' And Anne had to admit that she'd rather spend the morning sitting still with her thoughts than washing Mrs Farrington's delicates.

There was no denying it, the crown prince was quite something. Anne risked a surreptitious glance at him from beneath her long lashes. She looked in his direction, taking care not to move her head and incur Madame Amelie's wrath. His hair was thick and black, he had a fine nose and his fingers while he sketched were elegant, a bit like a pianist. She felt a flutter of some unidentified emotion as she realised that he was focused solely on her. With his pencil tip he was tracing her every line.

She gave herself a mental shake and could hear her mother's voice saying, 'Beautiful is as beautiful does.' She'd been referring to a man called Bill in the village rather the crown prince, but Anne felt the principle was sound. As her mother had explained to Anne when Bill had come round wanting to court her, 'I'll grant you that boy has looks but a pretty face won't put coals on the fire.' She regarded the prince intently as she wondered if a prince puts coals on the hearth or if they had someone to do it for them.

He looked up, a flash of mesmerising intensity, and their eyes locked for a fleeting second. Anne's stomach clenched and she felt a hot burning flush flood her body. She knew she was blushing and hastily stared down at the dog on her knee. She took slow breaths to calm her soul.

Her mind drifted back to their first meeting, in the garden. She checked herself; that may have been the first time they had actually spoken, but she had been acutely aware of him watching her, actually staring at her, when they first arrived at the château.

It had been a long journey. Nanny had complained for most of it, the princess had been pinch-faced, as well she might be, a lamb being led to slaughter with no say in the matter. Only Mrs Farrington had been unsullied by the travel; apart from a moment of queasiness crossing the Channel, she had been engrossed in some romance which Nanny had described as a 'penny dreadful'.

When they had eventually arrived at their destination, the château was magnificent and as pretty as any fairy-tale castle with its round towers and pointy roofs.

No sooner had Anne stepped out of car and onto the gravel, she had been aware of being watched. She'd glanced over to the reception committee, the debonair count, the rotund uncle in all his robes, and two extremely good-looking young men. The slightly taller of the two boys was looking not at his intended bride, Firuza, but over at Anne.

They did not speak to each other until the next day when they met, by chance, in the garden. Anne had found a small bench, hidden away in the corner, sheltered by blossom trees. She had felt certain no one would find her here and that she could safely indulge in a moment or two of reading.

She hadn't heard his approach and had no idea how long he'd been watching her when in a gentle voice he'd enquired, 'What are you reading?'

His tone and manner had been so natural that it hadn't occurred to Anne to be embarrassed until she replayed the scene in her mind later.

Quite carelessly she'd tossed the book down beside her and complained, 'It's T.S. Eliot's 'The Wasteland' but I can't say I'm enjoying it.'

A smile lit up his face, and his grey eyes sparkled. Sitting down beside her, he chuckled and commented, 'It's not exactly jolly.'

They had sat in companionable silence for a moment of two, listening to the birds singing and content in the surroundings, before he'd asked, 'Do you like Yeats?'

'The Irishman?' she'd enquired, glancing at him sideways as he sat beside her on the little garden bench. When he nodded, she shrugged. 'Can't say I've ever read him.'

The crown prince had smiled. 'I'll lend you my copy.'

Anne was about to say 'Ta' but corrected herself. 'Thank you.'

Once more they rested in an easy silence, both relaxed and serene.

Then in a soft voice, he'd stated, 'This is a good spot to read but I came out to sketch.'

He took out a small notebook and a pencil.

'May I see?' she'd asked, and he handed the small leather-bound book over. Anne, with the greatest care, began looking through it. She turned each page with deliberation. She allowed herself time to enjoy each image.

There was a plethora of exquisitely executed sketches, ranging from a morose gorilla in a cage to a tired charlady scrubbing a step. The very last sketch of all was of Anne herself as she stepped out of the car when she arrived at the château. She paused, regarding it, silently nodded, and without comment handed it back to him. Somehow, she had known that drawing would be there. It seemed only natural he would record the first time he'd seen her.

Her thoughts went to Firuza – she checked herself – to the princess. She must remember Firuza was a princess just as Dimash was a prince. She'd overheard Mrs Farrington complaining to Nanny how medieval and inhumane it was that the poor child, meaning Firuza, was to be deprived of an education and forced to marry someone against her will just because she was a princess. Anne wondered whether Mrs Farrington ever complained to Nanny that Anne couldn't get the education she craved or marry any man she chose just because she was a lady's maid. Somehow, she doubted it.

She abandoned her thoughts of the injustices of birth and brought her mind back to the studio by risking another peek at him. He was looking down intently at his sketchbook, his movements light and certain. She considered the unusual contrast of his dark skin and those dazzling eyes and wondered if one would ever get used to it.

Her mind flitted back to that morning when they had met by chance – or was it chance? Anne was beginning to think that perhaps they each had a sense, an instinct, about where the other was. Sometimes she even suspected they each knew what the other was thinking and feeling. So, it had been that morning when they had met after breakfast in the shrubbery. He had handed her his book of Yeats' poetry in a green binding. Their hands had touched, a soft brush, gentle as a spring breeze, but the jolt of electricity that passed between them made her draw in her breath. He'd looked into her violet eyes, half smiling, half serious. He'd felt it too. Confused, Anne had mumbled her thanks and hurried away.

She'd had an hour or two alone with her thoughts before Madam Amelie, loud and brash, had come and sought her out in the laundry of all places.

Madam Amelie, with her flamboyant clothes flapping and her wild red curls all over the place, had borne her off as if she was some hunting trophy. Anne was well aware of Mrs Farrington's many failings, but she was glad she didn't go around looking so unkempt. Anne would have been ashamed to have her mistress seen like that in public.

All the while, as Madam Amelie led Anne to the studio, she explained that she had Mrs Farrington's permission to draw her.

Mrs Farrington's permission? As if Anne's body wasn't her own to say who could and could not sketch it.

They were just exiting into the sunshine of the garden when

they had met Dimash. Anne didn't look directly at him, and she knew intuitively that he would avoid making things obvious to Madame Amelie. He would so fix his eyes and attention on the artist that she would never suspect that Anne and he were… What were they? Anne's stomach clenched and she bit her lip trying to label what she felt.

'Anne, dear, do relax your face.' Madam Amelie's crisp voice cut across the studio, bringing Anne back to the here and now.

Venus, that most voluptuous of Pekingeses, snuffled on her knee. Anne relaxed her face, careful not to smile as she thought of the way Dimash had exchanged pleasantries with Madame Amelie before enquiring where they were going. 'The studio? How interesting, do you mind if I join you?'

Madam Amelie evidently did mind and very much, but she could hardly decline. Anne had to suppress a giggle as she realised that it was 'a princely perk' – people had to agree to your smallest requests.

CHAPTER EIGHT

It was probably just as well that Flora wasn't privy to Anne's thoughts; as the saying goes, 'ignorance is bliss'. As she sauntered along the path to the château, she was able to admire the spring flowers and their light scent. She brushed aside worries about crown princes and ladies' maids. The memory of her recent encounter with the Venerable Uncle loomed in her mind.

The whole thing felt threatening – but to what end? Where is Busby? I could do with having someone to talk this through with. As a new thought struck her, she felt a wave of joy. *Not to mention the count confirming that he is a footman down – I will need to gloat a bit about that before we can discuss its implications.*

Dorothy was tugging on the lead, keen to go inside and have a little nap after her tiring morning.

Flora glanced up at the roof of the château. *It really is like something out of a children's book of fairy tales, with its medieval towers and pointy roofs – so romantic but I fear keeping the gutters clear would be a nightmare.*

The sun was bright in the clear blue sky. She blinked and raised her hand to shield her eyes. *Yes, there is Firuza, by the flag.*

The princess was leaning against the low balustrade, her hair fluttering, in the breeze. She was gazing out at the view. Flora's stomach turned over – she didn't like heights.

To hide her discomfort, she spoke briskly to Dorothy, 'Come on old girl – I think I ought to just pop up on to the roof and keep an eye on Firuza. I'll leave you in the room. You can have a sleep while I tackle all those stairs.'

Dachshunds have many skills, but surmounting hundreds of steps are not among them, and Flora didn't fancy carrying her up to the rooftop and then back down again.

Having deposited Dorothy happily in her basket, Flora braced herself for the climb. *Praise heaven for comfy shoes.*

It was with some difficulty that she found the correct door for the nearest stairs to the balustrade. It was small and low, hidden behind a smelly old tapestry.

The stone staircase spiralled round inside one of the smaller towers. There were occasional glimpses of countryside through slits in thick wall as she climbed. Flora stoically avoided thinking about how claustrophobic the compact stairs were.

It was with relief that she wheezed onto the final step and creaked open the heavy wooden door. Sunlight and fresh air greeted her. She took several deep breaths and stepped out onto a parapet. With the picturesque towers behind and a low balustrade in front, Flora viewed the rolling countryside. It was a side view, and she knew the princess was just around the corner on the terrace by the billowing flag. The count had proudly informed her that from this vantage point one could see miles of farmland and forest. Flora understood that the opposite side of the château offered an enviable vista of Paris. Her curiosity was piqued, and, despite her ambivalence to heights, she could hardly wait to explore.

Heavens, what a spot! thought Flora rapturously before taking an inadvertent glance down.

She had a fine glimpse of the garden laid out in geometric perfection. It seemed to spin before her, slanting at strange angles while Flora staggered back and found the security of a sloping roof. She tried to dig her fingers into the smooth tiles but, finding it useless, she contended herself with leaning her back against its warmth, shutting her eyes and taking some deep, steadying breaths.

Flora was so careful to avoid heights at all costs that she tended to forget the effect they had upon her. She also had some vague notion that she might grow out of the affliction.

She risked opening half an eye; if she kept her gaze on the horizon, the distant landscape did not spin quite so alarmingly. Even so, her legs seem to freeze, and her breath seemed to come in bursts. She swallowed. *If Boudicca can face the might of the*

Roman Empire, surely I can walk around this rooftop. Emboldened, she started edging her way towards the corner of the château where she hoped to find Firuza. She kept her back pressed against the meagre security of the sloping roof.

After what seemed an age of inching towards her goal, she finally turned the corner and was rewarded with a section of flat terrace and there, beside the flag, was Firuza. She seemed to be leaning into the gust, perilously close to the edge of the low stone balcony.

She blinked. The princess was not alone. Flora's breath was quick and shallow. She felt an instant flood of adrenaline and perspiration washed over her. She squeezed her eyes shut again but when she opened them the same terrifying sight greeted her.

There, just behind the oblivious Firuza, stood the Venerable Uncle. He appeared poised – one little push and Firuza would be over the balustrade and plummeting to her death. Flora had a sudden overwhelming sensation of dread. The flagstones below were beckoning and in her mind's eye she could see Firuza noticing the grotesque figure of the Venerable Uncle all too late, her eyes wide, her arms flailing in desperation, as she fell in slow motion to her inevitable death.

Hands shaking, body trembling, Flora let out a scream and saw both Firuza and her portly adversary swing round. Flora was in too much of a frenzy to take in much about their response, but she could see the whites of Firuza's eyes and her shocked open mouth. Demonic rage suffused the Venerable Uncle's features, his face was puce and his eyes little more than slits.

Flora's voice was a high-pitched squeak as she yelled, 'No! No! No!'

Suddenly her strong instinct for maternal protection outweighed all fear. She focused her eyes on the duo. All fear of heights vanished, and she ran full pelt at the Venerable Uncle. As she ran, she let out an animal-like wail that echoed around the rooftops.

The second before she collided with his portly middle, she saw his eyes widen in disbelief. He tried taking a step back, but he could not escape the impact. Flora herself was surprised by the force with which she hit him. She heard his sharp exhalation and knew him to be winded. As he crashed to the floor, Flora had a brief vision of Humpty Dumpty in her old nursery rhyme book, but she did not allow herself to be distracted.

He lay on his back, his arms and legs waving in the air like an exotic beetle. She leaped onto his stomach, straddling him, and pinning him to the ground.

'Quick, Firuza, help!' shrieked Flora but her young protégée seemed too stunned to move; she was standing immobile, staring with her mouth open.

Flora realised with triumph that the Venerable Uncle was too shocked or winded to put up much of a fight.

First, she thought she was going to cry with relief. *Firuza is safe!*

This feeling was swiftly followed by an emotion quite foreign to Flora. *I did it! I Flora Farrington rescued Firuza! I fought off an evil adversary. I can conquer the world!*

Busby and Roberts came dashing onto the terrace. They were red faced and breathing heavily having run up all the twisting stairs. She lifted her chin in triumph and faced them both defiantly. She knew her stocking tops were showing as she sat astride the bulbous stomach of Abbastan's royalty. *But what matter a flash of stocking in the face of such heroism?* mused Flora contentedly.

Feeling exultant, she was prepared to be modest, perhaps even humble in the face of the adoration she expected. Busby would look at her with admiration, the hint of a tear in one eye. Roberts would be awed and Firuza touchingly grateful.

There was a grunt from the Venerable Uncle; he appeared to be regaining his puff. His breath was gushing through his whiskers and Flora judged it best to vacate her perch.

Confidently and with the suggestion of the offhand, Flora said, 'I think you can take it from here, Busby.'

She slid off the sizeable tummy and, with her new-found dignity, stood up, bending briefly to smooth out the wrinkles in her frock.

She was ready for the praises to begin, but as she looked

from Busby to Roberts and finally at Firuza she had the sickening realisation that no applause was about to be forthcoming.

Busby's eyes were cold and hard while his lips were flattened. That vein on the side of his forehead that always pulsed when he was angry seemed to be working overtime. Roberts was shaking his head. Firuza's response was worse of all; her lip was curled, an imperious sign of displeasure. She even went so far as to avert her eyes from Flora.

While Roberts and Busby helped the spluttering Venerable Uncle to his feet Flora was left thinking, *I can't believe this. What exactly is going on? I have just saved Firuza's life from an evil villain, where's the adoration?*

With a flutter in her stomach, she began to experience her first quiver of doubt.

The Venerable Uncle was now standing. He glowered at Flora and pointed an accusing finger at her, declaring, 'That woman just attacked me.'

Indignation flared as Flora retorted, 'Because you were trying to kill Firuza – I only just stopped you from pushing her over the balustrade.'

The Venerable Uncle seemed to be having difficulty breathing. He went rather puce, and his mouth opened and shut rather like an engorged goldfish before he exploded with, 'You think I was trying to kill the princess? You stupid woman! I was preventing her from falling! And if you had been doing your job properly, she would never have been in such a precarious position or about plunge to her death from a rooftop.'

'But, but, but…' Flora's voice trailed away.

She briefly glanced at Busby for support, but his face was harder than the Venerable Uncle's. Roberts was busy dusting down the portly royal – the tumble had wreaked havoc with his stately robes – and Firuza had her arms folded in front of her and was looking down her nose at Flora.

Flora's shoulders slumped. She thought for a second she was going to be sick. She wished she was anywhere but on that rooftop with the policeman, the butler and two royals.

CHAPTER NINE

'Oh, do tell me again, that bit about how you jumped on top of that pompous twit!' said Nanny between gales of laughter as she mopped the tears of mirth streaming down her face with a hankie. Finally, she gave up all sense of propriety and rolled back on Flora's bed, laughing hysterically.

Flora eyed her coldly, then planted herself next to her. 'You are not helping, Nanny. Actually, it wasn't one bit funny, it was truly horrible.'

Nanny, sensing her sadness, sat up and, with only the hint of a smirk, said, 'Did he bluster?'

Flora sighed, 'No, it was far worse than that.'

'How?'

'Well, he fixed me with his little piggy eyes, one side of his wax moustache had got a bit battered in the struggle and, despite Roberts' ministrations, his robes were covered in dust. He might have looked rather dishevelled, but he was every inch an imperial majesty when he spoke. "Mrs Farrington," he declared, pointing a podgy finger at me.'

'How rude!' muttered Nanny.

'It gets worse. He went on, "To you it might all be some 'jolly jape'." And I must say he did a rather good mock-up of a posh English accent for the jolly jape.'

Nanny tutted, 'Do get to the point, Flora, dear.'

'So, he took a loud breath and announced, "But for some of us this is far more serious, it is a matter of life and death. The princess's wellbeing is of importance for the stability of my homeland. I, Mrs Farrington, was only seven when I witnessed my mother and most of the court massacred in a failed coup. And when I was eleven there was a famine that rendered a third of the population dead from starvation because we did not have the political alliances to bring us aid." By this time, he was well into his stride, his pointy finger was quivering, and he was spitting quite a bit when he spoke.'

Nanny grimaced at the thought.

Flora continued, 'So he glowered at me for a bit, then he puffed himself up like a Bantam cockerel and declared, "I have devoted my whole life to making sure these things never happen again, and you have just made a ridiculous accusation and attacked me."'

There was a silence before Nanny said, 'Gosh, I bet you felt quite a worm.'

'Positively maggot-like,' agreed Flora, her shoulders slumped with dejection and her voice low.

Even Dorothy had deserted her and had slunk under the bed, presumably unable to face her mistress's shame.

Firuza appeared in the doorway. She was still flushed with rage which gave her brilliant green eyes extra sparkle. She held her chin high as, in an authoritarian voice, she announced, 'I have come to inform you that our afternoon trip to Paris has been postponed and if the Venerable Uncle brings forward the wedding because of your stupid actions I will never speak to you again.'

Flora was on her feet. 'Look, Firuza dear, I'm most frightfully sorry if I made a blunder, but I really was trying to save your life. He's against the match anyway so surely he won't bring it forward.'

Firuza hissed a word Flora couldn't catch but judging from the tone she guessed it was a swear word in her mother tongue and a rather juicy one at that. 'Your understanding is pitiful.' Her voice dripped with contempt. She swept out of the room, slamming the door behind her with such force that the glass in the windows shuddered and the crystal chandelier vibrated.

'Firuza!' implored Flora, but her voice was lost in the young woman's fury. Flora's breath caught in her throat. She felt hot and knew she looked flushed as well as flustered.

Giving a bark of a laugh, she looked to Nanny for reassurance.

'Firuza must be being a bit dramatic about the Venerable Uncle bringing forward the official betrothal, don't you think, Nanny?'

Nanny was nonplussed and just shrugged her shoulders in a noncommittal way. 'Time will tell.'

Flora wrinkled her brow and bit her lip. 'I could hardly have acted in any other way.' Frowning and with a slight shake of her head she added, 'I don't see how I could have been mistaken.' With wide eyes she looked at Nanny, who was still resplendent on the bed. 'It certainly looked as if that pompous Venerable Uncle was about to push Firuza over the edge.' She glanced upwards trying to recall each second of the incident. 'I suppose it's just possible he was reaching to save her,' she conceded with reluctance. She gave Nanny a weak smile and with uncalled for jollity added, 'Hopefully it will all blow over. Storm in a teacup and all that.'

Nanny shrugged again but this time said nothing.

Flora slumped onto the foot of the bed. She sat there, the picture of dejection, wrestling with her thoughts until a deferential knock sounded at the door.

'Oh, rats! I really don't want to see anyone,' she whispered while looking imploringly at Nanny.

'I'm not surprised. If I looked like you nor would I,' commented Nanny, who was determinedly not moving from her comfortable position on the bed.

Flora twisted her fingers, in hushed tones she pleaded, 'Couldn't you be a dear and answer the door? Tell them I'm out?'

Nanny rolled her eyes. 'And what will you do? Hide in the armoire?'

Flora cleared her throat and tried to muster a fragment of dignity. 'Actually, I was thinking of the bathroom.'

The knock came again, a shade more persistent.

'You'd better get that,' said Nanny with what Flora thought was annoying insouciance.

Flora stood up, smoothed down her dress, took a breath and opened the door.

Roberts stood there, in all his butler finery. 'Sir Cyril Forsythe is on the telephone for you, Madame, calling from London.'

Flora gulped. 'Right oh!'

Obediently she followed Roberts down long corridors and many stairs. *Really, this walk seems unnecessarily long.* Their footsteps echoed. Flora lifted her chin high and composed her features into what she fancied was suitable for innocent martyrdom. *I can quite see myself as a noble aristocrat sauntering with dignity towards the guillotine.*

Eventually they entered a book-lined room with tall windows that opened onto the garden. Roberts indicated the imposing desk and the terrifying telephone. He threw Flora a compassionate look and murmured, 'His bark is worse than his bite, Madame,' before departing.

Flora stood before the desk for a moment, then rolled back her shoulders and picked up the handpiece. With undue jollity she gushed, 'Hello, Uncle Cyril. How's London? The weather here is simply heavenly.'

There was a crackle on the line.

'Flora, I am not paying a fortune to discuss the weather!'

From his tone, Flora could picture his puce face and contorted features, resembling a walrus with indigestion.

'Yes, Uncle Cyril,' replied Flora meekly.

I wish I didn't sound so much like a chastened schoolgirl.

'Did you or did you not assault one of the Stan's most powerful prelates?'

'Well…' she stalled for time, but Uncle Cyril used the pause for a further attack.

'I cannot believe that you could be so incompetent. Your task was simplicity itself; all you were required to do was to escort the princess as a chaperone and not to stir up a major diplomatic incident.'

Flora was relieved when his flow was disrupted by more crackles down the line.'Oh, dear, I seem to be losing you,' she shouted gleefully into the phone before thrusting the receiver down on its cradle.

She looked up to find the count smiling at her. *Oh, fiddlesticks! When did he come in? And how long has he been listening?* Flora cleared her throat and gave an embarrassed grin.

Oh my, his smiles are very... She lost herself for a moment in the intensity of his gaze – the greying around his temples and the fine lines on his face only emphasised his good looks. *Engaging. Rather like a cat before it springs on a mouse. My, he is standing rather close. Am I imaging it or is he leaning in? But goodness, doesn't his cologne smell heavenly? Sort of pine but manly. I wonder who his tailor is – he always looks so...dashing.*

When the count spoke, it was in husky playful tones. 'Do I gather you have just received a grilling from high office in Whitehall?'

Flora grimaced and side stepped away from him. 'You could say that.'

He gave her a compassionate look, soft with longing, and took a step closer. Flora wrinkled her nose. *Is that a hint of garlic with the pine?*

Her hand was resting on the desk, and she was surprised when he placed his hand over hers. She felt his warmth; her heart quickened, and her stomach knotted.

He stood still, gazing into her eyes. She gulped.

Sounding rather more French than usual, he murmured, 'Perhaps you should spend less time worrying about the princess and more time contemplating your own love life.'

'Oh! Er!' was all Flora could think to say while she blinked up at him.

CHAPTER TEN

'Excuse me! I hope I am not interrupting!' Busby's voice was loud, brusque, and unapologetic.

He stood framed in the doorway, a manila file in his hand and annoyance in his rust-coloured eyes. His tawny hair was more dishevelled than normal, a sure sign he'd been running his hand through the unruly curls while vexed.

Flora sprung guiltily away from the count.

Busby might have addressed them both, but his eyes were firmly fixed on Flora. He was standing extremely tall, taut in every muscle, and his knuckles showed white where he was gripping the folder.

The count looked languidly from Flora to Busby. He raised an eyebrow, and a hint of a smile played around his lips. With a low chuckle he winked at Flora and said, 'Not at all. Mrs Farrington and I can easily resume our conversation later. Now, if you will excuse me, I need to have a word with Roberts about tonight's dinner – it's going to be rather special.'

He brushed past Busby and could be heard whistling his way down the corridor as he went in search of Roberts.

Flora regarded Busby, his lips flattened into a thin line, his eyes flinty, and thought, *I have been berated by Firuza, scolded by Uncle Cyril, and I am certainly not in the mood to be told off by Busby.*

She returned his glare and coldly said, 'You must excuse me as well, I need to…' She couldn't think of anything to say but lifted her chin higher and strode towards the door.

He was considerably taller and larger than her in every way so when he squared his shoulders her route was effectively blocked. Short of pushing past him, she was trapped. Clenching her teeth with outrage and quivering with fury, she scowled at him.

He scowled back. He was breathing heavily and a vein on his temple was throbbing.

Flora's voice was both slightly raised and shaky when she hissed, 'Kindly move out of my way.'

Taking a step towards her and forcing her to retreat into the room, he spat back, 'Why? So, you can go and attack some other foreign dignitary and cause another diplomatic incident?'

Flora chose not to dignify that comment with any response; she simply filled her eyes with as much anger and derision as she could muster.

He clearly got the message and, taking another stride towards her, leant in so close she could feel his hot breath on her neck.

No hint of garlic, just sandalwood shaving soap.

He threw the folder onto the desk and papers, some typed and some handwritten, spilled out. 'Do you know how many months of research and preparation have gone into this mission?'

Well, no – my only preparation was to pop a new toothbrush into my case, but I'm hardly going to tell him that.

Tightening her fists, she aggressively took a step nearer to him; they were so close they were almost touching. 'And what may I ask was I supposed to do, faced with what looked like a life-and-death situation?'

'Call for help! For goodness' sake, woman, it was the obvious thing to do!' His chest was heaving and there was a sheen of perspiration on his flushed face.

'What? And watch Firuza be pushed to her death?' laughed Flora with derision.

'You might have been hurt! Even killed!' he shouted.

Flora shrugged her shoulders dismissively and turned to leave. 'I would have thought that my demise would simplify your professional life considerably, as you obviously have no respect whatsoever for my judgement.'

He grabbed her arm and pulled her towards him. She gasped in surprise. Staring into her face, he said, 'And did it never occur to you that I might be worried about you? When I saw you on that rooftop and thought what might have happened…' He broke off and released his grip on her.

Flora eyes widened, she took a step back and, feeling rather disoriented, she stammered, 'Well, er, no, not really.' While all the time thinking, *Gosh! Busby was worried about ME! What will Nanny say when I tell her?'*

She was just blinking up into Busby's hazel eyes, wondering what her response should be, when there was royal interruption in the shape of Crown Prince Dimash.

He cleared his throat, then, in his clipped upper-crust voice, he explained, 'Please excuse me, I didn't realise anyone was in here. I need to make a phone call.' There were tight strained lines around his eyes. His normally composed features were taut. 'My father, the emperor, wishes to speak to me.'

Once more Flora sprang away in guilty haste from a good-looking man. 'Oh?' she enquired.

She looked intently at Crown Prince Dimash; he looked back at her.

I was rather hoping the prince would spill all the diplomatic beans going, but, judging from his pinched face, he isn't in a chatty mood. I wonder if his father, the emperor, has heard about my little faux pas. I hope he isn't too miffed. I don't suppose it's appropriate to send him my love. With a sudden wave of nausea, she thought, *Gosh, I hope it's not in connection with bringing the betrothal forward.*

The prince was still regarding her, but she only took the hint that he wanted her to leave when Busby firmly took her arm and led her away, saying, 'If you will excuse us, sir, we will leave you to make your call in private.'

CHAPTER ELEVEN

Skeleton staff notwithstanding, Roberts has certainly outdone himself tonight, thought Flora as she entered the dining room and surveyed the long table resplendent with silver and crystal. Candles lit the whole room, sparkling like rare jewels. Roses added colour and scent to the atmosphere.

Busby's hand brushed briefly against hers as he passed, and Flora felt herself blush.

She was rather pleased with her frock. It was pink, showed a daring amount of leg, and had crystals on the front panel. Firuza had gone for a modern, fuller skirt. *But black? So inappropriate for a young thing. It's almost as if she's in mourning.* At the thought, Flora glanced from sombre Firuza to the two princes and was dismayed to see they looked equally tense. *As does Sister Claire, but then she is always stiff. Amelie seems unfazed, but, then, she is clearly in a world of her own. Interesting colour and costume choice; not many people would opt for turquoise and fuchsia with red hair.*

Sister Claire was explaining to the count that the priest was confined to bed with a headache and Roberts was silently removing the place setting.

Flora smiled at Busby and hoped he'd say something about her dress along the lines of 'Flora you look spectacular. A goddess of beauty and sophistication.' But he just nodded in her direction and remained professionally aloof.

The only two people who were in jovial form were the count and the Venerable Uncle.

I say, the Venerable Uncle may be ignoring me, but I have to admit he really does look magnificent. What amazing gold-threaded silk – he positively glitters. Crimson and gold are definitely his colours, and I'm so pleased he has waxed those spectacular moustaches of his. Gosh, and what I wouldn't give for all those pearls!

Flora was so focused on the resplendent man that she gave a small start of surprise when she felt the count take her elbow and murmur, 'Allow me to show you to your chair.'

His hands lingered longer than was necessary on Flora's bare arm before he departed for his other hosting duties.

When everyone was seated, the count beamed at the assembly. 'The Venerable Uncle would like to say a few words.'

Flora's pulse quickened, she tensed and scanned the room. Dimash's tight, stoical demeanour did little to calm her nerves. Parviz was looking anxiously at Firuza; she was the embodiment of dignified terror. Flora felt sick as she took in the deliberate way Firuza held her chin high while she struggled to stop the trembling of her lower lip.

Smiling, the Venerable Uncle staggered to his feet, his scarlet sash heaving under the strain. With great pomposity, he cleared his throat before gazing around the room with his piggy eyes. 'It is with great pleasure that I announce the official betrothal of the princess to the crown prince.'

On cue, Roberts appeared with champagne. The effervescent bubbles in the elegant flutes sounded loud in the shocked silence.

Feeling sick and with her heart racing, Flora glanced over to Firuza, who had paled and was gripping the table in front of her so tightly her knuckles showed white. She was trembling and biting her lip to hold back the threatening tears. Flora couldn't help thinking, *She is little more than a child.* Finding her own inability to help the young princess unbearable, Flora looked away, only to be confronted by the equally distressing sight of Crown Prince Dimash who was staring straight ahead with unseeing eyes and swallowing repeatedly.

Next, Flora's eyes alighted on Sister Claire who looked like a rather annoyed marble statue of an obscure saint. Her lips were rigid and her eyes steely. Flora thought she heard her mutter something about 'roof tiles' and presumed she was lamenting the loss of the funds Firuza would have brought to her abbey.

Prince Parviz was showing none of the dignified control of Sister Claire and his brother; he was evidently angry. He glowered at his uncle. Fire flashed in his brilliant blue eyes. Flora noted that beneath the table his fists were clenched so tightly his knuckles showed white. When she sensed he was about to leap to his feet, she instinctively put a restraining hand on his arm. He glanced at her; she gave a slight half-shake of her head. It was a small gesture, but it was enough to break his impetuosity. *And thank heavens for that! An angry scene isn't going to help anybody.*

A minor complication diverted, Flora frantically attempted to bring some order to her tangled thoughts. *Goodness, so the others were right! The Venerable Uncle will put aside all his misgivings about Firuza in order to secure stability in the Stans. At least Uncle Cyril will be happy.* She frowned at the thought. Her eyes flicked from Firuza to Dimash to Parviz and she added, *But at what cost?*

She looked to Busby for some reassurance, but he was avoiding making eye contact with her. His face was emotionless, totally neutral, and she could not fathom what thoughts were going on behind those hazel eyes.

Somehow, they managed to stumble through the evening. The conversation was stilted, to say the least. It was largely carried by Amelie, the count, and the Venerable Uncle.

Amelie, having downed two glasses of champagne with inelegant haste, had become both loud and animated. Her flowing robes threatened to send cut-glass and silverware crashing to the floor with each flamboyant gesture she made.

'How romantic!' she gushed with rapture. She waved her hands in the air with a vigour that caused her wild red curls to become even more untamed. She leant toward the Venerable Uncle, attempting an air of girlish coquettishness, and with much fluttering of eyelashes suggested, 'How about a life size portrait in oils of the happy couple to commemorate this auspicious occasion? You must have lots of palace walls at your home, or should I say *homes*, back in the Stans. I bet they are simply aching for a bit of art.'

The Venerable Uncle recoiled in horror, and the count, sensing an awkward social situation, intervened, 'The Venerable Uncle and I have already discussed making this wonderful news public.' He paused and smiled with satisfaction. 'We will hold a grand ball here, with all the dignitaries in attendance.'

The crown prince looked taken aback. He ran a hand through his thick black hair, his eyes took on an unnatural brilliance, and when he spoke his voice struggled to get past the constriction in his throat. 'When?'

The Venerable Uncle twisted the end of his moustache and in a low, almost threatening, voice announced, 'Soon, the sooner the better. We will all leave immediately afterwards for home. The festivities for your official betrothal will be extremely beneficial for the political stability in the Stans.'

The count jovially added, 'I was thinking we should be able to organise everything in ten days.'

Flora was horrified. *Ten days? That's not going to give me enough time to find a way out for Firuza! And what about that body in my bedroom? I need to get to the bottom of who killed him and then removed his body. After all, there is a killer somewhere loose in this château. AND, most importantly, how on earth will I find a frock to wear at such short notice?'*

Sister Claire brightened. 'We were scheduled to have returned to the Abbey by then, but perhaps we could delay our plans for a week.'

There was a wistful look beneath her wimple and Flora surmised, *Here is a cleric who likes a party.*

Amelie clasped her hand together in girly glee. 'A ball! How simply marvellous! It will be just like the old days! We used to have such spectacular balls before Mother died.'

There was a sudden chill in the air and Flora could not quite comprehend the looks exchanged between the count, Amelie, and Sister Claire.

Sourly, Sister Claire remarked, 'Don't be ridiculous, you were so young, you can't possibly remember.'

Amelie drew herself up and was about to retaliate. *Do I detect a sibling squabble about to erupt? Why is it that sisters fight with a fury that non-family members cannot begin to fathom?*

Fortunately, before blood could be spilt, the count interjected a lighter note, 'We will have champagne, flowers, and of course there will be dancing.' He fixed Flora with a flirtatious look and purred, 'And, Mrs Farrington, I must insist you dance with me.'

To her horror, Flora felt the heat creep up her neck, and she knew she was blushing an unbecoming crimson. With all eyes on her, she looked down at her lap and murmured something incoherent and noncommittal.

Not for the first time, Flora wondered, *Why can't I be cool and reserved in these situations rather than a gauche schoolgirl?*

Flustered, she glanced up just in time to catch Busby rolling his eyes, unimpressed by either Flora or the count.

He cleared his throat, 'Sir, there is a question of security with a ball.'

The count was unconcerned. 'Quite, quite. More champagne for the good inspector, Roberts.'

The Venerable Uncle nodded, but added, 'That is a discussion for another time. Tonight is for celebration.'

He was beaming but, as ever, there was a chilling coldness in his eyes. Looking at Firuza, who was silent and ashen, Flora couldn't see anything to celebrate.

Eventually, the evening ended. Flora hurried to Firuza's side.

She caught up with her on the stairs. Placing a hand on her arm, she said, 'My dear, I'm so sorry. Can I do anything to help?'

There were tears brimming behind the young girl's eyes as she swung around to face Flora. She spat out, 'I think you have already done more than enough.'

Firuza pulled away and strode up the stairs with determination, leaving Flora deflated.

It was Parviz who comforted Firuza.

'I thought I'd find you up here,' he said gently. She was leaning against the balustrade at the top of the château by the flagpole. It was the exact spot where the incident had happened that had precipitated the advancement of Firuza's doom.

By the light of the full moon, Parviz could see she'd been crying; her dazzling green eyes were puffy and red, and she clasped a limp hankie in her hand.

'Just leave me alone!' she hissed, glowering at him.

Calmly, he enquired, 'Are you always this rude or is it only when you have your future life laid out for you by a pompous oaf? I can go if you like.'

She sniffed, looked him in the eyes, and murmured, 'No, stay.'

Firuza was not sure how long they lingered there silently side by side beneath the stars with just the gentle rustle of the breeze in the trees far below and the occasional call of a distant fox, for company.

When a fresh wave of emotion welled up within Firuza and her gentle sobs grew into a cascade, it seemed only natural that Parviz should embrace her in a warm hug and let her cry against his chest.

Dimash rushed away from the dining room with the same urgency that Firuza had shown. He needed to find Anne, to explain – but what was there to explain? *I love you but I am going to marry someone else.*

As he had hoped she would be, she was sitting on the bench in that secluded part of the garden where they had met before.

She glanced up as she heard him approach but made no move to stand and greet him. She was pale and sad, with a shawl wrapped around her shoulders against the cool of the night.

Dimash felt his heart twist.

'You've heard, then.' He spoke softly and sat down next to her, so close their bodies touched.

A heaviness weighted in her stomach. In an endeavour to not even have the edge of her skirt touch him, she drew in her breath and shuffled a little further from him. She didn't look at him but stared blankly ahead. It took all of Dimash's self-control not to throw his arms around her. He wanted to hold her close and to never let her go but guilt tightened his chest and kept him immobile.

In a cold voice, she said, 'It's all the servants' hall are talking about. Congratulations, I hope you will both be very happy.'

'Oh, Anne, don't!' He tried to clasp her hand, but she pulled away and stood up.

'Now if you'll excuse me, sir, us servants have work to do.' Her voice was painfully frigid, and she held her body with a brittle rigidity.

Devastated, the pitiful Prince watched her stride away. The beauty of the cherry blossom in all its romantic night-time beauty and scent seemed to mock him. The magnificence of the moon and myriad stars only compounded his misery. For an instant, he thought about following her, stopping her retreat, and kissing her until she could only think of him, but what would be the use?

Flora was dejected when she reached her room. Each step took a Herculean effort, her arms hung at her side, her shoulders hurt, and a headache throbbed behind her burning eyes. A strange combination of emotions filled her mind; worry for all the young people whose lives would be irrevocably changed by the announcement of the betrothal and also an aching shame for her own part in it. Duty insisted she see Anne and offer a word of comfort, but Flora's emotional exhaustion made her want to avoid another highly charged interaction.

When she opened her bedroom door, there was no sign of Anne, but there was of Nanny. She was the picture of contentment, sitting with her boots on Flora's counterpane, propped against the many pillows, with a glass of whisky in her hand. Her profusion of grey hair was even wilder than usual, and she had undone the top button of her stiff black dress.

'You've heard, I presume,' said Flora wearily, while kicking off her kitten heels.

'Naturally.' Nanny took another sip of her whisky.

'One of the servants?'

'No, one of Le Brun's men.'

Flora flopped onto the bed. She lay looking up at the ceiling. 'Oh, Nanny, I feel simply awful. Poor Firuza.'

'Well, what are you going to do about it?' asked Nanny in her brisk, no-nonsense voice.

'What can I do?' wailed Flora.

'You can stop feeling sorry for yourself for a start!'

Stung by Nanny's words, Flora rolled onto her side and propped herself up on one elbow so that she could look at Nanny with her eyes wide and her brows furrowed.

'What?' Flora ejaculated. The word was enthused with so much martyred misery that Flora did not see how Nanny could not be flooded with remorse.

Nanny was made of sterner stuff and totally unperturbed. She continued, 'There is still the question of the footman. Don't forget someone in this château is a murderer and if they can kill someone once, they may well do it again. We don't know whether they were motivated by the politics of the Stans or the money the diamonds could raise. Either way, with the deadline of the ball coming up, he or she is bound to act soon. Firuza is in danger. First, we need to make sure her life is not in danger and then we can find a way to make sure that she isn't forced into a loveless marriage.'

CHAPTER TWELVE

The next morning, Flora awoke with a renewed sense of determination. As she lay in her comfy bed, enfolded in lavender scented linen sheets, a thought struck her. *Nanny is quite right, I can't lie around feeling sorry for myself, there is work to be done. I need to get to the bottom of the footman mystery, and I must find a way out for Firuza before the ball.* She paused. *I suppose, I actually need to find an escape for Anne's sake, not forgetting the princes.* She inhaled deeply. *Now, where to start?* Dorothy, sensing her mistress was awake, made small snuffling noises until Flora obediently leant out of the bed to scoop her up.

Dorothy sighed and mumbled, '*Flora is not a bad old stick – of course she is very lucky to have me.*'

As the small dachshund snuggled up to her, Flora continued to ponder the situation. *But where to start?* Bird song floated through her thoughts as did Dorothy's rhythmic snores. Happily dreaming of chasing French bunnies, the dachshund's back leg twitched. Flora smiled as she pictured Dorothy running through the undergrowth. The vision was fleeting; her mind came back to the problem at hand.

It has to be someone in the château. I have an idea. I wonder what was in that folder that Busby so dramatically tossed onto the desk? He said he had done masses of research. Surely, somewhere in all those papers there was a clue as who might be responsible.

'First things first,' she declared to an uninterested Dorothy as she slipped from the bed and softly padded over to her bathroom. She threw open the shutters and let the soft spring scents and the hopeful bird song in. She paused for a moment to breathe and enjoy before turning to run her morning bath. The hot water supply was erratic and the plumbing noisy, but neither deterred her from luxuriating in a tub large enough to accommodate a whole rugby team. With care, she decided to scent it with Floris jasmine oil, thinking it was fitting for spring adventures.

She dressed in a new – and to her mind, extremely becoming – frock. It was red, which suited her dark complexion, and simply cut as a lightweight dress coat, with lapels either side of the V-neck and buttons down the front. A faux camisole and the low-waisted belt added interest to its outline.

Surveying herself in the mirror, she pondered her wardrobe in general. *Much as I want to go long in the embroidered numbers that Madame Chanel has made all the rage, thanks to her army of White Russian refugees, I do feel that this dress suits me rather better than a square-cut Slavic costume.*

Nanny lumbered in just as Flora was admiring herself in the mirror. 'My, don't you look like the cat's whiskers?' she grinned. 'So glad that a bit of the old French *je ne sais quoi* is rubbing off on you.' The French idiom, spoken in Nanny's thick Irish blur, sounded unique. 'Now all you need is a bit of *oh là, là* to spice things up a bit. I wonder where that nice Inspector Busby is?'

'I don't know about *oh là là,* but I do want to have a word with Busby. I've been thinking about what you said last night – he has a rather interesting folder, simply stuffed to the brim with info about everyone here at the château. Surely, in all those facts there will be a clue as to who might have bumped off the footman.'

'Well done, my girl, and while you are questioning Busby, you might as well use it as an opportunity to practise your flirting.'

'Really, Nanny!' exclaimed Flora with a blush. Her high colour was largely due to her having been thinking exactly the same thing.

Nanny continued, 'I'm pleased that finally, after all these years as a widow, you seem to be ready to look forward. I haven't heard you talking to Roger the whole time we've been here so perhaps finally you are going to let the poor man rest in peace.'

Flora grimaced; mention of her long dead husband always did stir her emotions. She could hardly believe that it had been eleven years since his plane had been shot down in the last week of the war, leaving her a very young widow with two infants to care for.

Dorothy, tucked tightly under Nanny's arm, quietly growled, '*Hands off Busby – he's mine!*'

Flora never liked to dwell on unhappy things, so she enquired, 'Changing the subject, Nanny, what are you going to do while I'm questioning Busby?'

'I am going sweet-talk the butler, Roberts. Armed with the finest whisky, my best cigars, and a hot tip for the horse that's bound to win the Arc de Triomphe, I will find out all there is to know about that footman.'

'Gosh, Nanny, you are impressive. I know you are always on top of all the likely winners at English racecourses, but I didn't realise your knowledge extended to the French turf.'

Nanny looked complacent. 'To be sure, it's bound to be an Irish horse. Now you get yourself down to breakfast and Busby.'

Flora finished putting the final touches to her toilette with a dusting of powder and a smudge of rouge before following Nanny out but, while Nanny went to the garden, Flora followed the mouth-watering smell of bacon to the dining room. The dining room was inviting, with the morning sunshine streaming in through the tall windows. The sideboard heaved with silver salvers overflowing with breakfast fare. Fresh fruit and baskets of pastries stood temptingly on the table between small vases of flowers which still sparkled with the morning dew. To Flora's mind, best of all was Roberts. His grey hair pomaded, and his suit pressed to perfection, he was pouring out strong, black coffee.

Busby was at breakfast. *Oh bless, his russet curls are quite untamed by a morning brush. I think I rather like the boyish look.*

There was nothing juvenile about either Sister Claire or the count. *Are they rather heavy-eyed? I suspect one or three too many glasses of champagne last night.*

Sourly, Sister Claire commented, 'It appears that 'the young' – Firuza, Parviz and Dimash – have all elected to have breakfast in bed.'

Flora felt a pang of sympathy for them; last night's news

could not have failed to put them off more uncomfortable dining room meals.

The count languidly raised his coffee cup in greeting. His distinguished features were freshly shaven, and his salt and pepper hair was combed to sleekness. 'The princes have requested the use of a couple of my horses. I understand they plan to go on a long ride later on this morning.' He smiled at Flora. 'You ride, of course?'

'Oh, what, rather, love it,' mumbled Flora, trying and failing to summon up her inner French muse of sophistication and chic.

The count leant towards her, with a wicked twinkle in his eye and his voice low. 'Perhaps you and I could go for a ride later on in the week?'

Flora glanced over at Busby who was giving his croissant rather more attention than it merited. 'Oh, er, spiffing.'

She toyed with her own pastry and mused on what a skeleton staff actually looked like in the château. *So, we have a butler, that ancient chap in the garden, there is a cook and a skivvy and there must be at least one groom. I wonder if we should cast our sleuthing net a little wider.*

She looked up to find Busby's eyes upon her. By tacit agreement they both rose to head towards the sideboard. In honour of the English guests, there were several silver dishes overflowing with bacon, eggs, and sausages.

Flora felt a frisson of energy as their hands brushed against each other in her quest for a fried tomato. 'We need to talk,' she hissed.

He nodded. 'Meet me in the summerhouse in thirty minutes.'

She assented, took her tomato, and returned to the table.

Replete with bacon, eggs, pastries, and fruit, Flora was soon ready for the garden. It was as delightful as ever, with the sun glancing off the gentle spray from the fountain, creating delightful rainbows. The sound of falling water was relaxing and the spray refreshing. Some pink roses had freshly flowered, adding a burst of vibrant colour.

Goodness, what a heavenly scent – I wonder what variety they are? Jolly early to be flowering. Flora was always on the hunt for new plants to augment her already magnificent garden. She stepped over a rake left on the path and walked around a trug filled with weeds. *Traces of the ancient gardener, so he must be somewhere near but no time to search now. I need to press on to the summerhouse and my tame policeman.*

When she reached the summerhouse, she found that Busby was already there, but he was not alone.

Sister Claire, as stiff and prim as her wimple, was sitting upright on the bench, prayer book in hand. Her expression was cold; evidently, she did not appreciate her contemplations being interrupted by Busby.

Before Flora could break in on them with a bright, 'What ho!' she caught a whiff of cologne and felt the count take her elbow.

'Flora, you look quite enchanting this morning,' he purred. 'When I think of you, I always imagine you in a garden like this.'

Startled, Flora blurted, 'Why?'

'Because you are an English rose.'

Flora actually felt embarrassed for him – such an obvious statement she felt was a touch beneath a seasoned flirt like the count.

'I believe you are very fond of gardening,' he continued, his eyes sparkling. 'Just think what you could do with this place. You could bring it back to all its splendour.'

I suspect he is referring to my lavish bank balance rather than my ability with a trowel.

'Your garden is delightful,' she said, rather pleased with how diplomatic but noncommittal she was.

He may be very attractive in his dapper clothes with his distinguished features, but I don't really want to sign up to a lifetime of propping up his ancestral home.

The count was unaware that Flora was mentally putting her lavish cheque book under lock and key so he continued, 'I am so glad that you will be here for the ball; you will be able to see the château alive with people.' He tucked Flora's hand firmly into the crook of his elbow. 'Now, my dear, do let me show you around some more.' He gave her a smug smile. 'With a place like this, there is always more to explore.'

Dorothy gave a low growl which really expressed exactly how Flora was feeling. As he led the reluctant pair away, Flora glanced over her shoulder. *Where is Busby? Typical – just when I need a 'useful chap' he is nowhere to be seen. I just know the count is limbering up for another round of 'This château has been in my family since the dinosaur age.' And heaven forbid that he mentions fathering sons again!*

The count marched purposefully, leaving the flower garden and fountain behind them. With the main château to their right and the sleepy moat on their left, they skirted the side of the magnificent edifice until they were on the other side with the whimsical turrets of the medieval château before them, complete with its impressive portcullis.

The count paused. He evidently hoped the sight of the portcullis would weaken Flora's resolve. He pulled her closer to him and gazed down at her with what she considered to be a quite unnecessary degree of passion. She could see the count was moving in. *I really haven't got time for this!* she thought.

Annoyed more than inflamed, she looked at his smouldering, hawk-like eyes. She forcefully pushed him away while lightly declaring, 'Goodness, is that the time? I really must be going. I have a frightfully important appointment. You must excuse me.'

She almost ran along the gravel paths with Dorothy trotting beside her. To her great relief, he did not give chase. She retraced her steps until she was back on the other side of the main château. The fountain was still tinkling but now both Father Luke and Sister Claire were regarding it. Roberts was having a few words with the Venerable Uncle, and Amelie could be seen in the distance walking Venus.

Flora was delighted when she spotted Busby. He was coming towards her. She did not pause to examine the way she felt warm and happy at the sight of him. She was unaware of how amiably she was smiling.

She noticed a sparkle in his eyes. *And is that a mischievous expression? What is he up to?*

As they passed close to each other, he murmured, 'We can't talk here, this place is like Piccadilly Circus. Meet me out the front of the château as soon as you can – bring your hat.'

'My hat?' she queried, tilting her head on one side. *Goodness! How thrilling! I sense he's up to something.*

He smiled. 'I'm taking you away for an adventure.'

'An adventure?' she pressed, as her pulse quickened, but he was already walking away, whistling.

An adventure? What does one wear for an adventure? I suppose it depends on what sort of escapade he has in mind – after all, hot air ballooning is very different from hiking. Oh, well, I'll just do as he says and hope for the best.

She shrugged and fetched her neat red cloche, her white gloves, and her diminutive straw bag. In the absence of Anne, she entrusted Dorothy to Nanny and sauntered out to the front of the château.

Even here she was not alone, for there were Amelie and Roberts.

Flora quietly regarded them. With a sartorial sigh, she wondered about Amelie's fashion choices. *I know Amelie is an artist but is it really necessary for her to go around with her dress splattered with paint?* Flora's focus passed from fashion to the strange atmosphere that was evident even at this distance. *Roberts looks rather agitated. Goodness, Amelie seems to be giving him a bit of a berating. She is looking a tad Medusa-like with her hair even wilder than usual – and that's saying something, as it isn't exactly tame at the best of times. And poor Roberts may have a calm facial expression but just look at how tightly she's clasping his hand into a fist. I suppose it's not that surprising; she must be a good six inches taller than him!* Flora exaggerated by an inch or two, but she was accurate when she thought, *She is positively looming over him. I think I'll just creep a little closer so that I can hear what's being said.*

With impressive stealth, she manoeuvred herself to a pillar just by the door.

Amelie's voice was shrill, and her expression haughty and superior in the extreme. All her attention was focused on rebuking Roberts. She pointed her finger at him, and her mass of bracelets glinted in the sunshine. 'You thought you'd got away with it, didn't you? But I saw you struggling with that boy's body. Hats off to you – dead weight is never easy.'

Flora's heart was pounding, *Gosh! So, it was Roberts who killed the footman!*

Flora fixed her attention on Roberts and observed his eyes widened and his mouth fall open in a very undignified way. Flora felt a zing of elation. *I say, I'm getting rather good at this sleuthing business. Busby is bound to be impressed.* She allowed herself a moment of indulgence as she imagined him gazing at her with rapt admiration, but her reverie was cut short by Amelie.

'That being said, Roberts, I am prepared to overlook the matter.'

When Roberts spoke, he sounded as surprised as Flora felt, 'You are, Madam?'

Amelie expression was as complacent and as unpleasant as her Pekingese's. 'Yes – in exchange for one or two little favours.'

By this time, Flora's mind was racing with questions. Foremost was, *What favours? Surely more than his slipping her an extra sausage at breakfast?*

For now, Flora's curiosity remained unsatisfied as the sound of wheels on gravel heralded an approaching car and the conspirators scuttled off in opposite directions.

Needless to say, it was Busby. She only permitted herself the briefest of mental laments that his car was modest. She regarded it and swallowed down her disappointment. Even her dearest friends would have to admit that Flora was a car snob – she judged cars not so much by their grandeur but rather by their speed. *I do feel my rather dashing Morgan two-seater would be so much more fitting for an adventure, but still, I must be brave. The Morgan is in the garage at home and when in Rome – or, rather, Paris – one must make do.*

She leapt into the car with alacrity. With her eyes alight, she announced, 'I say, Busby, I know who did it.'

'Did what?' he queried with half a smile.

Exasperated, she babbled, 'the murder, the footman, the body snatching.'

'Who?' asked Busby, with one eyebrow raised.

'The butler!' she declared triumphantly.

To Flora's annoyance, he appeared amused rather than overcome with admiration.

'You can tell me all about it when we are on the road,' was all he said.

CHAPTER THIRTEEN

They swooped – or rather trundled, as the car obviously had very little power – around the drive. Busby nodded at the French gendarmes stationed at the exit.

As they passed through the majestic gates with their ornate ironwork emblazoned with the count's crest, Flora gave out a loud sigh. Busby glanced over to her.

'I didn't realise how oppressive I was finding that place,' she explained with a grin.

He smiled. 'It's good to get away.'

They rattled down the uneven road. The road had its early morning clean look, but Flora suspected that as the day wore on it would become dusty and unkempt. Streaks of thin clouds were scattered over the blue sky and there was a small plane flying far above. In the past, seeing a plane, unfettered and free, she would imagine it was her late husband, Roger, flying it but Nanny was right; she wasn't thinking about him nearly as much. Far from ruminating over her husband's untimely death on the last day of the war, she was surreptitiously looking at Busby.

Is the man not human? For a policeman he doesn't appear to have any curiosity. I offer him the butler on a plate and does he swoop in asking purposeful question? Not a bit of it!

'Alright, Mrs Farrington, tell me all.'

Happily, Flora commenced enthusiastically, 'Well, there I was just innocently waiting for you and who do you think I overheard as good as confessing to murdering the footman?'

Dryly, Busby stated, 'You already mentioned the butler.'

'Well, yes – Amelie confronted him about her having seen him lugging the dead body off. So, what do you know about the butler, Roberts? Surely you had lots of juicy info about him in that rather larger folder you were brandishing in the study the other day.'

'He has only been working for the count for the last eighteen months.'

Triumphantly, Flora exclaimed, 'I knew it! So, he isn't an old and trusted retainer?'

Busby's expression was impassive. 'No, but whatever Amelie saw, I can't believe Roberts can be guilty of anything illicit.'

Affronted Flora glowered at him and demanded, 'Why?'

'Roberts was personally vouched for by Sir Cyril Forsythe.'

'What? Why would Uncle Cyril put in a good word for the butler?'

Busby nodded while carefully slowing to pass a cart ladened with hay being pulled by a heavy horse.

'Oh, that explains it!' said Flora.

'Explains what?' murmured Busby thoughtfully, with a slight shake of his head.

She explained, 'When Roberts was escorting me to the study to get a rollicking from Uncle Cyril, he said that old Uncle Cyril's bark is worse than his bite – which I might say isn't true. Even so, I wouldn't necessarily go on what Uncle Cyril says.'

Busby raised an eyebrow, 'So, why exactly do you believe we shouldn't trust someone who has reached such dizzy heights in the Foreign Office?'

'Charades! He's a total fathead when it comes to charades. You should see the total hash of it he makes of it every Christmas.'

Busby was unimpressed. 'I'm not sure that we can equate diplomatic matters with charades.'

'Really?' replied Flora with a shrug.

Grazing cows were giving way to scattered hamlets. They were heading towards Paris and the closer they got, the traffic was getting heavier. Flora's mind was still racing with questions.

'Look, Busby, there must be something more in that folder of yours on Roberts. Where was he working before? He's pretty ancient; there should be a long list of employers. There is so much to know, like what did he do in the war? Why did an English butler choose to work for a French count in a crumbling château instead of a nice English widow in Bournemouth?'

Busby smiled. 'That's easy. His only relative, a niece, lives nearby. I didn't pay that much attention to his work history seeing as how Sir Forsythe was so for him. I gather he'd worked for one of your uncle's chums right up until his late employer died and I believe he served as that gentleman's batman during the war. Obviously, after what you overheard, I need to look into him, but I can't see why he would want to knock off a footman, especially when, by all accounts, he was very fond of the boy.'

'Money!' exclaimed Flora eagerly. She was leaning towards him and, had he looked at her rather than the road, Busby would have seen that her eyes were glowing. Speaking rather quickly, she continued, 'He was probably helping himself to the famous Abbastani diamonds and dreaming of buying a Panama hat and retiring to Monte Carlo when the hapless footman stumbled upon him.'

Busby was shaking his head, 'It just doesn't add up for him to have had a blameless character all his life only to turn to crime so late. But I will make further enquiries with Inspector Le Brun. The French Police force have been trying to track down Jean le Coeur but to no avail.'

'Who is Jean le Coeur?' asked Flora absently while gazing at some cows looking pleasingly picturesque in a green meadow strewn with buttercups.

Busby carefully slowed down to pass a boy herding some noisy geese. 'Jean le Coeur is the name of your missing footman. Inspector Le Brun has had his men searching for him all over Paris and beyond. They had thought he might have been with a girl he was sweet on, but they tracked her down and she's as baffled as they are. There's no sign of him – he'

Flora's attention was instantly both sparked and outraged. She spluttered, 'Of course, there's no sign of him. Roberts killed him and Amelie saw him disposing of the body.'

Busby nodded. 'So you say, but there is no body, which means no evidence that anything bad has happened to him.'

Flora sighed heavily, while thinking, *This is hardly how I expected Busby to receive my 'hot tip' on who the murderer was.*

Her eyes narrowed as she sourly inquired, 'Well, leaving aside the ridiculous notion that my testimony is not to be trusted, what did Inspector Le Brun tell you about Jean le Coeur? If there was a girl in the background, could it be that Roberts was also passionately in love with her and his motive wasn't avarice but lust?'

Busby laughed. 'You do have the most wonderful imagination.'

'Come on, Busby, tell me what you know about him.'

'He was young, about nineteen.'

Flora snorted. 'I could have told you that.'

'Both his parents worked for the count's family, but they died in the terrible flu outbreak just after the Great War. He was only a baby, and the count's parents took an interest in him – especially the count's mother – until her early death.'

'Not much of note there. Just out of interest, when and how did the count's mother die?'

They were approaching Paris, and the hamlets were growing into sizeable villages. Busby carefully negotiated a small boy whose ball had rolled into the road before answering. 'She fell from the château parapet at the last ball that was held there – hence the significant looks between the count's sisters at the mention of another ball.'

Flora thought of Firuza on that same parapet and shuddered.

'Now, can we stop talking shop and just enjoy the day?' enquired Busby good-naturedly.

'Just one more question, what did you find out about Amelie?'

Busby was dismissive. 'Nothing there.'

Flora was virtuously outraged. 'Nothing but her not being shy of a bit of blackmail!'

Busby suppressed a grin and nodded. 'Our records show that she doesn't make much money as an artist.'

Flora snorted. 'I gathered that – after all not many middle-aged women would voluntarily live with their brother.'

There was not much further to drive before they arrived at

their destination.

'Montmartre!' declared Flora with delight. 'Home to windmills, artists and a vineyard.'

'Not to mention a fairly sizeable cathedral,' laughed Busby as he parked near some shady trees to one side of the Sacré-Coeur.

'I've never been to this part of Paris, and I have always wanted to visit it,' exclaimed Flora, stepping out of the car and onto cobbles.

They wandered over to the front of the cathedral and admired the view of Paris from its hilltop vantage point, then they turned around to appreciate the cathedral's white domes, pristine against the blue sky. It stood proud and unapologetic.

Shielding her eyes from the glare of the sun, Flora commented, 'It's hard to believe this was build out of turbulence and war.'

'Shall we go inside?' asked Busby, reaching for her hand, and leading her up the steps.

As they pushed open a heavy side door, their nostrils were assailed with the scent of incense and polish.

Busby paused to dip his fingers in holy water and crossed himself.

'You're Catholic?' blurted out Flora before she could check herself. Busby flushed and she stammered, 'Of course you are, your mother was French.'

A slight embarrassment hung in the air between them. There was still a stigma attached to being Catholic rather than good old Church of England – another black mark against him, as well as his class.

'Nanny is Catholic,' announced Flora, making the situation worse.

A couple of improbably-young priests walked past. They were fresh faced and sleek in their robes.

Ever quick to admire beauty, Flora smiled. 'I always think your lot wins out in their get-up – so much more sophisticated than our sack-like vestments.'

Busby gave a wry smile. 'I don't think that's the point.'

Flora shrugged. 'Shall we look round?'

He nodded and they quietly wandered through the cool of the cathedral. Flora found the subtle light filtered through the narrow stain glass windows calming. Glorious blue and gold colours were repeated around the building. Divine organ music surrounded them. Flora craned her neck to look at the angels high above. She drew in her breath at the beauty of the mosaic in gold and rich red which adorned the central dome.

'More than a hint of the Byzantine,' whispered Busby, and she nodded.

At a side altar, she dropped a coin in the donations box and lit a candle for Roger. Busby watched, understanding, but said nothing.

When they left the sanctuary of the cathedral, they were assailed by the bright sun and the exuberant yelling of a group of children running around, excited to make their bright balloons float behind them.

'Let's explore,' suggested Flora, and Busby nodded.

She gave him an appreciative glance. *He's very easy company. Thank goodness he doesn't find it necessary to be forever explaining things to me. I do get so tired of men feeling I am there to be pontificated at.*

There were the usual relics of the war, women in widows' black, men sitting idly on benches with trousers or sleeves pinned where limbs should have been, but there were also vibrant flowers on a market stall, a canopy overhead to keep them fresh. Vibrant tulips of red, yellow, pink, and white stood in buckets along with flamboyant, frilly-edged parrot varieties. There were pillowing clouds of yellow mimosa which reminded Flora of the warm Mediterranean. She lingered over the delicate bouquets of lilies of the valley, exquisitely cool, fresh, and fragrant. The blooms' mingled scents hung in the air. Nearby was a vegetable stall. The stallholder had every possible vegetable, from red tomatoes to cool cucumbers to orange carrots with their curly green tops still intact, and had arranged them with all the artistry of a grand master.

They meandered up and down steep cobbled streets, pausing to admire a windmill here, a languid cat there, and eventually they came to a halt by a vineyard where the vines curled elegantly and a small man in dark blue tunic and pantaloons was working steadily, his head protected by an old straw hat and his feet in sturdy boots.

'Time for some refreshments?' suggested Busby.

'You read my mind,' laughed Flora, leading the way to an inviting café she had spotted earlier.

Over a glass of wine and with the sound of SacréCoeur's Savoyarde bell ringing, Busby enquired, 'Who is your favourite French artist?'

Flora considered for a moment before saying, 'Sitting here, I want to say van Gogh, but I think really it's Monet. And you?'

'It's a bit like music – it changes depending on the mood I'm in.' He took a sip of his wine while he considered his answer. 'Van Gogh's colours are so vibrant they do rather stir the soul.'

Flora nodded. 'Like his depiction of Montmartre's famous windmills, eye-catching to say the least. I must say I adore his sunflowers; they are so happy.'

He looked at her intently, smile lines emphasising the sparkle in his auburn eyes. 'Much as I admire van Gogh, I think if I was choosing a work to live with—'

Flora interrupted, 'On one's kitchen wall, so to speak.'

He cocked an eyebrow and grinned. 'Interesting suggestion, as I don't suppose you spend much time in your kitchen, but I know what you mean. So, for my kitchen wall it would have to be Renoir. My favourite is his depiction of that open-air dance.'

Flora nodded happily and leant forward. 'I know the one, frightfully jolly.'

His gaze was direct as he mirrored Flora and also leaned in closer to her across the spindly table. Flora felt her stomach tighten at his proximity. His voice was low and had a hint of being husky as he added, 'I've always rather liked how he paints women.'

Flora was lost for a moment in his gaze. *Gosh! Is that pounding my heart? I do hope he can't hear it. Come on, Flora, pull yourself together! Try to pretend you are unmoved.*

She laughed lightly. 'How funny, I've always thought that if I could ask one artist to paint me it would be him.'

She broke off as she suddenly realised, *Goodness, Busby really is VERY close. Talk about intimate.* With a start, she sprung back in her chair and looked away. Flushing, she stammered, 'Silly, really.'

A heavy silence descended between the pair, which, rather to Flora's annoyance, appeared to bother her more than him. While she tapped her toe and frantically looked around for a new topic of conversation, he simply leant back in his chair and took a sip of his wine.

Somewhere close by someone was cutting grass.

Keen to break the silence, Flora commented, 'I always love the smell of grass being cut – it's a real sign of summer.'

'It makes me think of my father,' commented Busby as he took another sip of wine.

At the mention of a hint of horticulture, Flora perked up. 'He was keen on gardening?'

Busby laughed. It was a deep, rich, relaxed belly laugh and, when he'd regained his composure, he explained, 'You could say that; he was head gardener for Lord Sanbury in Norfolk.'

'Oh,' said Flora wishing that she didn't feel a trifle perplexed. 'And your mother?'

'She was a French governess to Lord Sanbury's daughters.'

'Oh,' said Flora again and then, before she could check herself, she murmured, 'That explains it.'

To her consternation, Busby had heard her. 'Explains what?'

While she struggled to think of how to phrase her thoughts in an inoffensive way, he chortled, 'Why I'm not a total Philistine?'

Flora flushed and muttered, 'Well, yes.'

'My mother was a big influence, it's true, but then I was very fortunate. Lord Sanbury took an interest in my education and even paid for my scholarship to the local grammar school.'

CHAPTER FOURTEEN

While Flora and Busby were relaxing in Montmartre, the two princes had found their own amusement and their own companions. Far from Parviz riding with his brother, he had stolen away with Firuza while Prince Dimash had carried off a small craft from the boat house and Anne from the laundry.

Firuza had been standing on the parapet, with her shoulders drooped and eyes swollen. She glowered at Parviz when he approached, his face brimming over with mischievous glee. She was not in the mood for boyish enthusiasm. She felt as old and cold as the Himalayas and a million miles removed from anything that could be thought of as light-hearted.

He called her name, and she curled her lip and lowered her eyebrows. A small worry line edged between her brows as she pinched them together and said nothing. Undeterred, he grinned, his blue eyes sparkling like the sun on the Mediterranean Sea.

'You can glare at me all you like but I've come to take you away.'

Firuza was confused but Parviz pulled her by the arm towards the staircase. He laughed quietly and whispered, 'The count thinks Dimash and I are going for a ride together.'

'And you're not?' asked Firuza without much interest.

Parviz chuckled, 'Hardly – Dimash has his own adventure planned.'

Despite herself Firuza's curiosity was pricked. She glanced over at Parviz. He was grinning broadly. 'It's all arranged, I just need you to put on riding togs and to sneak out to the stable gates without letting anyone see you.'

Firuza hesitated for a moment and then gave herself over to being carried away by Parviz. Within twenty minutes, she was clad in breeches and boots with her long hair hidden by a cap.

The number of horses the count owned was small in comparison to the lavish size of his stables but there were a couple of magnificent animals. The moment Firuza sat on the bay, she knew she was in for a glorious morning. Her mount was excited to be off and would have jiggled around as Firuza adjusted girth and stirrups, but he calmed as she uttered soothing words. Parviz was on a towering sixteen-hand grey.

As they walked side by side away from the château, their hooves clicking on the cobbles, Firuza felt her worries floating away with the wisps of clouds overhead. They turned off the road and trotted up a tree-lined track, the sun filtering through the new, translucent leaves. The air smelt fresh with no hint of the château's mustiness. Everywhere Firuza looked there were signs of the hope of summer: a pair of butterflies danced their courtship; the birds were singing, and she felt a glimmer of hope somewhere deep in her heart.

She felt a surge of total certainty in herself, supreme confidence in her own abilities, as she urged her horse into a canter.

Parviz was smiling, encouraging his animal to keep pace. Firuza was laughing now as she pushed her horse to gallop, the sound of their hooves changed to the familiar rhythm of thunder, and over that sound, she could hear Parviz was laughing too. The wind in her face refreshed her soul. When her hat flew away, leaving her long hair streaming like a banner behind her, she only laughed more.

They crested a hill and, puffed, they pulled up.

As they and their mounts regained their breath, Firuza looked out at the view. Parviz regarded her, though perhaps 'regard' is too mild a word to describe the rapt concentration with which he took in the line of her face, her every feature and gesture.

He felt a ridiculous surge of pleasure that he had been able to lift her out of her turmoil even if it was only for a moment.

Eyes still gleaming, Firuza indicated to the far horizon where black, threatening clouds were gathering. 'Looks like we are in for a storm.'

Parviz didn't want her to suggest that they ought to go back to the prison of the château. Relieved, he spotted below them an isolated barn nestling by some trees. 'Let's shelter there until it passes. It will only be a shower.'

They walked their horses slowly down the hill, allowing them to cool off. They reached the cavernous doorway just as the first rumble of thunder rolled across the valley. The barn was light and airy with the scent of old hay, and a surprised mother hen was the only resident. She clucked indignantly and hurried her fluffy brood away.

Parviz leapt from his horse and was at Firuza's side before she had time to dismount. 'Madam, allow me!' He clicked his heels together in a military salute before reaching up his hands towards her.

She hesitated, noting that his eyes were an extraordinary, vivid blue and right now they were twinkling. She felt the rising danger within her and, in a moment of decision, slid down from the horse and into his arms.

He held her.

Briefly, she allowed herself to enjoy the sensation of being safely cradled in his strong arms, but the nagging voice in her was too strong to be ignored for long.

'I think you are taking liberties.' She spoke lightly but there was an edge of seriousness in her tone.

He looked down into her green eyes. She saw surprise followed by anger.

Abruptly, he dropped his arms away from her. He said coldly, 'If you don't want me to,' and turned to walk away.

Confused by her own tangled feelings and by his reaction, she hurriedly made the few steps it took to stand in front of him, barring his retreat. He stopped and the corner of his mouth quirked into a half-smile.

Her hair fell in cascades around her shoulders and her cheeks were rosy from the ride. She raised a teasing eyebrow and, looking him directly in the eyes, stated, 'I never said I didn't like it.'

He swallowed, not sure what he had unleashed.

She took a step closer, their eyes locked, and then she took another step, and suddenly they were so close their toes touched, and he could feel her breath on his face.

He closed his eyes as she leant in towards him. He could feel his heart thumping in his chest but, instead of gently placing a kiss on his lips, Firuza cracked a laugh and pushed him away. Her voice ringing with mirth, she triumphantly declared, 'I got your hopes up, didn't I?' while running away towards the safety of an empty stall.

Opening his eyes, he blinked in surprise. She glanced back at him over her shoulder, challenging him, teasing him as she ran away.

Outside, the thunder rumbled, and the gentle pitter patter of rain gave way to heavy pounding on the barn roof and the dry earth outside the door. Inside, the horses moved restlessly; one gently whinnied.

Parviz paused, for a moment unsure, before, with a surge of excitement, he gave chase, calling, 'Hey Firuza, you'd better hope I don't catch you.'

Firuza laughed and dodged behind some hay. Parviz lunged at her, missing by a whisper, and stumbled. She guffawed with mirth and ran outside into the rain. He gained on her as they both ran across the parched ground towards a gnarled oak tree. He caught her hand and spun her round to face him.

Pressing her back against the tree trunk, he leant against her, and she reached her arms up to encircle his neck. With heaving breath and eyes open, she gave him a smouldering smile. 'What now?'

Was that momentary surprise she read in his Mediterranean blue eyes? She let her arm slip from his neck and rest on his upper arm, taut beneath its thin covering. She briefly wondered when her spindly playfellow had metamorphosed into a man. She felt her heart quicken as he firmly encircled her waist and pulled her against him, squeezing the breath out of her. As a small gasp escaped her lips, his hand cupped her cheek and then he kissed her.

Anne had been even frostier than Firuza when her prince found her. She was in the laundry, amid the smell of soap and dirt.

She knew he was there before he spoke. Sensing his presence, she felt a wave of humiliation at being found at a menial task.

Her face impassive, her violet eyes cold, she looked to the soiled items she was washing in a small ceramic bowl filled with suds.

Filled with rage she thought, *My hands will soon be as red, swollen and cracked as my mum's and I will be old before my time. What right has he to come and dangle hope in front of me?*

'You have lost your way, sir. You have no business here.' She spoke softly but with disdain rang out of every syllable.

He took a step closer to him and she could smell his expensive cologne over the harsh scent of her fabric soap. She felt his warmth against her back as he leant into her. Putting his strong arms around her, he gently lifted her hands out of the water. Despite all her intentions, she found herself responding to his touch and tingles of electricity coursed through her treacherous body.

She sensed his warm breath in her ear as he whispered, 'Come with me on an adventure.'

Reluctantly, she allowed him to lead her by the hand away from the laundry and her labours out into the bright sunshine. They crept along the garden paths, careful not to be seen. When they reached the moat, Anne was surprised to see a punt.

She looked enquiringly at Dimash through lowered eyes and long black lashes; in answer to her look, he murmured, 'It's quite safe, we can easily cross the moat and get onto the river beyond.'

'But the guard?' she whispered, frightened of being heard.

Dimash grinned. 'All arranged. Nanny is acting as a distraction. She said something about sharing a smoke with the lad and a flask of potcheen, which will render the boy lifeless for the afternoon.'

He didn't add that Nanny had clapped him on the back, wishing him well in his quest to win a fair lady's heart.

She heard the river beyond the moat before she could see it. It was really little more than an eager stream. Despite wanting to remain aloof, the sight of the shallow-bottomed boat nestling in the reeds filled her with anticipation.

'I love messing about in boats,' she murmured as he held her hand and helped her onto the rocking craft.

He grinned. 'Like Mole and Ratty.'

'*Wind in the Willows* is one of my favourite books,' she confessed, all hint of seriousness banished by a boat and a river. 'I haven't been on a river for ages.'

'It's something I miss about Oxford,' said Dimash, taking up the oars.

Anne took his hand to steady herself as she lightly stepped onto the craft. 'When I was younger, I used to take my little brothers out in an old rowing boat.' She settled herself on the seat at the stern before continuing, 'We would be gone for hours.' She smiled and he noticed a wistful look come into her lavender eyes. 'Sometimes, Ma would pack us some bread and butter – biscuits if we were lucky.'

Her whole being seemed to come alive at the memory and his heart turned over.

Eagerly, he gestured to a wicker basket under her seat. 'I hope we fare a little better than bread and butter.' He saw her wince at the slight to her mother's poverty, which had only allowed for a meagre picnic. Inwardly cursing his clumsiness, he rushed on, 'I persuaded the cook that after a long ride we would want a feast. That is our cover story – everyone thinks Parviz and I are off riding.'

She was looking pensively at her feet and did not appear impressed with the subterfuge.

He pushed off into the mid-stream. Picking up the oars, he made easy strokes and they cut through the water. A leggy heron took off, disturbed by their arrival. Anne relaxed back, allowing the cool water to caress her hand as she trailed it over the side. The water sparkled where the sun hit its ripples and eddies. The tall grass on either bank swayed and murmured in the breeze. Bright yellow irises and delicate shinning buttercups dotted the greenery while midges hovered overhead.

Absently, Anne murmured in voice so low that Dimash only just caught it above the sounds of the river, 'I always dreamed of being able to study at Oxford. I cannot think of anything more glorious than to be able to read and study as much as I wanted and then to drift away on a punt.' She thought of her reality, of laundry and pressing frocks, and her face hardened.

Dimash caught the change in her mood and guessed at the cause. His heart twisted. It was so unfair that Anne, for all her intelligence and loveliness, had so few options in life. Then he thought of himself and his upcoming betrothal ball and realised he was as trapped as she was by the accident of his birth.

The river took them beneath some overhanging trees. The sudden chill made Anne shiver but also recalled her to the present.

As my Ma would say, there is no point in mourning what can't be helped. And I may as well enjoy the moment. She smiled. *After all, I don't reckon I'll have many more times when I'm taken down the river by a handsome prince.*

His grey eyes were on her, he'd been watching her, alert for any change in expression. Her skin was smooth with the gentle bloom of youth and when she was happy, he felt his spirits soar.

She gazed back at him quite unabashed, her violet eyes openly raking over his face and his arms, muscular in the art of rowing.

It was hot and within fifteen minutes he stopped rowing and leant against his oars. 'Do you mind if I take my jacket off?'

Her boldness a moment before evaporated. She blushed at the idea of a prince asking her permission to do anything. She nodded then regretted it. It felt strangely intimate, the pair of them alone within the confines of a small boat while he shrugged one arm out of his jacket and then the other. She looked away and focused on a dragonfly hovering in the reeds. When she heard him take up the oars once more, she glanced back at him. He had removed his tie and rolled his sleeves up, his muscles bunched with each stroke. For a second, her breath caught. Realising she was staring, she flushed. He was gazing directly at her and, catching her eye, he smiled in understanding.

He said lightly, 'You really need a parasol to keep the sun off your face.'

Anne almost laughed. She could hear her Ma saying, 'And what would the likes of us be doing with a fine parasol?' But she checked her thoughts. *Just for today why can't I be a fine lady? Even a princess?*

They rowed on a little before he indicated a grassy area beneath a willow tree. 'Let's pull in there. I have a rug, and I've brought a book of poetry.'

She laughed. 'How romantic.'

He smiled. 'I'm trying.'

As he helped her out of the boat and spread the rug in the diaphanous shade of the willow, she enquired, 'Keats?'

Dimash surveyed the moss and grass that surrounded their bier. 'It would be appropriate. "*And when thou art weary, I'll find thee a bed, of mosses and flowers to pillow your head.*"'

'So, it is Keats,' said Anne with triumph as she helped him with the wicker basket.

He shook his head, 'No, I've chosen a poet full of wisdom.'

'Rumi?'

He chuckled. 'You will have to wait until we've eaten.'

Inside the wicker basket there was a feast of crusty baguettes, soft cheeses, cured meat, and fruit accompanied by lush fruit and a bottle of wine. They spread it as a banquet on the rug. A gentle breeze rustled the willow's fine leaves, and the river provided a tinkling lullaby. Occasionally, the restful scene was punctuated by the plop of a fish or a quack of a duck.

Anne sipped the red wine and felt mellow. She leaned back on the rug and watched the clouds scudding across the blue sky. She was drowsing when she remembered the promised poetry book.

She looked at Dimash through half-opened eyes and long lashes. 'Read to me,' she murmured.

He grinned and, with a flourish, took out a slim volume. 'As promised, a book filled with profound thoughts.'

She leant up on her elbows. 'So, what is it?' she queried.

In a sombre voice he commenced reading, '"*The owl and the pussy cat went to sea in a beautiful pea-green boat ...*"'

Anne exploded into laughter and only just recovered enough to splutter, '"*They took some money and plenty of honey ...*"'

He hadn't seen her laugh so wholeheartedly before and his heart soared.

When, between them, they finished the poem, they were both laughing. Dimash regarded her dancing eyes and relaxed smile and commented, 'So you approve my choice?'

She nodded. 'I can't think of anyone better than Edward Lear to entertain us on our picnic.'

Dimash smiled and, turning the page, he read, '"The Courtship of the Yonghy-Bonghy-Bo."'

Anne gushed, 'That's one of my favourites.'

With a voice filled with gravitas he began to read, only faltering when he got to, '"*Lady Jingly! Lady Jingly! Sitting where the pumpkins grow, will you come and be my ...*"' He faltered to a stop and swallowed. Their eyes met. Barely above a whisper he continued, *'"... my wife, said the Yonghy-Bonghy-Bo.*"'

Regaining his composure, he declared the next line with more gusto than it warranted, '"*I am tired of living singly, on this coast so wild and shingly".*'

As he finished the sad tale, he was aware that Anne was sitting very still, looking out at the river, not at him. She was so close he just had to lean down to place a gentle kiss on her lips but, with his face very near to hers, she seemed to snap to.

She pushed him away and angrily snapped, 'We can't! You shouldn't behave like this.' He had never seen her eyes wild before or her delicate fists clenched. 'Have you forgotten you are engaged to be married to the princess?' She nodded to the horizon and, hastily throwing the remains of the picnic into the wicker basket, she declared, 'There are storm clouds over there, we should get back as soon as possible.'

They rowed back in silence, both brooding in their isolated misery.

CHAPTER FIFTEEN

There was nothing brooding or miserable about how Nanny spent her afternoon. After rendering Inspector Le Brun's young and naïve watchman senseless with the generous use of a flask of potcheen – a lethal Irish spirit home brewed from potato skins – she gave the boy's inert figure, which was now propped up against a tree, a compassionate look.

He won't be bothering anyone for a while. Those lads and lasses can come and go as they please and he will be none the wiser. She turned to face the path to the château. *Now to ditch the potcheen and equip myself with a bottle of good whisky and a couple of cigars and I'll be ready to tackle that dignified butler, Roberts.*

The luck of the Irish was certainly with Nanny that day. Upon reaching the château, she went in search of Roberts and found him not industriously cleaning the silver but sprawled in an old comfy armchair in front of a modest but cheery fire in his equally modest butler's pantry. He had so far forgotten himself as to take off his coat, tie, and shoes. The shoes, shining to perfection, stood neatly side by side with military precision while his bunioned feet were loving encased in a pair of battered slippers. He was wearing what, on a gentleman from a different social class, would have been called a smoking jacket. Close at hand was a steaming teapot.

Startled by Nanny's sudden arrival, he started to struggle to his feet, but Nanny quickly stopped him. 'There, there. Don't you go troubling yourself, I can see you need to rest those old bones of yours. And it's not to wondered at! What with a houseful – and royalty at that – and you having to manage with a skeleton staff and now being a footman down. It's hardly to be wondered at that you need a little sit down.'

Roberts looked less than thrilled as she firmly plonked herself in the adjacent chair, but he instantly mellowed as she produced a bottle of whisky and two fat cigars with a cheery, 'Normally I prefer a raw Woodbine, but a change is always welcome.'

Woodbines were the smoke of the men in the trenches – the moment of pleasure before destruction. They both knew the implications – the shared memory of a hideous war – and there was no need to mention the trenches.

The whisky was peaty and warm, especially sipped in the scandalous afternoon rather than the acceptable evening.

'You keen on the horses?' enquired Nanny casually with her feet propped up a handy footstool.

Roberts sipped his whisky and eyed Nanny speculatively over the rim of his tumbler, one eyebrow raised. He knew a horse shark when he met one. Here was a woman who, beneath her respectable Victorian garb, would know every likely winner from Paris to Cork, taking in Newmarket and Cheltenham. She would fleece him of his last sixpence if he was naïve enough to accept any wager from her.

He chuckled and they talked about various recent winners and losers at a variety of horse races.

It was peaceful sitting side by side with the crackle of the fire and the room slowly growing thick with cigar smoke.

Roberts took another puff of his cigar and closed his tired eyes.

'Do you miss home?' asked Nanny.

The question surprised him. He thought a moment, then said, 'I'm not sure where that is.'

'No family?' she asked in the same languid almost uninterested tone.

'Just a niece living in Paris – she met her husband in Ramsgate and the rest, as they say, is history.'

Nanny took another puff of her cigar, savoured it, and said, 'So you hail from Kent?'

'You could say that.' Robert's cigar swayed and she let a silence follow.

The whisky, the cigar and the company were making him feel pleasantly mellow. He gave out a long, satisfied sigh and shut his eyes.

Nanny commented in an unhurried way, 'As I was saying, I reckon you must be in need of a break, given as how you have more than one man's workload and now you are without a footman.' She smiled to herself. 'It's not even as if you or I are spring chickens either.'

'I've had easier billets,' murmured Roberts, not opening his eyes.

'That lad, the footman ...' Nanny made the sort of questioning sound that indicated she was searching for a name.

Roberts supplied it. 'Jean le Coeur.'

'Yes, him. Good worker, was he?' Nanny enquired, staring into the fire.

'Aye, young and strong.' A smile played about Robert's mouth. 'Bright as a button – one of those that sees a thing needs doing before you have to tell them.'

Nanny nodded. 'Anne's like that. His family must be devastated what with him vanishing like that.'

'He doesn't have one. He was orphaned young – both his parents died of the influenza just after the war.' Nanny tutted sympathetically and the fire crackled and spat out a spark which Roberts hastily stamped out before resuming his seat. He added, 'Both his parents worked for the count, and I believe their forebears had been retainers for the family for time immemorial.'

'So, you knew him from a tot,' stated Nanny and was mildly surprised when Roberts shook his grey head.

'Not really,' he said, 'but I like to think I am a father figure.'

Nanny's voice remained casual but inside her heart raced with glee. 'So, you haven't worked for the count for decades?' Roberts made a noncommittal guttural grunt and took the opportunity to top up Nanny's glass but, like a terrier, she refused to be distracted. 'You were saying that you haven't worked for the count for long. Who did you work for before? The world is such a small place, I am bound to know them.'

'Here and there,' said Roberts, gazing into the fire.

There was a silence which Nanny recognised was not going to be breached by any more questions about his past employment.

She took a long, satisfying inhalation on her cigar and savoured it. The fire crackled. Eventually, she commented, 'This ball is going to be quite something. Goodness knows how many ambassadors there will be here and you're having to manage with hardly any staff.'

Roberts nodded. 'I feel sorrier for Inspector Le Brun; he's the one who is in charge of keeping everyone safe and, with all that's been happening, I fear there is bound to be trouble.' His lips pressed into a firm line before he smiled and said, 'Actually, the good Inspector is loaning me several men to act as temporary staff and protection officers.'

Nanny chuckled. 'Let's see how that works. I foresee a lot of spilled champagne.'

Roberts laughed in agreement.

Nanny took advantage of the relaxed atmosphere to touch on the missing footman once again. 'You could do with Jean le Coeur being here.'

Roberts nodded. 'He is a fine lad and has all the makings of an admirable young man.'

Nanny raised an eyebrow. 'Don't you mean "was"?'

His faced clouded. 'Yes, was.' He shifted in his seat, still looking at the fire when he added in a flat voice, 'There was a girl he was keen on who moved to Paris, so he might have followed her there.'

'Do you think it's likely?' asked Nanny looking intently at him.

Roberts shrugged. 'Who knows? The police are looking into it.' He levered himself up from the chair. 'But now, I must get back to work.'

Dinner, that evening, was a silent affair and when each went to bed there was little recourse from their various worries.

In the sanctuary of his parlour, Roberts relaxed with another whisky. Shoes off, he noticed that his right big toe was poking through his sock. *I need a wife! No chance of that, though, with this job.* He took a sip of whisky, warm and peaty. It made him homesick although why, when he was English, not Irish like Nanny, he didn't know. *After this job, I'll pack it all in, go home and grow marrows.* The thought made him smile but then Madame Amelie's wild curls and curled lips came to mind. *I fear she is going to be a problem. Now, how can I take care of her?*

Father Luke regarded his opulent room with its rich fabrics, ornate furniture, and lavish proportions. He was enjoying the break from his austere priory. *It's a relief not to be looking at bare walls and not to have to sleep on a hard bed. It reminds me of happier times.*

He instantly felt a wave of shame for his thoughts. He had a duty to God and his communist comrades to live a life of hardship. Kneeling on the hard wooden floor, he relished the biting pain of the unyielding surface on his bony knees.

Before him was the beautiful, bejewelled icon of Madonna and Child. Glistening with gold, it was a precious gift he knew had been looted from the late Tzar's treasures. Like all things Russian, he considered it above reproach.

A wave of pain shot through his joints, but he didn't flinch. *I need inspiration about what I should do next. This engagement is not good, and the ball is so soon. I need to tell my contact – how can I visit Paris without arousing suspicion?*

He had a new contact; there had been so many changes in the turbulence of the past decade and a half. He sighed and tried to concentrate on the Madonna's halo, to let its quiet majesty seep into his bones. Try as he might, his soul would not soar. Matters temporal would keep popping into his mind.

It had all seemed so simple back in those heady pre-war days! Lenin had been so clear, so magnificent. He swallowed. *Now Lenin was dead, and the old order had been replaced not by a shiny utopia but by...* he pushed away the word 'chaos' and tried to look deep into the Madonna's eyes, seeking refuge.

Was I wrong? I truly believed back then that Marx declaring, 'Religion is the opium of the people' was only a statement expressing a short phase as the people embraced a new way of living – that, given maturity, everyone would come to see that the church and communism are one and the same, but…

Sister Claire was far more focused on her evening prayers. Rosary in hand, she recited her Hail Marys and dedicated them to a way to pay for the convent roof. The thought, '*How annoying; there is going to a ball and a 'betrothal,'* was a mere passing distraction.

Her sister, Amelie, in flamboyant wide-legged pyjamas, was dancing around her room to a creaky jazz song on her wind-up player with its enormous horn of a speaker. She had a glass of champagne in her hand and her trademark long-stemmed cigarette holder with its smouldering tip firmly clapped between her teeth, a lipstick smear at the base and a precarious length of ash at the end.

'How fortunate it is, my dear Venus, that I know where my brother keeps the keys to the wine cellar.' Her voice was only slightly slurred. She took another sip, emptying the glass, and replenished it from the small amount that remained in the bottle. Venus, on her plush red cushion, watched her mistress with indulgent affection. The gramophone was winding down and Amelie vigorously turned the handle.

'A ball!' she exclaimed with glee, twirling around to the music. She pouted. 'So unfair! I missed out on so much fun! Christoff and Claire went to so many of them and, just because I was younger, I only got to go to the one!' She skipped over the grim thought that that ball had been the night her mother had plunged from the balustrade and died. Stroking Venus under her chin, she looked her directly in her black beady eyes and smirked. 'I wonder just how much money that butler has? Or rather what he can steal and sell from my miserly brother. After all, I *must* have a fabulous frock for the ball!'

She paused in her happy musings of silk and jewels. 'I wonder if I should bypass Roberts – after all, he is only the monkey to my brother. A count has to be a more promising blackmail prospect than a butler; perhaps it would be better to apply a little touch of blackmail directly to Christoff.' Considering the idea, she frowned and bit her lip. 'He may hold the wealth, but he has a nasty vicious streak.' Even in her own mind she didn't add, 'Like our father.' She chuckled and pushed a wayward red curl out of her eyes. 'Yes, that's what I'll do! It's the life of luxury for us from now on. After all, I know enough about my dearest brother to have him hanged.' She laughed exuberantly and swirled Venus around the room making the poor Pekingese's eyes bulge even more.

Her miserly brother, Count Christoff, was standing on the balustrade looking out at all he owned. The sight brought him great joy. He breathed in the night air then took a long drag on a fat and particularly fine cigar. He savoured the taste.

An extravagant purchase thanks to the generosity of that fool Cyril Forsythe. Who'd have thought the Foreign Office would pay so well simply for me to host this little marriage market. He chuckled. *And now this ball! I wish Father could see me bring back the château to all its glory; he would be so proud of me. The ball will be no expense spared thanks to the Abbastan coffers, and after that...* He took another long slow puff on his cigar and smiled. *I won't let anyone stand in my way! After all, what really matters is maintaining the château and that takes money. If there is one thing I learnt from my father, it's that a count needs to be ruthless.*

He watched Prince Parviz far below, angrily striding along. It was the third time the count had observe Parviz marching past. It was evident that the young man was walking laps of the château's grounds trying to exercise away his vexation. *What a fool! All caught up in his passion for the princess.*

Then his hooded eyes came to rest on a spot near the old château. He could just make out two figures, standing very close. From their body language, he guessed they were discussing something of importance. He frowned. *So, Inspector Le Brun and*

Busby are having a little tête-à-tête? I hope they don't make things difficult for me.

Inspector Le Brun and Busby were going over recent events. They spoke in low rapid French.

Le Brun was frowning. 'This ball raises all sorts of security issues.'

Busby nodded.

Le Brun continued, 'There are plenty of powerful people who won't want this marriage to go ahead – the Soviets, for example. I must admit I have fears for the princess's safety – her untimely death would solve a lot of problems for some people.'

Busby frowned. 'It's unfortunate that there are already rumours of the upcoming union in diplomatic circles so we can't rely on the element of surprise at the announcement.'

Le Brun was shaking his head, 'All those people – it will be very difficult for us, if not impossible, to guarantee anyone's safety. It would be all too easy to hide a small pistol in one of the ladies' evening bags.'

'Or a stiletto blade in a cummerbund,' sighed Busby.

'It's not even as if we can insist on searching the guests as they arrive,' lamented Le Brun.

Busby laughed at the notion. 'Hardly! That really would spark a diplomatic incident.'

Le Brun's shoulders sagged even further, and his face sank into melancholy. 'To make matters worse, word on the streets of Paris – that is among the criminal classes – is that the famous Abbastani diamonds will be worn by the Princess.'

Busby cocked his head to one side. 'And you are worried someone might try and steal them?'

'Quite. It would be easy enough for some mafia type to pose as a diplomatic private secretary and kick up a fuss if we demand to see his papers.'

Busby was nodding. 'But I fear the greatest threat is not from a guest but from one of the château's present house party.'

'I agree.' A hint of a smile played about Le Brun's lips. 'What we need is to have the place overflowing with my finest officers.'

'Hardly possible when we have been told that discretion is of the highest importance,' sighed Busby.

Le Brun grinned. 'My dear Busby, I must confess that I have not told you of some of the steps I plan to take, have already set in motion.'

Busby raised an eyebrow and looked quizzically at the inspector. He did not like surprises. 'What have you been planning?'

'If I get my officers to pretend to be waiters…'

Now Busby was also smiling. 'I take it you have already spoken to Roberts?'

Le Brun nodded. 'Let's thrash out the details over a bottle of wine.'

The two men wandered off.

Crown Prince Dimash, in his silk pyjamas and elaborately embroidered dressing gown, stood at his window, gazing out at the moonlit garden with its long blue shadows. He couldn't appreciate the airy beauty of the night-time garden; his mind was too filled with thoughts of what was to come.

He could not get out of his mind the image of Firuza when the Venerable Uncle had made his announcement. He had never seen anything so tragic as the look in her eyes. The memory of it made his heart tighten. *Poor Firuza, she doesn't want to marry me any more than I wish to marry her.*

He exhaled and attempted to steady his emotions by looking through the window at the serenity of the garden. Even here there was no respite from his troubling thoughts. He spotted Parviz coming out of the shadows. From his rapid strides and the way he held himself, Dimash knew his brother was distressed as well as angry. The breath seemed to catch in Dimash's throat. *I have never seen Parviz so elated as when he came back from riding with Firuza.* Feeling sick with anxiety he wondered, *Can my relationship with my brother survive my marrying the woman he loves?*

He sighed, his mind struggling for a solution.

If there is any hope of escaping from this marriage it must be done before the official engagement announcement at the ball. But it's so soon that we have virtually no time.

Defeated, he leant his forehead against the cool glass of the windowpane. His mind went back to the afternoon with Anne. *Such a strange mix of happiness and misery.* His mind then settled on their last moment together.

It was Anne's final words that haunted him.

He had wanted to explain, to make thing better between them, and struggled for words as he helped her out of the punt. She was composed and poised as she allowed him to steady her step onto the riverbank.

With a desperation alien to his normally calm demeanour, he suddenly gripped her hand tightly and blurted out, 'Anne, if I could… It's not just us I have to think about… My life is not my own – I have to think of my people. I was born to rule.'

Now she looked at him, with such ice in her violet eyes that his heart shrank. 'How can you rule a nation if you can't even command yourself?'

For the first time the expression 'the crushing weight of a crown' seemed real and intolerable.

Without another word, while his heart broke, she had walked away from him, her head help high and determination in every stride.

Parviz was too filled with restless energy to even contemplate sleep. He did not bother to get ready for bed but rather went outside. He strode several laps of garden, confined by the moat. The exercise did not bring him any relief but rather emphasised his entrapment. He felt like a pitiful tiger he had once seen in a zoo, driven demented by its endless futile pacing.

His mind went to how Firuza had looked, free and exultantly happy as she galloped across the countryside. His body ached for the feel of her. He relived her passionate kisses, felt again his quickening heart, his dry mouth, and swore. He couldn't let her go. But what could he do?

Flora sat up in bed, her oyster silk pyjamas soft and cool and her feather pillows deliciously malleable. She had hoped reading letters from home would distract her from her worries about Firuza, Anne, and the fate of the Stans, but they had done little but add to her concerns.

Her housekeeper wrote:

> Ma'am,
>
> Problem with range, will call sweep. Although as I said to yourself before there was no need to get rid of the old cooker – if you ask me all your concern about keeping it stocked with wood being too much work for the young maids is a load of rubbish. The only problem with Mavis and Gladys is plain laziness and if you weren't so lenient with them, they would be far less trouble. (If you'll forgive my boldness.)
>
> *As if dear Mrs Wilkes has ever cared a fig about whether she receives my forgiveness or not.*
>
> I was totally scandalised just after you left, to find that both those silly girls had gone and had their hair cropped short – would you ever credit it? I said as you would have a stern word with them on your return and they had the cheek to say that you would probably tell them they look like that actress, Mary Louise Brookes. Girls today have their heads full of that 'silver screen' and are just workshy that's what I say.
>
> And speaking of 'workshy', young under-maid Mavis and Gladys who is meant to do the scrubbing but doesn't, are both complaining about the wage and say they can get more down the factory.
>
> *I keep telling Mrs Wilkes to raise their wages and she will insist that 'You shouldn't go spoiling them!' I can see I need to write her a stern missive insisting she pays them more – goodness knows what her reaction will be but at least those girls will have a decent wage.*
>
> I hopes as you are having a nice holiday – must be

lovely to have a holiday not just to work still mustn't complain and I need to get back to that dratted range.

Well, really, as if I'm not forever asking her to have a little holiday!

Your humble servant,

Mrs Wilkes

She turned to a much-blotted script she guessed was from her gardener. It was a simple note.

Ma'am,

Don't like the look of the potatoes – reckon its blight and them roses look like black spot.

Yours,

Mr. Bert

She put household matters to one side and with maternal hope picked up the missives from her children.

She started with her letter from Tony. His strong, forward slanting penmanship always reminded Flora of Roger's.

Dear Mother,

I hope you are enjoying France.

I have been giving my education and future a lot of thought. I have decided that school is a lot of tosh and holding me back. I keep getting 100% in all my maths and science exams and the masters don't like it.

He's so like his father – mathematics is in his veins, whereas I find it tricky to add up my household accounts.

In consequence I propose we get me a tutor so I can prepare take the Oxford entry exams early.

Best wishes,

Tony.

Oh dear! Should I be proud or alarmed?

She hoped Debo's letter would be less worrying. It began well enough,

Dearest Mummy,

Thanks for your letter – I must say I wish I was with you! It sounds too topping you finding a dead footman in your bedroom and then losing him again. Do let me know what happens.

Thrilling news – the tennis courts are open. This year I am really going to show silly Susan a thing or two – she really does think she's the bee's knees.

May I have a new tennis racquet?

That's odd, she had a new racquet at the beginning of term.

Lots of love,

Debo xxx

P.S. Please ignore the letter from Miss Crawford saying I hit stinky Susan over the head with my racquet.

Dutifully, Flora took the missive bearing Debo's school crest and dropped it in the wastepaper bin with a sigh.

Flora sighed. Perhaps she'd been wrong. Could it be that solving the problems of the Stans was less troublesome than her domestic worries?

She tried turning out the light and settling down to sleep but her mind would not stop going over and over the unresolved issues.

There must be something I can do to help Firuza. I really can't see how to get her out of this wedding but what's more pressing is I need to find out who killed that young man before they do Firuza any harm. Then the ball is so close and, after the official engagement is announced, there will be no turning back for either Firuza or Dimash. She sighed. *The ball is so soon. It will change those young people's lives for ever and what is more I don't have anything to wear. I must make an appointment at Madame Chanel's. I will take Firuza with me; as she's come straight from school, she won't have anything suitable either and she can hardly wear her tennis kit. Monsieur Fortuny's too. Those velvets! Perhaps I should take Anne along too, she can help carry the parcels and it would be good for the child to see a bit of Paris. And there's always Worth. Now, what colour should my dress be? Beaded or embroidered? And the cut? Then of course there are the shoes to be considered, not to mention the jewellery.*

With her mind filled with happy thoughts, she knew sleep would come.

Dorothy was the only one who was sleeping cheerfully from the moment she closed her eyes. Flora had failed to evict her to her basket, so she was comfortably snuggled up to her mistress under the covers. She was having a particularly happy dream whereby she had managed to steal a particularly fine marrow bone from Venus.

In Princess Firuza's bedroom, two young women sat side by side on top of the lavish bed. They sat so close their heads almost touched, one golden and one dark as a raven wing. Both in wrapped in their dressing gowns, one silk and one cheap cotton. They spoke in whispers even though there was no one to hear them.

Anne said something and Firuza nodded. 'Yes, that might work.'

Anne bit her lip. 'It HAS to work – or both our lives will be ruined for ever.'

Firuza sought to comfort and encourage her friend. Gripping her hand tightly, she said, 'I think it will work! I knew if we put our heads together, we would come up with something.'

Anne nodded. 'We will need help.'

Firuza smiled. 'Nanny would be delighted to assist us.'

Anne grinned too. 'Can you imagine her glee when we tell her what we are planning and ask her to be a part of it?'

They both laughed, smothering the sound in their hands.

Suddenly a new thought struck Anne, and she stopped giggling abruptly. For the first time she looked unsure. 'What about the Venerable Uncle?'

Firuza frowned then whispered something unintelligible to all but Anne.

CHAPTER SIXTEEN

Flora had such high hopes when she awoke the next morning. Her first thought was much the same as her last thought the night before: *I need to get something to wear for the ball.* Somehow the notion of shopping had the ability to put her life into perspective.

Dorothy was nestling next to her, so she gave her a loving pat and said out loud, 'I think, Dorothy, my dear, that Descartes had it wrong. It isn't "I think therefore I am" but "I shop therefore I am."'

Unfortunately for Flora that was the pinnacle of happiness that day.

Having given Dorothy a brief walk around the garden, she glanced at her watch. It was still early. 'Dorothy, shall we risk bringing you into the dining room for breakfast? It is so early I very much doubt that Amelie and that pesky Venus will be up yet, let alone ready for breakfast. This way I won't need to trail back up to my room or to find Anne or Nanny to look after you while I have my breakfast.'

Dorothy looked up at her, head cocked on one side, tail wagging furiously and black eyes sparkling. In doggy-speak she was saying, '*Oh yes! Rather! I'd just love to see Busby – he probably won't be able to resist tickling my tummy; after all I am irresistible. And should you see fit to slip me a bit of bacon, that would be a bonus.*'

The dining room was empty when they arrived.

Finding that Busby was not at breakfast was enough to dampen both Dorothy's and Flora's spirits a touch.

Firuza wandered in just as Flora was finishing her scrambled eggs. To Flora's pleasure, she seemed to have lost some of the pinched expression around her eyes and tentatively she made her suggestion. 'Firuza, how about you and I pop into Paris to look at dresses for the ball?'

Flora half expected the child to greet the suggestion with much the same alacrity and joy as the proverbial lamb when told to shine up its fleece for the slaughter but instead she looked at Flora for a steady second before smiling warmly and clasping her hands together in a very un-Firuza gesture of girlish glee. 'That would be wonderful!'

Flora blinked. *I know shopping has miraculous powers for restoring one's spirits, but I wasn't expecting this degree of success.*

She blinked some more when Firuza added, 'Can Anne come too?' As the princess registered Flora's surprise, she added, 'To help carry the bags.'

'Good idea,' nodded Flora.

The night before she had been thinking a visit to town might give Anne something else to think about rather than that her handsome prince, who was on the cusp of being married, while she was about to return to Blighty and a life of drudgery. Now, it dawned on her perhaps it was a little tactless to invite Anne on a shopping trip whose objective was to purchase a frock for her rival in love to wear when her betrothal was announced to Anne's own prince. *And to rub salt into the wounds, Anne won't even get a dress out of the outing.*

She might have queried the suggestion, but Firuza was already more or less skipping out of the room while saying over her shoulder, 'I'll go and tell Anne now; she'll be thrilled.'

'But what about your breakfast?' called Flora, suddenly feeling both maternal and responsible.

'Not hungry,' came the reply before she disappeared out of the door.

Flora watched her depart. There was no sign of Roberts but there was a coffee pot on the sideboard which was being kept hot by a small flame. She was just pondering if a third cup of coffee would be wise when Busby wandered in, looking heavy-eyed and with a hint of stubble around his chin. Flora barely registered his dishevelled appearance; she was suddenly absorbed with the thought that she could discuss the situation with him. *After all, as Uncle Cyril said, he is a 'useful' chap and perhaps he has some new ideas about finding the killer of that poor footman, or even inspiration over how to get Firuza out of a political marriage. Buying some new dresses, however stylish, probably should not sway me from what should be my main focus.*

Dorothy, like Flora, was too absorbed in her own thoughts to register all the obvious signs that Busby hadn't slept and was exhausted. She rolled over on her back, wantonly exposing her bare tummy, wagging her tail, and staring adoringly at Busby. Every inch of her screamed, '*Go on! Tickle my tummy! You know you want to!*'

Busby chuckled and obligingly rubbed her tummy. He gave her a final pat before saying, 'That's your lot, mutt, until I've had some coffee.'

Flora was struggling to get his attention but sadly had to admit to herself that her charms were not a match for Dorothy's superior allure.

The moment he stood up, Flora took her chance. In a rush she enquired, 'Busby, please tell me you have had some thoughts as to who might have killed that young man? Until we apprehend the murderer, Firuza is in terrible danger. And there must be some way we can stop this betrothal.'

Busby regarded her through bloodshot eyes and sourly remarked, 'Mrs Farrington, if you could kindly allow me a cup of coffee before bombarding me with questions.'

Flora looked and felt affronted but allowed him to procure some coffee in stony silence.

He sat down, took a long sip, shutting his eyes while the caffeine did its work, before looking across the table at her. Without a softening smile he stated, 'Mrs Farrington, for your information there is no "we" in apprehending anyone, let alone a murderer. May I remind you I am the police professional, and you are a civilian. Secondly, it is not either your or my business to get involved in political alliances, let alone those of a foreign country and—'

While Busby had been speaking, Flora had been staring at him, her fury growing with each word. Now she cut him off, 'But Firuza is just a child and—'

Now it was his turn to rudely interrupt her. 'I am here in my professional capacity, not to interfere in politics. For your information, Inspector Le Brun and I have been up all night discussing the safety issues surrounding this ball. My job is to make sure none of the extremely high-profile guests are assassinated on my watch. Your job is to get yourself a frock.'

It took Flora a moment to register what Busby had said. Thrusting her chin up, she glowered at him. Only now did she register that the man did look sleep-deprived and probably not in the mood to focus on her woes, but she was by now too wrapped up in her own outrage to care.

Involuntarily, her fists clenched, and her body tensed. Her heart was pounding and her head felt as if it might explode. Standing up with a force that sent her chair crashing to the floor, she took a stride towards the door.

Her intention of storming out and slamming the door was impeded by the count, who, judging by his expression, had heard everything. He had one quizzical eyebrow raised, no doubt prompted by the noise of his furniture being thrown around. Amelie was by his side; she looked as dishevelled as Busby but from too much champagne the night before rather than from lack of sleep due to professional duties. Close behind were the religious element: Sister Claire and Father Luke. Sister Claire bore her habitual curled lip and wrinkled nose, denoting disapproval of the world in general and Flora in particular. Father Luke was uninterested in his surroundings and simply blinked behind his pebble-thick glasses.

None of this would have mattered, apart from it all being slightly embarrassing, had Amelie not been accompanied by Venus. That imperious pooch lost no time in attacking Dorothy with all the fury of Genghis Khan invading China. Dorothy had never been one to flinch from a good old scrape so with a, *'Take that you pampered hound of hell!'* she bit Venus squarely on her flattened nose. Simultaneously, Amelie and Venus gave out screams of horror, at which point the two dogs took off at high speed out of the dining room and down the corridor, barking all the while and narrowly avoiding sending Roberts flying, along with his tray bearing fresh coffee.

Amelie, with her broad shoulders and greater height, squared up to Flora, towering over her. She was obviously well aware of how intimidating her formidable figure could be. Flicking her flowing silk scarf over her shoulder (much like a pantomime villain), Amelie opened her mouth to give Flora one or two well-chosen words.

Flora was already wound taut by her exchange with Busby. She felt a headache coming on and her neck was intolerably stiff. Amelie, in bullying mood, was the final straw. She exploded, 'I wish you would keep that poisonous dog of yours under control. If she has hurt my poor Dorothy in the slightest, you will regret it!'

Flora was only vaguely aware of everyone's shocked expressions as she ran after the dogs. Out of the corner of her eye, she registered Sister Claire's mouth drop open and Father Luke's rapid blinking. She thought she heard a bark of laughter from the count.

The sound of Dorothy's and Venus's hysterical yaps were easy to follow; unsurprisingly, they led down the corridor and out into the garden where they abruptly stopped with a squeal.

Flora gave chase, ignoring the sun on her face and the morning garden scents which normally so enchanted her. Rounding the corner, she saw the ancient gardener in front of the fountain, his gnarled features crooked into a wry smile and an empty bucket in his hand. Both Venus and Dorothy were soaked with water and shaking vigorously. Dorothy's shorter coat gave her an advantage whereas Venus looked less regal and more like a wet mop. Mentally commending the gardener's swift action in stopping the fight by throwing a bucket of water over the pair, Flora scooped her wet hound up into her arms.

Venus can find her own way, thought Flora sourly. *Now what? We could both do with a walk but, without a lead, Dorothy will just go in search of Venus to finish the fight. I have no intention of going back to the dining room to get the lead. I can just imagine what Amelie would say, and I really have seen quite enough of Busby for one day.*

Dorothy was trembling with excitement and proving to be a very wet and wriggly package. Flora carefully put her down on the bench and examined her for bites; much to her relief, the dog seemed fine. She looked up at Flora with sparking black eyes and wagged her tail vigorously. Even Flora could tell she was saying, '*Wasn't that great fun! I showed that pampered pooch a thing or two! Now if you will just let go of me, I will go and finish what I started.*'

Flora frowned as she regarded her diminutive hound. 'Judging by how you look, you certainly have no intention of becoming a meek and amenable pup and walking quietly to heel. Nothing for it but to go all the way up the stairs and fetch the spare lead from my bedroom.'

She carried Dorothy up to her room, pleased not to run into anyone in the spacious hall or on the imposing staircase. It took a moment or two to find the much-needed lead because, as both Nanny and Anne could tell you, Flora was not the tidiest of souls.

Clipping the lead firmly onto her dog's collar, she once more descended the grand staircase and went into the garden. The combination of the exertion of climbing the stairs followed by having to concentrate on looking for the lead had calmed her agitation a bit. She marched down the gravel path towards the medieval petit château with quick strides. Dorothy trotted happily at her side.

As she thought about Busby's cutting words, her eyebrows pulled close and down, creating a forehead crease. *Your job is to get yourself a new frock! As if that's all I'm capable of.* Shaking her head she muttered, 'He really is an odious man. Just where he thinks he has the right to lecture me in that patronising way is beyond me.' She gave the French police officer staffing the gate a tight smile and turned left along the path that followed the line of the moat. 'Well, I'll show him! I'll work out who killed the footman and who knows, I might even find a way to help Firuza - and I'll do it all without his help.'

As they paced by the water, with dragonflies buzzing over the surface and a pair of black swans gliding past, Flora allowed herself a moment of indulgence. She joyfully imagined herself apprehending a masked villain while receiving accolades from all, with Busby watching admiringly from the sidelines.

This happy scene was destroyed as her mind returned to the dining room and her rudeness to Amelie. She felt a tightening knot in her belly, and she slowed her speedy walk to a slow amble. *She may be a vile woman of limited talent but perhaps I was a shade ... brusque.*

A flush of embarrassment crept across her cheeks and her shoulders slumped. *Oh, help! I really don't want to apologise to her, but I can't see a way out.*

She and Dorothy had wandered down the side of the main château with the formal garden, complete with fountain and hidden summerhouse, to their left. Amelie's studio was close by and – *speak of the devil* – there was Amelie accompanied by Venus. Amelie appeared to be confronting Roberts. As ever, she loomed over the butler, gesticulating in a threatening manner, and Roberts was looking down at his immaculately shiny shoes. To Flora's surprise, Roberts suddenly lifted his head and, in a low voice which was the nonetheless strong enough to reach Flora and Dorothy, said, 'Madame, let me caution you. Do you really think you can get away with this?' Amelie's cackle of a laugh pierced the air followed by Roberts' firm, 'You don't know who you are dealing with.'

Oh Lord! I really don't feel up to seeing Amelie just now! However intriguing that little tête-à-tête might be, apologies can wait, as can my curiosity! Flora turned 180 degrees and swiftly retraced her steps. Dorothy, although bemused, followed along. She marched back along the side of the moat until she once more passed the much-turreted old château and again gave the guard a tight smile. She looped by the stables before returning at a saunter to the fountain. The gardener had gone but he had absentmindedly left the bucket and a rake. Flora stepped over them before moving them to one side in case someone, such as the short-sighted Father Luke, should trip over them. *And that would never do.* She was just straightening up when she spotted Roberts scuttling back into the house from the side path. *I wonder what he's been up to.*

She did not have long to wonder as she was distracted by the sudden appearance of Venus who, much to both Flora's and Dorothy's embarrassment, had sidled up to them, whimpering. With highly uncharacteristic behaviour, she was showing every sign of doggy submissiveness, positively bowing before them. She virtually crawled on her belly up to Flora before rolling over on her back and looking plaintively up at the dachshund with lolling watery eyes.

Even Dorothy was too much taken aback to do anything but stare. She was not so lost in surprise as not to be horrified when Flora bent down and scooped the hated Pekingese into her arms and held her tight, all the time cooing, 'What's wrong, Venus? It's alright, you are quite safe now. Oh, you poor little thing, you are terrified. What can have happened?'

Ignoring Dorothy's low growling, '*Cut the cooing! Stop fraternising with the enemy this instant!*' Flora continued, 'Much as I dislike your mistress, I think we had better go and find her for you.'

All Flora's comforting did not seem to be helping to soothe Venus much, so with Dorothy reluctantly following on the end of her lead, she carried the Pekingese towards Amelie's studio.

As they drew close, Venus's whimpers of distress grew louder, and she wriggled to get free of Flora's arms.

Flora tried calming her with a soft, 'What is it?' Another few steps and she was alerted to what was frightening the dog by the sight of smoke billowing out from the studio. She froze for a moment and simply stared as the thick smell assailed her nostrils. A jolt of apprehension run through her. Her heart was beating rapidly, and she gasped for air as fear rose up in her chest.

She dropped Dorothy's lead and put Venus on the ground. Flora was too agitated to notice that, far from attacking each other, the two dogs seemed to glean comfort from cowering closely together.

In a voice that came out shrill and high-pitched, Flora screamed for help. Without thinking through the wisdom of her action, she threw open the door and was propelled backwards by a gust of heat and smoke that made her eyes water and her skin flush.

The dogs took refuge under a nearby bush.

Flora regained her footing and standing by the doorway, shouted over the sound of burning wood and canvas, 'Amelie!'

Her call went unanswered but for the crackle and pop of the fire. As she squinted into the inferno, she saw canvases and drapes burning. She tried to focus her watery burning eyes. *What's that mound on the floor?* She could make out the flamboyant colours Amelie liked to wear. *No! It can't be! Surely not?*

She blinked, not quite believing what she was looking at. There was Amelie, sprawled on the floor amid an upturned easel and scattered brushes.

Her body looked ungainly with her arms and legs splayed. She lay face down.

Flora screamed again, 'AMELIE!' but the body did not move; the flames licked higher up the surrounding walls and the crackle of the fire turned into a roar as it reached the oil paint and turps on a side workbench.

Suddenly Flora's rising panic was replaced by calm. *Come on Flora! Get a grip! You know what you have to do!*

Taking a gulp of fresh air, as if preparing to dive under water, she plunged into the studio. Heat, flames, smoke, and the crashing sounds of burning engulfed her but she was beside Amelie in a few strides.

Coughing from the smoke and desperately calling her name, Flora tried turning her over. She was heavy. *A dead weight,* she thought.

With one final heave she succeeded, and Amelie was on her back, her glassy eyes staring unseeing at the flames. Her vibrant red curls had slipped from her head. *A wig? There is no dignity in death.*

While Flora was stunned into stillness by the sight of Amelie, she felt a tremor shake her and she was engulfed by a deafening sound. *This must be what it is like to be in a cloud when it's thundering.* She scanned the scene for what was causing the noise. *It must be that heavy brocade drape Amelie likes to use as a backdrop – but why are the flames rushing up it like that?*

The noise reverberated over the crackle of burning, alerting Flora to the danger she was in. Her breathing became faster and shallower. All her muscles spasmed taut. Adrenalin flooded her body, and she felt both faint and as if she was about to vomit. Too late, she heard a crack and, looking up, saw a beam falling. For some illogical, but very human, reason she threw her own body over Amelie's to shield it.

When the beam hit, Flora thought, *That didn't hurt.* It was a brief sensation before pain and panic consumed her.

Against the smoke, she cried out the names of her children, 'Tony! Debo!' but the sound was eaten up by the flames as surely the studio was being destroyed.

Perhaps she swam out of consciousness for a second for the next thing she knew was that the count was looming over her. She felt a wave of relief. *Thank goodness! I am safe! He has come to save me!* but then through the smoke and with her eyes stinging, she registered that his face was contorted with anger and his eyes filled with hatred. *But why? I don't understand.*

Roughly, he kicked the smouldering beam away and pulled Flora off Amelie's body, all the while screaming, 'You've killed her!'

Flora opened her mouth to protest but nothing come out.

Through half-shut eyes she could see the count dragging Amelie's lifeless body towards the door and safety.

'Don't leave me!' screamed Flora in her head but no sound came out. She tried to move but her limbs wouldn't obey. The flames were creeping close to her head.

Her last thought was, *No! Not like this! I can't die like this!*

And then she slipped once more into oblivion.

When she roused, she was aware of being carried away from the smoke and flames and towards the green of the garden. *I say, so this is what heaven is like, floating into the strong arms of a capable angel. Gosh! Well, I will miss the children, of course, but if this is a taste of eternity…* here she draped an arm around her rescuing angel's neck and nestled into his firm chest, *I will probably manage.*

There was a bright light that made her blink, and her eyes hurt. *It's like the sun,* she thought in wonder. She took a mouthful of fresh clean air and started to cough. Looking up again, she realised that it *was* the sun, and she hadn't been saved by an angel. *It's better than a heavenly body, it's Busby* and she nestled against him, burying her head in his chest and thinking, *Uncle Cyril is right, Busby is a useful sort of a chap.*

She was on the grass now. It felt cool. Busby was kneeling beside her, still holding her. Dimly, she could see Inspector Le Brun with his men and Roberts forming a chain to ferry buckets, jugs, and chamber pots filled with water from the moat to the studio in a vain attempt to quench the flames. Firuza and the two princes were in the middle of the line. She idly wondered, *Where is the Venerable Uncle?*

Flora was slowly coming to and making sense of world as it was now, when an accusatory shout roared across garden, 'MURDERER!'

The shout made her turn the other way. There on the grass lay Amelie, no longer flamboyant with cascading red curls but inert with a meagre crown of thin grey locks. Next to her knelt Sister Claire and Father Luke, both reciting a prayer that Flora couldn't catch. But what was all too clear were the count's words. He was cradling Amelie's head in his lap with tears streaming down his soot-smeared face. His finger was pointing directly at Flora and, above the fire and the confusion, what he said rung out distinct in every syllable. 'She killed Amelie! I saw her with my own eyes, in the studio!'

Sister Claire jerked her thin face up. She stopped her murmured prayer and fixed Flora with cold, tearless eyes. Father

Luke glanced up for half a second but did not stop intoning his prayers.

Flora felt a crushing pressure in her chest. She couldn't breathe, winded by his words. Her mind whirled. *He can't really think that I killed her. But he's so angry. What if the others believe him?*

She coughed, struggled to sit up and spluttered, 'I didn't do it! I didn't do it!' as she started to cry.

Busby held her tightly. 'Shh! Don't try to speak.'

CHAPTER SEVENTEEN

A few days later, after the dramatic fire and Amelie's tragic death, Flora was hiding from the world by insisting she needed to stay in bed. As the weather had turned inclemently cold, accompanied by unpleasantly heavy showers, Dorothy was happy to join her. Dressed in a becoming silk pyjama set in oyster pink she was whiling away the time re-reading PG Wodehouse's *The Inimitable Jeeves*. She feared it would wreak havoc with her vocabulary, but the pleasure was worth the risk.

She laughed as she read a bit where in awe Wooster enquires, 'Good Lord, Jeeves! Is there anything you don't know?' to which Jeeves replies, 'I couldn't say, sir.'

Putting the book down on her covers, she stroked Dorothy's head and commented, 'I really could do with a Jeeves in my life – a reliable factotum who could sort out all of life's little problems, like finding a dead footman in one's bedroom or being accused by one's host of murdering his sister. I mean, Nanny is a dear, but she doesn't exactly have Jeeves' reserve.'

She sighed and glanced at the rain splattering against the window while Dorothy rolled over to have her tummy rubbed.

Flora decided to tackle her correspondence which lay by her bed. There were two from her Cotswold home, Farrington Hall, and two from her children. She decided to put work before pleasure and look at the ones from her staff first.

> Ma'am,
>
> Sweep says range useless, and you need to be getting a new flue. Far be it from me to say 'I told you so' but I did say at the time that I thought you getting a new range was madness.

Further to your last letter where you insisted that (against my better judgement) I increase Mavis and Gladys' wage. I did so. They were thrilled. As you know I am never one to say, 'I told you so' but both girls have used their riches to buy new frocks and have left by the morning bus to seek fame in them film studios in London. So now Ma'am you are without staff.

Your humble servant,

Mrs Wilkes

P.S. Hope you are still enjoying your holiday.

Flora sighed and decided not to think about these domestic woes for now. She picked up a rather battered envelope. *Could Mr Bert have spilled his tea on this?*

Ma'am,

The roses is worse and the potatoes be done for and now we have carrot-fly in them carrots,

Yours,

Mr Bert.

Oh! thought Flora, picking up her letters from the children, starting with Debo's.

Darling Mummy,

Thanks for the new racquet – it's whizzo!

Susan is positively green with envy. We have called a truce and even competed together in the doubles against that other school. We smashed them!

All my love,

Debo xxx

P.S. Just ignore the letter from Miss Crawford saying that Susan and I nobbled our opponents by putting laxatives in their juice.

Once more, Flora dutifully picked up the crested envelope, no doubt from Miss Crawford, and popped it, unopened, in the wastepaper basket. She slid the letter opener into Tony's envelope.

> Dear Mother,
>
> I placed an advert in the Times, on your behalf, seeking a Mathematics tutor. I addressed replies to me here as I knew you wouldn't be able to vet them properly.
>
> Love,
>
> Tony.

Flora swallowed hard and decided to return as quickly as possible to the tranquillity of Jeeves and Wooster.

Before she could resume reading, Nanny waddled in. In a totally un-Jeeves-like manner, she unpinned her dripping black boater hat and flung her mackintosh on a chair before flopping inelegantly down on the side of the bed.

She regarded Flora with her black beady eyes. 'How long are you planning on staying in bed? There's nothing wrong with you apart from a bruise or two. Talk about the luck of the Irish! How you could be trapped in an inferno and come out only slightly singed is beyond reason!'

Flora looked complacent. 'Yes, it was rather fortunate, and I admit I'm physically fine, but I really don't want to have to face everyone. How was the funeral, apart from wet?'

Nanny's wrinkled face morphed into a smile. 'Grand! I do love a good funeral! Especially one with proper wet rain and black umbrellas aplenty.'

Flora frowned. 'Rain doesn't really seem fitting for someone as flamboyant as Amelie – there should have been sunshine or at least a rainbow.'

'Rubbish! Rain is always perfect for a funeral. The only downside was that no one wailed, "Please forgive me!" as they threw themselves onto the coffin.'

Flora raised an eyebrow. 'Did you think that was likely?'

Nanny shrugged. 'Well, a girl can hope. Someone must be feeling guilty – after all, I doubt it was an accident. Busby caught me as we were coming in and said he'd be visiting us with some new information.'

Flora felt herself blushing. 'Is that entirely proper? After all, I am in bed and only wearing my pyjamas.'

Nonplussed, Nanny assured her, 'Fear not my girl! If your carnal desires prove too much for you to control, I will defend poor Busby's honour with my life!'

Outraged, Flora expostulated, 'Really, Nanny!'

But Nanny was already moving on to a new topic. She indicated the enormous vase filled with red roses and the generous bunch of plump grapes, complete with ornate silver scissors, which lay within easy reach on her bedside table.

'They are from the count,' said Flora. 'He popped in just before he left for the funeral. The poor man, he really is grief-stricken. He had dark circles under his eyes, he can't have been sleeping and he seemed totally deflated. Strange, as he never appeared particularly fond of Amelie. I really felt quite sorry for him. He left the dearest little letter.'

Nanny's face was impassive, her lips a firm line and her brows slightly puckered as she enquired, 'What did the letter say, "Sorry I accused you of arson and murder"?'

Flora felt a little flustered, 'Well, not exactly, you can read it for yourself – it's just there by the grapes. He does quite a bit of begging for forgiveness and mentions regrettable hasty words spoken in extreme circumstances.'

There was a quiet but firm rap at the door. Nanny levered herself up with a brisk, 'That will be Busby.'

Flushing, Flora sat up a little straighter against her pillows and ran her hand through her curls. 'Wait a moment, Nanny; where is my compact and my lipstick?'

'Wherever you left them,' stated Nanny unsympathetically as she continued lumbering towards the door.

Dorothy rolled over and started wagging her tail, eagerly asking, '*Did someone mention Busby? How do I look? Is the tip of my nose moist and shiny?'*

Busby was ushered in. He smiled at Flora, and she blushed and looked away, pretending to be looking for her notebook. He pulled up a chair next to the bed and, delighted, Dorothy jumped from the bed and onto his knee. Obligingly, he started to stroke her as she looked up at him with total love.

Nanny plonked herself back on Flora's bed – the springs creaked under her considerable weight.

'You are looking well, Mrs Farrington,' he commented, his brown flecked eyes sparkling.

'Oh! Well, Er...' muttered Flora, 'ah, here's my notebook – I was … er … looking for it, so I can, er, make notes, you know facts, clues, culprits, evidence and the like.' Her voice trailed off and she blinked at Busby.

Nanny rolled her eyes and butted in, 'So, young Busby, what is this new information you have?'

Busby frowned, instantly serious. 'Madame Amelie's death was definitely not the result of one of her ubiquitous cigarettes unfortunately uniting with all the turps in her studio. From the burn pattern, someone had liberally sprinkled the accelerator all over the studio and – more to the point – the back of her head was bashed in.'

Flora pursed her lips. 'But couldn't that be from when the timber fell? I know I'm pretty bruised from it.'

Busby shook his head. 'No, the doctor says there were no wooden fragments in the wound.'

Nanny swung her legs. 'So, who did it?'

Busby shrugged.

Flora exclaimed, 'Roberts! For goodness' sake, how obvious does it have to be? Amelie nailed him with the poor lamented footman—'

'Jean le Coeur,' interrupted Nanny.

Flora frowned. 'What?'

'Jean le Coeur was the footman.'

Flora gave her a withering look. 'As I was saying, Roberts was implicated in the footman's demise and disappearance and he had all the motivation in the world, with Amelie blackmailing him.'

'No! You are wrong,' said Nanny firmly.

Flora, wide eyed and incredulous, expostulated, 'Why?'

Nanny smiled; her eyes twinkled. 'Because I like him,' she explained before settling down comfortably and folding her arms over her ample bosom.

'Really, Nanny, that's hardly a reasoned argument!' snipped Flora.

Busby looked up from stroking Dorothy. 'We haven't been able to verify his movements before the fire, but I hardly think someone who comes so highly recommended by Sir Cyril Forsythe could possibly be guilty of such a heinous crime.'

Flora looked from Busby to Nanny and back to Busby. 'So, if neither of you think it was Roberts, who do you think it was? We really do need to get this sorted – I feel that Firuza is in danger with every moment that goes by.'

Dubiously, Nanny said, 'I suppose there is a possibility the Venerable Uncle might wish to remove Firuza so some relative of his own might take the role of consort to the crown prince. He did mention thinking some other girl would be more suitable. That would be a pretty good political reason to want rid of the princess, but why would he want to kill Amelie?'

Flora was instantly energised by Nanny entering into the speculation. Scribbling in her notebook, she declared, 'If Amelie was happy to blackmail Roberts, I don't think she would be shy of getting money off a foreign dignitary, but what would she have to blackmail him over? What evidence would she have that he was trying to dispose of Firuza?'

Deflated, she stared at her scribbles; she couldn't read her own writing, let alone draw any deep conclusions from it. 'It's all so confusing – I mean we have two clear possible motives for foul play.'

'We do?' queried Nanny.

Flora nodded. 'Firstly, the political motive – someone who doesn't want the marriage to go ahead. In which case, that footman was just a chance casualty and, if Amelie did see Roberts disposing of the body, then our butler is in the pay of some foreign government.'

Busby drew in a breath to speak but Flora cut him off. 'Please spare us your oft-repeated, and if I might say slightly naïve assertions, that Roberts is above suspicion because my Uncle Cyril vouches for him.'

Busby grinned at her good-naturedly. 'Alright, let's hear your second motive.'

'Greed! Plain and simple! Those diamonds are worth a fortune.'

'Always a good motive for murder,' piped up Nanny. 'So, the boy caught someone trying to steal the diamonds from your cami knickers – leaving Roberts to one side, who else is desperate for money?'

'Sister Claire!' blurted out Flora, excited by her sudden inspiration. 'She was positively crestfallen when she heard Firuza would not be joining her convent and paying for the new roof. If her sister caught wind of it, she would happily have tried blackmailing her. I think Sister Claire is more than capable of killing off any number of people; if looks could kill, she would have slain me any number of times. She could have killed the footman then paid Roberts to get rid of the body!'

She beamed triumphantly from Nanny to Busby.

Busby dryly said, 'Or Sister Claire and Father Luke could be having a torrid affair and Amelie found out about it and tried to blackmail them, so they needed to get rid of her.'

Flora let the idea float around her mind for a moment and was just getting excited by this new possibility. 'You could be right,' she murmured thoughtfully. 'Goodness knows what dark thoughts go on under that stiff wimple? I shouldn't think for a moment Sister Claire would allow sibling relationships to get in the way of what she wanted.' Then she caught the gleam in Busby's eyes and the amused look he exchanged with Nanny, and she realised they were teasing her. 'Well, really! You two are no help at all with your outlandish motives!' she exclaimed indignantly while the two of them started laughing.

Between chuckles, Busby said, 'It's no more fanciful than your other theories.'

What Flora would have replied remained a mystery because at that very moment Firuza burst through the door.

She was neat and trim in her tennis flannels with her racquet in hand. Her long hair was tied back in a thick loose plait and her deep green eyes were gleaming.

'Hello,' she gushed in a rather overly-loud voice. 'I thought I'd just pop in and see how you were doing, Godmother Flora. I didn't expect you to be holding court in your boudoir like some French queen at Versailles.'

Flora was a little taken aback by both the comment and the enthusiasm, but she smiled and said, 'I can see you are off to play tennis.'

Firuza took a few practice swings with her racquet, narrowly missing a vase of flowers. As the mother of two, Flora was used to such horseplay and didn't flinch. 'Yes, the boys and I are going to have a bit of a knockaround. But what I really called in to find out was how soon before you are going to be up and about and able to take me into Paris to get my dress for the ball? After all, we don't have much time.'

Flora looked at her with no small degree of surprise and said with a slight smile, 'As soon as is humanly possible.'

'Wonderful,' exclaimed Firuza, as she headed out the door. 'I'll tell Anne.'

In the quiet after she'd left, Flora looked at Nanny and Busby and wrinkled her forehead. 'Am I the only one who doesn't understand the child's enthusiasm, given that the ball is when her not-wished-for betrothal will be announced?'

Busby rose to his feet and shrugged. 'I don't know anything about young ladies, but I thought they were meant to get rather giddy over balls and new dresses. I'm glad someone is looking forward to it. Inspector Le Brun and I aren't. Speaking of which, I am late for a meeting with him to discuss security at the ball.'

Nanny was also on her feet and heading towards the door, but

Flora stopped her. 'Nanny, surely you find her enthusiasm odd.'

Nanny picked up her carpetbag and flung it over her shoulder, saying, 'Just youthful high spirits.'

CHAPTER EIGHTEEN

When Flora did venture outside, she was pleased to find that she was the only person enjoying the morning sun on the dew-spangled greenery. *I really don't feel like making small talk, especially not along the lines of how I am feeling or about recent tragic events.*

She tilted her face to the sun and allowed its warmth to caress her skin. She hadn't bothered with a hat so now she ran a hand through her short curls and enjoyed the slight breeze. Simply attired, in a chic navy frock with low heels, she was ready for action. *Chanel's use of flannel is so liberating; so different from the dresses I had to wear as a child.*

She had been forced to leave the cocoon of her bed and visit the garden for more than her own well-being. Naturally, Dorothy needed to go outside but, added to this responsibility, Flora had somehow found herself as the quasi owner of Venus. She glanced down at the snuffling mop of a dog by her feet. 'Poor little thing, you are missing your owner, aren't you?'

Venus looked up at Flora with black watery eyes and uttered a pitiful whimper. Flora bent down and gave her a pat before standing up again and resuming her perusal of the garden.

Dorothy threw Flora an angry glance and growled in disgruntled dog, '*Utterly ridiculous! If you ask me, all this fuss over that pampered pouch is totally unnecessary.*'

Venus was quick to retort, '*You bratwurst, you have no notion of romantic loss and how sensitive souls like me are slaves to our emotions. Take that, you Liverwurst!*' She gave Dorothy a quick nip on her ear and then looked the picture of innocence when Flora glanced down again.

'Dorothy, I heard that, now don't be such a meany and a grump! Poor Venus is grieving and needs to be treated with love.'

Dorothy fell into a sulky silence after whispering to Venus, '*Just you wait until I get you alone!*'

The garden's beauty soothed Flora. So much had changed there in the few days she had been confined to her room. *I do believe there is even more blossom out since I was last here and all those tulips have bloomed spectacularly – I wonder how they keep the slugs from eating them all?*

As the three of them approached the fountain, Flora noticed a discarded hoe, evidence once more of the often absent, ancient gardener. *One so rarely actually sees the count's gardener, just the traces he leaves behind – rather like when one has a mouse in the pantry.*

As Flora gazed at the hoe, she found it necessary to take a deep breath to steady her emotions. *Dandelions! Goodness, as if leaving the implement lying around as a tripping hazard wasn't bad enough.* She regarded the bright yellow, squat flowers with mounting horror. *If the man uses the hoe on those, the count will never be rid of them; if he cuts the dandelions off at base, lots more will grow up from the roots. They need to be dug up, ensuring you get all the roots.*

Scanning her surroundings, she spotted a wheelbarrow in the distance, deserted by the summerhouse. She was pleased to spot, more usefully and closer to hand, that next to the bench was a towel and a bit of old sack.

Leaving the dogs to sniff around, she set to, making things right. Using the sack to cushion her knees and with the trowel in hand, she was soon careful digging the offending weeds out by their roots.

Half an hour later, with her stockings ruined and her nails a disgrace, Flora had happily moved on from the dandelions to some pernicious ground ivy she had spotted under a bush.

She was so absorbed in her task she did not notice that she was no longer alone in the garden. How long the count had been watching her she didn't know, but when he spoke, she looked up in surprise.

'I used to help my wife with the weeding,' he said as he

discarded his jacket and joined her on his knees.

Flora gave him a brief nod but, as she was intent on getting a particularly deep root out whole, she didn't comment. She was aware of a certain tangle in her emotions at seeing him. *After all, do rather delicious grapes and some flowers really make up for screaming 'murderer' at one?* Even with the briefest of glances she could tell he had regained his normal vigour. *His grief seems to have been short-lived.*

They worked steadily side by side and between them was a silence that Flora found strangely companionable. When she happened to glance over at him, she noticed he had rolled up his sleeves and opened the top button of his shirt. *Goodness, there's a surprise, he doesn't look nearly so ...* The adjective eluded her.

He caught her eye and smiled, not the dangerous smile of a sexual predator, just a run-of-the-mill kind of smile and Flora found herself smiling back. His hair was slicked back, and his features were sharply drawn against the morning sunlight.

'We are doing rather well,' he commented, surveying the heap of weeds on the pathway. They were already starting to wilt in the morning sun. 'I'll just go and get the wheelbarrow.'

Helpfully, Flora gestured and said, 'I think your gardener left it by the summerhouse.'

The count chuckled. 'I'm afraid he's getting rather absentminded but he's been with us since he was a boy so I couldn't possibly get rid of him.'

Once more they exchanged smiles, and Flora watched him speculatively as he walked away. She thought about his comments on his ability to father sons and flushed. Hot and agitated, she returned to her weeding with renewed effort.

Dorothy and Venus looked up from their sniffing and regarded the count, then Flora.

Venus enquired, '*Is your mistress always so soppy around men*?'

"*Fraid so,*' sighed Dorothy, resuming some enthusiastic sniffing. Momentarily forgetting her animosity to Venus, she exclaimed, '*Goodness, something smells good here.*'

Venus joined her. '*Yes, whatever it is, it is definitely dead.*' She gave another sniff and ecstatically added, '*And wonderfully decayed. Let's dig it up and roll in it!*'

Dorothy wagged her tail in agreement, '*Exactly what I was thinking but we'd better wait until my mistress is distracted – she's rather odd about dogs digging and is bound to stop us.*'

Venus wagged her tail and replied, '*Humans are so illogical – after all, she clearly adores digging herself.*'

Dorothy snuffled back, '*Tell me about it! But we just have to wait for the count to come back and then she won't give us a second thought. We will be able to dig to our hearts' content.*'

They went back to their important sniffing under all the bushes.

The wheelbarrow squeaked as the count trundled it back along the gravel path. He stopped by the little mound of weeds.

'Here, let me help you with that,' said Flora as he stooped to pick up the debris.

She hurried over and bent to collect a handful of bindweed. As she straightened and tossed them into the wheelbarrow, she found she was a mere dandelion's width apart from the count. She couldn't help but notice how the fine lines around his eyes only emphasised how extremely good looking he was. He was regarding her intently, a faint smile playing around his lips.

Feeling herself flushing, she hastily looked at her feet.

He took a step closer and murmured, 'You have a smudge of soil on your face.' As he said the words, he very gently brushed his thumb over her cheek.

Gosh! thought Flora. *Am I outraged at him for taking such a liberty? Or was it actually rather nice?*

Before she could decide, they were both startled by a cough.

There was Busby, standing by the fountain and observing them both. His face was devoid of expression. His rusty curls caught in the sunlight. As was his norm, he was standing straight and strong and observed them with keen, knowing eyes.

Flora glanced guiltily at the weeds, the barrow, and the count. Her hands fell limp, and a weed dropped from her grip. She shuffled her feet and sought for something to say.

Dorothy and Venus were displaying no such inscrutability. They were sitting at Busby's feet, and both the canine ladies were gazing up at him with total devotion.

'*He's dreamy!*' cooed Venus.

'*Paws off!*' growled Dorothy. '*He's mine!*'

'What ho, Busby!' said Flora, then wished she hadn't.

There was a distinctly uncomfortable silence as the two men eyed each other warily. Flora was extremely relieved when Roberts appeared. Dignified in his tailcoat with his silver white hair, he was carrying a tray of crystal glasses and lemonade, and this broke the tension.

'If you will excuse me, there is a telephone call for the count and I thought Mrs Farrington could do with a beverage, given the weather and her exertions.' He gave her a knowing, almost fatherly, look. 'I also brought a damp cloth so Madame can wipe the soil from her hands.'

'Topping!' exclaimed Flora while vowing to herself *I must stop reading so much PG Wodehouse!*

The count strode back to the château, his jacket and tie flung over one shoulder.

Roberts deposited the tray on a nearby table which was shaded by a cherry blossom tree and departed. Flora eyed the inviting drink. She screwed her face up and briefly waged an internal battle. *If Roberts is the wanton killer of footmen and the shameless disposer of artists, should I shun the offering?* She focused on the delightful opaque liquid with the droplets of condensation frosting on the glass, promising chilled refreshment within. She licked her lips and gave up the fight.

Flora and Busby both sat on the notably uncomfortable wrought-iron chairs that were by the table.

The silence was uncomfortable in the extreme. She stole a glance at him, he was gazing across at the fountain, glass in hand, his long legs crossed in front of him. *Basically, he is the picture of relaxation, detestable man. Why am I the one who feels like I'm a naughty schoolgirl caught having tuck in the dorm at midnight?*

Flora took a sip of her lemonade; it was ice cold and tart.

The ancient gardener with arthritic joints tottered by. He didn't register any surprise at finding the wheelbarrow full and his work done; he simply trundled it away. The two dogs had positioned themselves devotedly at Busby's feet. Their twinkling black eyes were looking at him full of love and admiration.

Flora was finding the silence oppressive, so she broke it by saying, 'It's getting rather warm.'

Without looking at her and in an infuriatingly bland yet accusatory tone, Busby replied, 'You are rather pink.'

Silence fell again. Flora took another sip of her lemonade and ventured, 'I didn't know the count was so…'

Once more, she just couldn't think of appropriate word.

After a slight pause, Busby made a suggestion. 'So sleazy?'

Flora gave him a keen-eyed stare, but his face remained inscrutable as he gazed over his glass of lemonade at the fountain.

'No! That's not what I meant at all. When one gets to know him, he is surprisingly…'

'Egotistical? Obnoxious? Self-centred?'

Flora swivelled round in her chair, so she was square on to Busby and leant in towards him until he was compelled to look at her. His russet eyes were intent.

'Why do I get the impression that you don't like him?' she enquired.

Impassively, Busby corrected her. 'Like has nothing to do with it. I am just making a professional observation as a police officer.'

There was a silence before Flora said, 'Firuza and I will be visiting Paris for gowns for the ball.'

Busby maintained his lack of interest while gazing not at Flora but at the fountain. 'I know; I will be escorting you.'

'Right oh,' said Flora toying with her glass. She couldn't quite keep the excitement out of her voice as she commented, 'It's going to be quite a bash – lots of posh frocks and diamonds.'

'More like a security nightmare,' sighed Busby.

'Well, if you would listen to me and lock up Roberts, that

would be one less thing to worry about. After all, Amelie didn't bash herself on her head and spill turps all over the floor before setting it on fire.'

Busby smiled. 'Mrs Farrington, you really do have a thing about "The Butler Did It".' He eyed her speculatively for a moment before saying with certainty, 'Red.'

Thrown by the sudden change of conversational tack, Flora stared at him and blinked. 'What?'

'You should get a red ballgown.'

'I should?' gasped Flora, feeling her heart beating a little faster as confusion battled with elation in her mind. Busby had returned his gaze to the fountain, so Flora found herself staring at his profile. Well-chiselled though it was, with his fine nose and firm jawline, she did not find it totally satisfactory as she tried to assess his mood.

Still looking at the picturesque fountain rather than Flora, he cleared his throat and, with only the hint of a flush around his neck, he said, 'Yes, red suits you.'

CHAPTER NINETEEN

'I can't wait to see the Eiffel Tower!' exclaimed Anne a day or so later.

To Flora's eye she was looking especially beautiful that morning. Excitement added a faint pink to her porcelain cheek and her eyes gleamed. In her sensible, not to say austere, coat befitting of a lady's maid, she was striking. *Even the drabbest of clothes can't hide her fine figure – what a shame she was born to be a maid. If not, she would have taken London society by storm. She would look most becoming in a costume like the princess is wearing. The cut is youthful while not being childish.* Flora regarded the pair for a moment longer before, in her fashion-conscious mind, adding, *but with Anne it should be a vibrant purple, to set off her unusual eyes.*

At that point in her musings Firuza surprised Flora by grasping Anne's hands affectionately and exclaiming, 'What fun we are going to have today!'

Flora coughed. 'Sorry to burst the bubble of your enthusiasm but we are not going to the Eiffel Tower – we are going to Madame Chanel's in the Rue Cambon. That's at least a forty-minute walk along the river to the Eiffel Tower.'

Firuza faced Flora and with pleading eyes, quite unlike her normal haughty self, exclaimed, 'Oh, Flora, we simply must go to the Eiffel Tower.'

Unused to her goddaughter being a supplicant as opposed to a youthful dictator, Flora fudged the issue, 'Well, we'll see, perhaps if there's time after our dress appointment.' There was the sound of car engines and tyres on gravel. 'But now here are the cars, so it's time to go.'

The girls both squealed and hand in hand, ran to the vehicles.

The transport was courtesy of Inspector Le Brun.

Mystified, Flora watched their departure, then turning to Nanny she enquired, 'What has got into those two?'

Nanny dismissed her with, 'Just girlish high spirits. Now, have you got a clean handkerchief?'

'Really, Nanny, I am not twelve.'

Nanny indicated Flora's handbag, which was a rather whimsical straw affair woven in the shape of a bucket. Flora was extremely taken with it and wrongly, in Nanny's opinion, thought it gave her a youthful air. Nanny, if asked, would have suggested it was more likely to give Flora a comic air than the impression she was still in her salad days.

Nanny fixed Flora with a look and Flora harrumphed.

She checked in her bag all the same and found she hadn't, which gave Nanny the satisfaction of smugly handing her one from out of her ever-present carpetbag.

Eyeing Nanny's bag, Flora commented, 'The idea of your carrying around the priceless Abbastani diamonds in that old thing beggars belief.'

Wrinkling up her black hedgehog eyes with her broad smile and with a voice brimming with complacency, Nanny said, 'That's why it's the safest place for them. Now you hurry along; you are keeping that nice Inspector Busby waiting.'

'Really, Nanny!' exclaimed Flora once more, suddenly checking the slant of her hat in one of the many magnificent mirrors that graced the spacious hall. All in all, she was pleased with her reflection. It was too warm for a fur stole but too cool for a simple summer frock, so Flora had opted for a tawny patterned dress with a light plain coat the exact same shade of golden beige.

Absentmindedly, Flora remarked, 'I would really have liked to wear that rather dashing hat I recently acquired from Madame Agnès, but as that lady is an arch-rival of Coco Chanel I decided it would be tactless, hence this dull, neutral cloche.'

Nanny raised a bushy eyebrow. 'What? That thing that makes you look like you've got a flowerpot on your head?'

Nanny, quite rightly, took Flora's indignant look as

confirmation and said, 'Just as well you didn't, my girl! Now get away with yourself.'

She physically propelled Flora out of the front door and into the driveway.

When Flora reached the fleet of three large cars, she couldn't help but pause for a moment of admiration. *Goodness the French Police believe in travelling in style! Or is it just another 'Princess Perk'? I'm not quite sure what the car at the back is, but the yellow and black beauty in the front is a brand new La Buire Saloon. Goodness, what lines – how frightfully up to date. While the one behind I do believe is a red Citroen Type A – a little dated but still rather splendid.*

Upon allowing a smartly uniformed French policeman to open the door of the first car for her, to her horror she found not just 'that nice Inspector Busby' but also the myopic Father Luke and the austere Sister Claire sitting inside. Flora instantly surmised that the two girls had wisely opted for the second car. For an instant she wondered if she could join them, but she wasn't fast enough.

'Do hurry up and get in, Mrs Farrington; we really don't want to miss Mass at Notre Dame.' Sister Claire was pinch-faced and irritated.

'Oh, right – so sorry to keep you waiting,' she apologised, while trying to squeeze herself in. Unfortunately, Busby had opted to sit in the front seat beside one of Inspector Le Brun's men who was acting as chauffeur. After all, since she was only human, Flora would have found the trip far more enjoyable had she been forced into close proximity with him rather than with Sister Claire, who was all starch and bones.

Parviz watched them depart from the top of the main staircase. The enormous windows gave him an excellent view of the courtyard, the cars and the people. Seeing Firuza smiling and her eyes sparkling as she exchanged a word with Anne, his fists clenched. He stared at her, his eyes boring into her, willing her to look up, to look at him, but she was oblivious. *How can she laugh when she is going to buy an outfit to wear for the moment when her betrothal is announced? She must realise that it will be the end of us.*

His head was pounding.

'They seem happy enough,' murmured Dimash.

Parviz swung round, startled by his brother's sudden arrival. Through narrow eyes, he flashed Dimash a glance of pure venom. He took in his furrowed brow and the grim line of his mouth, both sliced through by the crown prince's scar. In that instance, Parviz' frustration boiled over and he snapped, 'I don't know what you're looking so tragic about! You are getting to marry Firuza!'

Dimash reacted immediately to Parviz' barbed comment. His head jerked up and his nostrils flared as he took an aggressive step closer to Parviz. He was eye to eye and toe to toe with his brother when they were interrupted by Nanny, wheezing up the stairs.

As she crested the top step, she puffed, 'What are you two boys doing here? You are glowering at each other like a couple of fighting cockerels. It's a lovely day so get yourselves out on the tennis court and use up some of that surplus energy.'

Dimash stepped down, disengaging from the brewing fight with his brother as he murmured, 'How about it?'

Parviz hesitated; he was still scowling at his brother as he nodded his assent.

They both changed into their tennis whites in record time. When Dimash reached the court, he found Parviz was already there, practising his shots on the sun-dappled court. He unscrewed his wooden racquet from its press.

When Dimash finally went to his side of the net, he barely had time to look up before the first ball from Parviz whistled past his ear. He didn't even attempt to hit it; he simply dodged it. Eying his brother with surprise, he stated evenly, 'Steady on!'

But Parviz was in no mood to listen.

The next ball came at Dimash with just as much force but this time he was ready for it, and he was able to return it with equal strength.

The ensuing rally was energetic and powerful. Both young men threw themselves into each stroke with total focus. Dimash was more measured in his strokes than Parviz but soon both had rivulets of sweat snaking down their faces and their muscles strained beneath their lightweight tennis whites.

Parviz lobbed a ball in a high arch to Dimash's back line, forcing him to run backwards. He did manage to return the ball – just – but he was wrongfooted so that when Parviz sprinted up to the net and, with all his strength, smashed the ball straight at the crown prince, there was no time for Dimash to get out of the way.

With a thud, the ball impacted Dimash's chest, and he crumpled like a rag doll.

Parviz stood motionless, too stunned to react. Heaving to catch his breath, he looked at the crumpled heap of a man that lay inert opposite him.

Then reality hit.

'Dimash!' he screamed as he dropped his racquet to the ground and raced to his brother.

Reaching Dimash's inert body, Parviz fell on his knees beside his older brother. Dimash was deathly pale beneath his chestnut complexion. Parviz placed his hand on his brother's chest and was greatly relieved to find he was breathing. After, what seemed an age to Parviz, the crown prince blinked open his blue-grey eyes and then, after a moment more, he was able to roll onto his side.

Parviz helped him to sit up while muttering, 'I'm so sorry!'

Dimash looked at his younger brother with eyes that looked far greyer and sadder than Parviz had seen before. His shoulders slumped as he shrugged and, his voice heavy with apathy, murmured, 'It's alright. It's what I deserve.' He let out a couple of rasping breaths before adding, 'After what I've done to Anne, I deserve a lot worse.'

'Anne?' asked Parviz sharply.

Dimash didn't answer, he just hung his head and Parviz wondered if he was fighting back tears.

Finally, Parviz stated, 'I've never seen you like this before.'

Dimash raised his head. 'I've never been in love before.'

A slow smile spread across Parviz's face. 'So, you don't want to marry Firuza?'

Startled, Dimash glanced over to Parviz, exclaiming, 'No! I mean, she's a fine girl and all that but I want to spend the rest of my life with Anne.'

Parviz let out a peal of laughter that rang across the court. Relief flooded his body for an ecstatic minute before the reality of the situation struck him and he sunk down next to Dimash.

'We are in a mess, aren't we?' he said.

To Flora, the journey seemed interminable, and it was with some relief that the car came to a jolting halt upon the cobbles in front of Chanel's boutique on the Rue Cambon.

With the rustle of her stiff robes, Sister Claire majestically disembarked from the car the moment Le Brun's chauffeur-policeman opened the car door for her. Flora slipped out next.

Excitedly, she scanned the scene, the bustle of people, the cobbles, the shutters, the faintly unpleasant smell of rubbish – it was all so French.

She spotted several overly thin young women; they scurried, with bent heads and in dilapidated clothes, into a side door by the illustrious Chanel main entrance. Chanel was renowned for employing the impoverished aristocratic girls who had fled the Russian revolution with nothing to commend them but their prowess with a needle. *Poor things!* thought Flora. *To be born into the riches of Imperial Russia and to then find yourself reduced to being a seamstress.*

'Flora, isn't this exciting!' exclaimed Firuza with shining eyes as she hurried across the cobbles towards her with Anne just behind.

Father Luke had eased himself out of the car with Sister Claire's help.

Sister Claire imperiously announced to Flora, Busby, and the world in general, 'We will return here at four o'clock promptly.'

With deference, Father Luke coughed and said, 'Could we make it five? Or five-thirty?' In response to Sister Claire's outraged, wide-eyed stare, he added, 'I am meeting someone, on, er, papal business.'

At the mention of the Pope, Sister Claire looked suitably impressed and almost curtsied in awe.

'Five-thirty?' beamed Flora, trying to keep the excitement out of her voice.

The focus had been on Father Luke so none of them had even notice the elderly woman, still ramrod straight despite her shabby clothes, who had been staring at the group. At her side was one of Chanel's little seamstresses, hollow eyed and painfully skinny. Her long, elegant neck and statuesque bearing as well as her striking facial features marked her out as being related to the elder woman – perhaps her granddaughter?

Instantaneously, Flora felt the hairs on the back of her neck rising. There was an alarming tension in the air which Flora struggled to make sense of. She intercepted the look the old woman was giving Father Luke; in it was a depth of inhuman passion that Flora had never before witnessed. Flora's heart seemed to freeze and then pound. As if in slow motion, Flora watched the old woman stride up to Father Luke. Energised by obvious anger, with her chin held high, the lady looked him in eye for a full thirty seconds. Father Luke blinked back at her through his thick pebble glasses.

With extreme dignity, she said something in Russian and then spat directly in his face.

All apart from Busby were too shocked to move. He stepped between Father Luke and the old woman, the bulk of his body separating them.

The young woman grabbed the old lady's arms; her eyes were wide, terror evident on her every feature. In fluent French, she gabbled, 'Please excuse us. I apologise. Please forgive Grand-mère; she has seen many, many horrors.'

Father Luke took a large white handkerchief and wiped the spittle off his cheek.

With many apologies, the girl dragged her grandmother away and hurried her down the cobbled street, murmuring in a low urgent voice all the while. The grand-mère's face was as iron, her lips were pressed together, and she remained silent.

Sister Claire quite unnecessarily took out her own starched white handkerchief and began dabbing at Father Luke's thin, pale cheek.

A flicker of anger crossed his face and, before he had time to regain his composure, he snapped, 'That is quite enough, Sister!'

Surprise registered on her pinched face. Then she pulled her eyebrows down and drew her lips into a thin line of annoyance.

Father Luke drew himself up to his full height, made a point of looking at his watch, and with great dignity announced, 'Sister Claire and I need to leave now if we are going to be in time for Mass.'

With that, the two marched purposefully away, leaving Flora staring open-mouthed and Busby looking puzzled. Anne and Firuza seemed to be less interested in the incident and more concerned with getting into Madame Chanel's emporium of delight.

Busby nodded to Flora and said, 'We will wait here.'

Flora grinned. 'So, being Firuza's bodyguard does not include dress shopping?'

Busby smiled back. 'Thankfully, no! And I hardly think she can come to much harm there.' He looked over to the entrance where the two young ladies were anxiously waiting for Flora to hurry up and join them.

As Flora walked towards them, she felt a frisson of excitement. *For half a sixpence I could squeal with girlish glee, just like Firuza and Anne. What is it about shopping?* Looking at Anne, Flora's old worries resurfaced. *She's being quite extraordinarily generous towards Firuza. I mean on a scale of socially tricky situations, going on a shopping spree to buy the girl who is about to be formally engaged to the man you love a dress to announce their engagement can't be easy.* She regarded the two girls, both young and pretty and neither showing any signs of concern, but Flora was not swayed from her convictions and decided, *I must buy her a little something and make time for her to see the Eiffel Tower.*

Once inside, Flora was not surprised to find that Madame Chanel was waiting for their appointment. *After all, a princess is a princess!* Flora smiled to herself as she watched Coco Chanel take Firuza's hand. Chanel, thin in the extreme and with swift, bird-like movements, was very much in command. Firuza had easily shed all the girlish exuberance she had been showing only moments later. She had transformed from a frivolous child just out of the school room into the regal princess she was. Anne stood demurely to one side.

Firuza, with Anne in her wake, was ushered away by Madame Chanel while Flora was taken by a competent, willowy lady who had introduced herself as Mademoiselle Something that Flora did not catch. She was secretly rather pleased to be relieved of chaperone duty and able to devote herself to the next interlude, solely to her own enjoyment.

Standing before the young, neat, and beautiful Mademoiselle, Flora was aware that this capable assistant was assessing her. As Mademoiselle's eyes scanned Flora from head to toe, Flora knew that Mademoiselle would be appraising, down to the ha'penny, how much Flora liked to spend on her clothes. Mademoiselle smiled; today she would make a healthy commission.

'So, is Madame looking for evening or daywear?' Mademoiselle inquired with false innocence.

They both knew that the appointment had been clearly made for buying a gown suitable for a lavish evening gala. They regarded each other.

Flora felt her heart skip a beat or two. 'Well, I do need a ballgown rather urgently but while we are here, I may as well look at everything.'

Mademoiselle smiled the knowing smile of a woman who is already spending her commission.

Within moments Flora was sitting in a comfy chair, an elegant coffee pot complete with a macaron to one side. Impossibly tall, slim and beautiful models glided in front of her.

As each model swished and swirled, Mademoiselle gave a running commentary: 'Perfect for a lunch out' or 'Ideal for a stroll around the Tuileries.'

In Flora's mind she could see herself, elegant and svelte;

Dorothy would be walking obediently to heel. Admiring glances would be forthcoming on all sides which Flora would accept graciously with a modest smile.

When Flora found herself in the neat changing room, the reality did not live up to the vision. Flora felt her earlier excitement deflate rather like the air out of a balloon. Even elevated by the small stool seamstresses use for pinning hems, Flora looked dumpy.

Flora observed her reflection and pressed her lips together. 'It's a bit—'

Flora wanted to say 'sack like' but Mademoiselle swiftly declared, '*Oui*, Madame, you look *très chic*.'

Flora looked dubiously back at the mirror. She bit the inside of her cheek as visions of herself looking ethereal evaporated in the harsh reality of her reflection. Folds of material seemed to hang all about her. She struggled with how to word her thoughts. 'It's rather shapeless.'

'*Mais non*!' smiled Mademoiselle. 'All it requires is a pin or two or a tuck put in.' She put her head on one side. Flora's eye followed Mademoiselle's eyes and rested on the heap of fabric at Flora's feet. 'And perhaps the hem needs shortening a little.'

Flora smile was unsure, and she felt slightly lightheaded. 'Yes, perhaps.'

Is the woman totally blind? I must be at least six inches shorter than any of your leggy models! Of course, the hem will need taking up – a lot!

Mademoiselle set to with her pins and Flora's hem. During the next half an hour Flora felt a range of emotions from desperation to despair. After half an hour of pinning the dress still looked like a sack, only of a slightly smaller variety.

Eventually Mademoiselle stood up and triumphantly declared, '*Voilà*!'

Poor Flora looked with dismay at herself. She looked less like a chic elegant lady and more like a toddler who was playing at dress-up with her mother's dress. She regarded herself some more and wished she hadn't. *Yoke neck, Slavic, and shapeless (or at least not the shape the Good Lord has made me) I fear this dress does not flatter me. I am more likely to illicit giggles rather than admiring glances should I ever be rash enough to venture into the Tuileries Gardens.* She twirled a bit and allowed the light to fall on the tunic. *And this colour looked so amazing on that blonde, blue-eyed model yet it gives me a decidedly sallow complexion.*

Mademoiselle was looking expectantly at Flora.

'*Voilà* indeed.' Flora smiled weakly.

'We will amend it and have it sent to you,' beamed Mademoiselle. She had no intention of losing this dress sale, however uncomfortable Madame obviously was.

Flora nodded. Internally she wailed, *Why, oh, why can't I clearly, but firmly, look her in the eye and say, 'Mais non!' Come on, Flora – get a grip! You are mature lady of a certain age! You can do this!*

'Mademoiselle, I think … perhaps…'

'*Oui, oui*, Madame we must move on to ballgowns.'

'Oh, right ho!' murmured Flora sadly. *Well, perhaps it won't look so bad when I get it home. I just need to be sure Nanny doesn't see it. I really don't think I could stand her laughing and wanting to know how much money I've spent and then she is bound to offer to get me a burlap sack from the stables and run up a whole wardrobe for me.*

The ballgown portion of the appointment was far more enjoyable, largely because both Flora and Mademoiselle agreed that the most expensive dress on offer was 'the one'.

It was the first dress that Flora's eyes had alighted on. As luck would have it, the dress was as striking on her as it had been on the model. It was red and heavily beaded. Its silhouette was simple, but the daring scooped back and faux drape gave it a dramatic flair.

'Exquisite needlework,' commented Flora as Mademoiselle helped her step out of the dress.

Mademoiselle smiled in a modest yet exultant way and murmured, 'We pride ourselves on the skill of our seamstresses.'

'And even with all this intricate beading it can be ready in time for the ball?'

'The date *encore, s'il vous plaît*?'

Flora gave it and Mademoiselle raised an eyebrow. 'It will be difficult but not impossible.'

Flora felt a brief pang of guilt over the sleepless nights of toil in poor light her rush order would give those poor overworked Russian immigrants, before beamed broadly and declaring, 'Excellent!'

CHAPTER TWENTY

Excitement dissipated as the dress-finding mission was completed and Flora realised she was actually extremely hungry. She glanced at her watch. 'Goodness, it's two o'clock already and we haven't had any lunch! I must collect up the girls.'

Casually, Mademoiselle explained, 'Mais, Madame, the princess and her companion left an hour ago.'

Flora dropped the stocking she had been teasing up her calf. 'What?'

'*Mais oui!*' affirmed Mademoiselle casually.

Flora swallowed down her panic and with false calmness, she said, 'Busby and Inspector Le Brun's men are waiting outside by the front entrance. They will be waiting in the cars.'

With infuriating serenity, Mademoiselle folded the garment and stated, 'No, I think not – they specifically asked to leave by the back door.'

Flora stared at her in disbelief and in a strained voice said, 'You must be mistaken.'

Mademoiselle, pretty, young, and unshakeable, stated, 'Why no, Madame, I am quite certain, I saw it with my own eyes when I went to get the bag that went so well with the robe.'

The very small amount of French chic which had managed to rub off on Flora during the many hours she had spent in Chanel's boutique evaporated in a rather rapid heartbeat. Moments later, with her clothes dragged on rather than carefully arranged, she burst out of the main entrance. She spotted Busby and the assortment of Inspector Le Brun's men. The mere sight of him lent Flora hope.

Breathlessly, with wide eyes, she grabbed Busby's arm and blurted out, 'The girls have gone!'

Busby blinked, a moment of surprised registered in his creased brow but he maintained the appearance of calm assurance.

'Are you sure?' he enquired.

Flora did not dignify the remark with a verbal response, but her glance said all that needed to be conveyed. The only sign of the potential seriousness of the situation was a slight flush beneath his rusty freckles and the clenching of his firm jaw.

Busby nodded, gave some instructions to the men, and strode into Madame Chanel's establishment. Presumably, Flora's tale was confirmed as he was back in minutes.

In Busby's absence, Flora's mind had had enough time to spiral out of control. *Abducted! The girls must have been kidnapped – there will be a ransom note soon – we will need to get those diamonds off Nanny although quite why they voluntarily left the boutique I can't imagine? Could they have been lured out under false pretences? Or worse, could some Soviet assassin have taken the opportunity to bump Firuza off to stop the wedding? Gosh! I do feel rather peculiar – lightheaded, rather dizzy. Is it the stress?* Her stomach rumbled. *Or am I just hungry?*

It was fortunate that Busby returned at that moment. 'I spoke to Madame Chanel. The princess and Anne were talking about the Eiffel Tower, and she mentioned how delightful the walk along the Seine is to the Eiffel Tower at this time of year, with the cherry blossom out.'

'What? But why didn't they ask me?' exclaimed Flora.

Busby gave her a half-smile. 'Weren't you ever young? You know how much the princess craves freedom.'

Flora was aware that what he was saying was true. She had several rather roaming flashbacks to her own youth which did nothing to calm her anxiety. For form's sake she made a few blustering incoherent sounds.

Busby spoke to Le Brun's men. There was quite a bit of manly nodding and looking serious before they all dispersed. When he came back to Flora, he had taken his hat off and run his hand through his rusty curls – presumably to aid his thoughts. Despite the seriousness of the situation, Flora could not help thinking how much she liked the way he was able to control everything but his own hair.

Through a concerned frown he explained, 'There is no getting around what a dangerous situation this is. Firuza may well be being watched and there are plenty of people who would like to take advantage of her being unguarded to do her harm. Even aside from her position, I don't relish the idea of those two young girls wandering around Paris alone, especially down by the river. The place is overflowing with pickpockets and ruffians.'

Flora felt a wave of nausea. Once more, she wasn't sure if it was hunger or fear, but Busby was still talking.

'The Parisian police are being notified, and I have sent one of the cars straight to the Eiffel Tower. I suggest you and I walk along by the river; if we are fast, we may catch them up. There is no need to panic yet.'

He spoke calmly and firmly but Flora was still concerned, and clarified, 'I don't like your use of the word "yet".'

He glanced down at her, half-grimacing and half-smiling. 'Well, the sooner we get going, the sooner we will find them.'

They set off at a brisk pace, dodging cars, vans and laborious heavy horses that were pulling carts noisily along cobbled streets. On either side of them stood the elegant façades of tall houses with their attractive shutters and ornate wrought-iron balconies.

After a few minutes of this vigorous exercise, Flora puffed, 'I may be wearing comfortable shoes, but, even so, let me latch onto you for support.'

She took his arm and felt his muscles tense. *I hope that reaction is due to surprise not displeasure* she thought as he paused for half a stride then pressed on.

They both knew Paris well and reached the Seine in rapid time.

The river looked murky and grey despite the spring sunshine. On this water highway there was frenzied activity, with numerous ladened barges and men shouting. The glimpses of the Eiffel Tower spurred Flora on.

They passed by the Pont Alexandre III with its magnificent

columns and elaborate candelabra.

Flora commented, 'This is my favourite bridge in Paris.'

'Because it's overly ornate?' queried Busby, not slackening his pace.

'No, because it's regal and spectacular.'

They hurried down the steps and onto the walkway that ran along the side of the river.

Glancing around, Flora commented, 'They have recovered remarkably well from the great flood.'

'Uh?'

'The flood – you must have seen it in the papers – Paris was underwater just a few months ago when the Seine burst its banks.'

'Hmm!' was all Busby said as they hurried along. They passed a group of men in tatty clothes; one had his empty sleeve pinned up where his right arm should have been, and another was on crutches and had only one leg. They were passing a bottle from one to the other, each taking a swig. Flora regarded them with both compassion and fear. *After all, they didn't choose to go to war, but they don't look very savoury.* She thought of Anne and Firuza.

Tentatively, she enquired, 'Busby, do you think the girls will be alright?'

He grunted.

Sharply, Flora enquired, 'What does that mean?'

'What does what mean?'

'You grunted.'

'I didn't.'

Flora was righteously indignant. 'You did!'

'Well, that was a rather nonsensical question.'

Affronted she challenged him. 'I don't see why.'

He stopped with the river surging beneath them and a sea of humanity rushing around them. Facing Flora with one eyebrow raised and his mouth quirked with what turned out to be black humour, he said, 'Well, we would hardly have mobilised the whole Parisian police force and be striding by the Seine if I was confident about their safety.' As he finished speaking, he continued walking in silence.

After a minute of two, Flora rather grudgingly muttered, 'There are times when a little considerate fabrication would be both comforting and appreciated.'

'Noted,' came his neutral reply.

They were approaching the Pont d'Iéna and hurried up the steps. To their right was a busy road with the Jardins du Trocadéro beyond and to their left, beyond the bridge, the Tour Eiffel.

Flora tugged on Busby's sleeve. 'Busby?'

Cautiously he said, 'Yes?'

'Have you had lunch?'

Surprise evident in his voice, he replied, 'No.'

Sadly, Flora said, 'Me neither. I am rather hungry.'

Busby pressed on until Flora exclaimed in excitement, 'Do you smell that rather delicious smell? Of crêpes cooking?'

'Crêpes?' queried Busby in disbelief.

Flora sniffed some more. 'I think I smell melted chocolate too.' She suddenly stopped and, elated, cried, 'Oh yes! Look over there!'

Busby looked and there was a moveable crêpe stand box with a man in a beret and apron skilfully smoothing golden batter on a hot plate. Flora released his arm and hurried over, all the time reaching in her neat basket bag for a coin or two. Within the space of a breath, she was placing her order in rapid French.

Busby stood slightly dazed. He watched her with eyes wide in disbelief.

'Really?' was all he said as she returned to his side with two neat paper-wrapped crêpes and a broad grin.

'I need to keep my strength up!' she replied with both a smile and an air of dignity.

He cocked his head on one side. 'With the princess and Anne missing, you want to stop for food?'

Taking a generous bite, she looked up at him with her mouth full. 'Not for mere food, for a Parisian crêpe with chocolate.' She looked up innocently at him through long lashes and enquired. 'Does that mean you don't want the one I bought for you?'

He smiled, taking his proffered crêpe. 'Alright – I suppose a five-minute break won't make much difference.'

After a little happy munching, Flora smiled mischievously. 'It's so wonderfully illicit and dangerously naughty to be eating on the street. My sainted grandmother would have a fit if she could see me now, brazenly eating in the Jardins du Trocadéro so close to the Pont d'léna.'

Busby grinned back and nodded towards all the tourists in their Sunday best milling around them. There was a constant stream of happy holidaymakers going to and fro on the bridge toward the Tour Eiffel. That iconic landmark, with cars driving through its legs, boasted further throngs of sightseers.

'What, even eating a crêpe in Paris?' he teased.

Emphatically, Flora answered, '*Especially* in Paris.'

He raised an eyebrow, and a broad smile creased his face. 'You do live a scandalous life!'

She laughed lightly catching the twinkle in his eye. She savoured another mouthful with her eyes shut before sighing, 'Delicious!'

As she spoke, her gaze wandered over two nuns walking with an immaculate crocodile of small pupils heading towards an educational visit to the Tour Eiffel. Then she could not help giving an admiring look at a glamorous lady walking a pair of haughty Afghan hounds. But it was two men sitting on a nearby bench that caught and held her attention.

One of them was Father Luke. Beside him sat a man who was as round and corpulent as Father Luke was spare and lean. Apart from his size, Father Luke's companion's most notable feature was a large fur hat on his bald head. The two men were talking and whatever they were discussing it didn't appear to be making either of them very happy. Flora nudged Busby and nodded in their direction.

Busby got as far as whispering, 'How curious, I wonder what he's up to? I think we should just hang back and observe.'

Poor Busby was not quick enough. Barely had he got the words out, when he realised Flora had not listened to a word he'd said. She lost no time in striding over to the two men and greeting them with a jolly, 'Father Luke, how amazing seeing you here.'

Busby muttered something about saints rushing in where angels fear to tread before following her over to the bench.

Father Luke blinked myopically behind his thick pebble glasses as was his habit. His skinny body stiffened, and he shifted ever so slightly away from his companion. The other man opened his large, broadsheet newspaper.

Flora observed them with mild consternation. *Goodness, our resident cleric seems to be quite away with the fairies today – he has so far forgotten his manners that he hasn't even made the weakest attempt to stand at my arrival. I wonder who his companion is? He must be quite something to distract our Father Luke to such an extent that he abandons even basic courtesies.* Surreptitiously she eyed the pair. The ungainly bulk of the stranger only served to add emphasis to just how painfully thin Father Luke was.

Putting aside his etiquette faux pas, she pressed on. Glancing around, she inquired, 'No Sister Claire?'

Hastily he explained, 'We lost each other.'

'What? At Mass?' queried Flora, surprised.

He nodded.

Flora stared at him and commented, 'How curious.' She regained her focus quickly and continued, 'No matter. Have you or your companion seen the princess or Anne?'

Both Father Luke and the other man visibly started. Busby rolled his eyes heavenwards.

Father Luke blurted out, 'We are not together – I don't know this gentleman.'

Innocently, Flora said, 'Oh really? I thought you were chatting?'

Father Luke cut across her. 'The princess is missing?' He struggled to his feet. 'I haven't seen her. Should I help you look?'

Busby, who had joined Flora, said, 'No need, Father Luke. We have mobilised the Paris police.'

The large man buried himself deeper behind his paper as Busby took Flora's elbow. 'Mrs Farrington, we should be going.'

'Oh! Right oh!' said Flora, bidding Father Luke goodbye.

Flora could not help feeling a surge of excitement as they strode across the bridge towards the magnificent Tour Eiffel. Surrounded by gaily dressed tourists in holiday spirits, it was impossible not to have some of that enthusiasm infuse her steps.

After her momentary elation, she checked herself. *Goodness Flora, get a grip on yourself! Here we are searching for two defenceless girls, and you are so wanting in finer feelings that you are excited by a visit to the Eiffel Tower.* Instantaneously, the crêpe felt heavy in her stomach and her body prickled with apprehension. *What if the phantom footman killer has followed the girls to Paris? Or what if some political adversary of Abbastan has been spying on Firuza and just waiting for an opportunity to assassinate her?*

Flora's rather vivid imagination conjured up the image of Firuza and Anne as the heroines in a melodramatic film at the local pictures. In flickering black and white, the girls clung desperately to each other, wide eyed and terrified. All the while the theatre organist played dramatic music and a menacing figure in a black mask and cape advanced on them, step by step, like a pantomime villain.

Flora felt sick. Everything swam before her eyes. Then, as if emerging from a fog, she made out two girls walking towards them with carefree smiles. They were almost skipping arm in arm in their happiness. The approaching girls' joy only increased Flora's sense of despair. *That's how young girls should be – without worries or fears. If only we can find Anne and Firuza safe and well, I will cherish them and shower them with love.* Flora looked again. *They look vaguely familiar – no – it can't be.* She blinked trying to clear her vision. Even on a closer look there was no doubt about it, here were the two missing souls. Disbelief gave way to anger in less than a second. *Of all the cheek! It is Firuza and Anne! How dare they be sauntering around so full of joie de vivre!*

They were only about a third of the way across the bridge when they came face to face with Firuza and Anne. They both appeared flushed and happy.

Outraged, Flora stopped, stared, and stammered, 'Firuza,

Anne, where have you been? I was *so* worried!'

Anne had the grace to look shamefaced, but Firuza was merely surprised. Firmly and with no hint of remorse, the princess said, 'But we finished early and when we peered into your changing room you looked as if you were having so much fun, we didn't like to bother you.' Flora was too angry and relieved to speak, but Firuza still had more to say. 'We are ravenous. We thought we would wait for you before we ate.'

She batted her long eyelashes around her dazzling green eyes and coquettishly entwined her arm around Flora's. Flora was reminded of Dorothy, when she had eaten Flora's new fan and wished to ingratiate herself back into her good books. Speechless, she looked from one young woman to the other.

While Flora was without words, Busby was not. 'Princess, apart from causing Mrs Farrington distress, you have caused Inspector Le Brun's men a great deal of trouble.'

Flora tried to look the picture of martyred innocence while hoping there was no tell-tale trace of chocolate or crepes around her lips.

The journey back to the château was uncomfortably silent. Sister Claire appeared to feel that Father Luke had been most remiss in mislaying her in the cathedral. She had spent several hours in a futile search for him. Flora was far too occupied with her own grievances to engage in conversation with anyone. She didn't even respond to Busby when he murmured, 'I wonder what the Princess and Anne have been up to – it's not like either of them to behave like this.'

CHAPTER TWENTY-ONE

It was inevitable that the Venerable Uncle would hear about the princess's exploits, and it was equally inevitable that he would make his displeasure known. It was not until the following morning that the unavoidable confrontation took place.

Nanny, Flora, and the dogs were just going for a gentle post-breakfast perambulation and observed it all. They wandered on to the forecourt of the château and found the Venerable Uncle, the princess, and the two princes already there. The Venerable Uncle had his hands on his ample hips with his fists pressed into the folds of his silk cummerbund and his magnificent moustache quivering with rage.

'Make no mistake about it, Princess, you *will* marry the crown prince, and you *will* conform to a life of circumspection, service, and obedience. This reckless behaviour gallivanting around Paris alone will never happen again.' His voice was frightening in its calm certainty, his steely eyes boring into the young Firuza.

In her simple jersey frock and with her hair in a long plait hanging down her back, Firuza looked ridiculously young. In an act of youthful defiance, she put her shoulders back and snapped, 'I wasn't alone – Anne was with me.'

Somehow his podgy face became hard like granite in its unyielding expression. Flora could see the impossibility of such youth being able to withstand his aged determination. His moustache twitched as he continued, 'For people like you and me, our lives are aligned in the stars. We do not have the luxury of indulging in our personal whims and wishes like any common peasant. Think on my words and think well.' He drew in a breath, turned, and gave a half-bow to Flora and Nanny which the ladies ignored while Venus and Dorothy united in a low growl. 'Excuse me, I need to go and attend to affairs of state.' He fixed Firuza with a hostile eye and added, 'Matters that affect the lives of your people and mine.'

As the Venerable Uncle strutted off, he reminded Flora of an imperious Bantam cockerel she had once owned. She switched her gaze to Firuza. Her body was taut, and her fists clenched so tightly that her knuckles showed white. She was biting her lip.

Flora felt a wave of despair as she regarded Firuza. Her eyes misted with futile compassion for the Princess. Flora was struck by the worry lines on the girl's face. *I wonder how many years it will be before the cares and stresses of courtly life, as Dimash's wife, etch those fine lines on Firuza's brow, between her eyes and around her mouth into deep trenches of misery, permanently marring her beautiful features? How I wish her mother was still alive and could advise the child. After all, she too had faced similar dilemmas whereas my biggest decisions are less about international relations and major life sacrifices and more along the lines of, 'Should I have that second slice of cake, or should I resist?'*

Dorothy and Venus were uninterested in the human drama unfolding and both made slight mewling noises to encourage Flora to take them on their promised walk.

Nanny ignored the dogs and screwed up her beady black eyes. 'Well, now, he's a pompous twit and no mistake. I may have to slip a generous serving of laxatives into his night-time cocoa.'

She took a step towards Firuza and clapped the girl none too gently on her shoulder with her paddle of a hand. 'Cheer up, my old duck! I know just the thing to improve your spirits. While Flora walks the dogs, why don't you and I go and explore the medieval château's dungeons?' Her voice took on an excited lilt. 'If we're lucky, there may be a torture chamber – perhaps even an oubliette.' Her eyes sparkled. 'And while we look, we can think of all the people who came to a terrible end in those dim halls.' She sighed in contentment. 'There's nothing like contemplating the misery of others to buck up one's mood.'

Flora gave Dorothy's lead a gentle pull to remind the hound of her manners and to discourage her from tugging on it, impatient for her walk, and then looked up at Nanny and Firuza. 'The count says there is a lot of work going on in the medieval château, so all the interesting bits are inaccessible.'

'Stuff and nonsense,' declared Nanny as she tucked one arm into the crook of the princess's elbow and hitching up her carpetbag in her other hand before stalking off towards the fairy-tale turrets of the old castle.

Flora watched the incongruous pair depart with some amusement. Firuza was willowy and walked with easy graceful strides in her becoming, sporty dress whereas Nanny was small and square and creaked with every step she took in her sensible shoes. As Nanny walked, her dated black starched dress crackled even more loudly than her joints. *All in all, Nanny's outfit is far more suited to the Victorian era than life in today's rather racy 1920s.*

Venus, as well as Dorothy, was now jerking on the lead and making little whimpering sounds just to remind Flora that they were desperate to be off.

'Alright, my darlings, you have been very patient,' declared Flora as she set out on a brisk walk.

Much to the dogs' dismay, they had not gone far before they rounded the summerhouse and came face to face with Sister Claire and Father Luke, both of whom had their prayer books in their hands.

Flora smiled, as she was wont to do, only to have the gesture rebuffed. Father Luke blinked myopically in her general direction while Sister Claire looked down her narrow nose at her.

She spoke without warmth. 'Mrs Farrington, I thought the princess was with you.'

Flora continued smiling but felt small and foolish beneath Sister Claire's perusal. 'Well, she was, but she and Nanny have gone off on a jolly to explore the medieval château.'

Sister Claire looked more imperious than ever and through

tight lips asked, 'Whatever for? That place is full of dust and cobwebs.'

Sister Claire clearly did not actually want a reply as, without even a second's pause, she glided past Flora, Venus, and Dorothy, with her head held high and her personal cleric at her side.

Flora only had a moment to ponder on the pair as the dogs really had reached their patience limit. As she obliged them by striding off in the opposite direction, she mused, *Father Luke is less of a man and more of a shadow.*

CHAPTER TWENTY-TWO

To begin with, Flora was not concerned when Nanny and Firuza failed to show up at lunchtime. Her only thought was, *They must be having a spiffing time.*

Everyone else, apart from the count, assembled in the dining room, eager to eat. Parviz was restless. He murmured to Dimash, 'Where can Firuza have gone to? I am starving.' Dimash grinned and shrugged his shoulders.

The Venerable Uncle twitched his moustache and looked at his watch frequently. Flora glanced at him. *I bet that miserable old goat is counting each second as yet another black mark against Firuza.* Father Luke was quite detached from his fellow guests and seemed untouched by the temporal inconvenience of hunger. *No doubt his mind is on higher spiritual things than lunch.*

Sister Claire was far more human. 'Mrs Farrington, where is your ward?'

Flora smiled at Sister Claire in response to that formidable lady's stern query and pleaded ignorance. She refused to flinch under the nun's withering gaze across the salad and ham decking the luncheon table.

Sister Claire coldly stated, 'I don't think we can delay grace or luncheon any longer.'

'Quite! Quite!' agreed Flora, eyeing the mashed potatoes and feeling rather peckish.

She was secretly pleased that the count was absent from the dining room table. *I suspect he'd make rather a fuss about the medieval château being dangerously inaccessible due to work being done on it.*

It was only as she embarked on some delicious hothouse strawberries and sorbet that the words 'dangerously inaccessible' began to penetrate her thoughts.

Perhaps I'll just have one more mouthful and then I'll nip down to those jolly dungeons and remind Nanny and Firuza that life isn't all about fun in torture chambers and that they need to attend to real life and lunch.

With great self-restraint, she demurred when Roberts offered her coffee. Tempting though its aromatic scent was, she excused herself.

Pausing only to pull on her light coat she hurried across the majestic front hall, through the grand front door and down the gravel drive.

Of course, there won't be an issue – I'll barely have time to call a jolly "Coo-ee!" and there will both Nanny and Firuza, speckled with cobwebs and laughing happily.

Even in her agitation, beholding the medieval château with its romantic turrets lifted her spirits.

After all what could possibly happen to them? This place is as secure the Tower of London. I know Inspector Le Brun brought in extra men after Amelie's death.

The sight of two of Le Brun's men patrolling by the moat confirmed her surmise.

Soon she was creaking open the heavy door in the nearest tower. The interior was dark and musty. She shivered, partly from the chill but mainly from the eerie atmosphere.

Her cheery cry of 'Coo-ee!' was met with an empty echo and an unnerving scuttling sound which Flora feared was a rat.

Her eyes became accustomed to the miserly light that the three arrow slits in the thick stone walls and the open door offered.

'They probably just can't hear me,' she said out loud in her brightest voice, in the vain hope that the assertion would give her courage.

She had two options: either to explore the narrow stone staircase to her left that spiralled up the turret or to push on through the arched wooden doorway straight ahead.

She eyed the doorway directly in front of her.

That door is against the wall; on the other side is the portcullis's driveway.

Mentally she summoned up the image of the first time she had driven across the rattling bridge that breached the moat to be met by the magical turret's medieval château either side of the driveway. There was a lofty portcullis arch that led through to the newer château. Above the arch, the sturdy castle walls were punctuated by more small slit windows.

'I suspect that door must lead down to the dungeons.' Flora smiled to herself. 'They are probably just on the other side.'

Losing no time, she strode over to the door and tried the ornate handle. The door was stiff, but to Flora's relief it was not locked. The metal door handle and the ancient hinges creaked but swung open under a bit of pressure.

There before Flora all was black. This was not the darkness of night when, even if there is no moon, the stars offer a glimmer of light, but an impenetrable void. She experienced a moment of doubt.

The open doorway let in just enough day to show the first shadowy step. Flora surveyed the scene in front of her and swallowed down a rising terror of the sheer unknown emptiness before her. She took the first step down and inhaled the cool, damp air. The sensation reminded her of a cave she had once visited. She hadn't enjoyed the cave exploration. As she breathed in, she was assailed by the dank and unappealing whiff of stagnant water.

'Nanny? Firuza?' she called in her loudest voice.

There was no reply apart from an ever-repeating echo. It was an echo that suggested the dungeon was cavernous, which was hardly surprising given that it probably extended under the expanse of the whole medieval château.

Flora took another step down towards the abyss. She placed one hand on the stone wall for balance, flinching from the cold and damp.

She called again and once more she was greeted not by an answering cry but by a mocking echo.

For the first time, her lingering anxiety about Nanny and Firuza threatened to bubble up out of control. Her heart was beating fast, and, despite the chill air, she felt hot and sweaty. She steadied herself with a couple of deep breaths.

Come on, Flora, get your act together! You are only on the second step – if you are going to heroically find Nanny and Firuza you at least need to be brave enough to get all the way down these steps and into the dungeons.

With determination she took another step down, but instead of the next step there nothing but air. Panic shot through her and instinctively she threw herself backwards. With an involuntary scream she crashed down on her bottom.

Winded, she sat for a moment before realising she was bruised and shocked but otherwise alright. She pressed her hands against the damp wall and managed to stand. Gasping to control her breath, she peered over the precipice. As her eyes adjusted, she could just make out another stone step beyond the broken one, but her nerve failed her. Her thoughts raced with a gory vision of Nanny and Firuza lying in a crumpled mass of broken bones at the base of the stairway.

To give herself courage, she spoke out loud. 'If they were down there, surely they would have answered me.' She swallowed and bit her lip, despair washed over her as she wailed, 'Oh, Nanny, where are you?'

Once more paralysed by fear and indecision, she stood immobile until in her mind she heard Nanny's Irish burr. She knew exactly what she would say. 'Well, standing there like a stuffed dodo isn't going to help! For goodness' sake, girl, pull yourself together and do something!'

She drew herself up to her full height and declared, 'Right, Flora Farrington! Get a grip! What now?' She looked around her. 'I need to face the facts. If something has happened to Nanny and Firuza, it won't be by accident. Nanny is far too canny to have an accident and Firuza is fit and feisty – there's little chance of her coming to harm unless someone had a hand in it. The best thing I can do is to go back to the main château and get some help and, more to the point, a torch or three to throw some light on things.'

She turned to leave, aware of the back of her dress clinging to her; it was wet and no doubt grubby. *But a mucky dress is the least of my worries.*

Leaving the dungeon door open, she retreated to the welcoming light, however dim, of the hallway.

As she crossed the entrance portal, she glanced at the corner where a narrow stone staircase spiralled up to the tower. She raised her eyebrows and paused. Hope flickered in her heart. *I wonder whether could they be up there? I had better check before I charge into the château demanding a search party and torches.*

She headed towards the arch of the narrow stone stairway. Taking two steps at a time, she wound her way up the narrow steps. At each turn, an arrow slit in the thick stone walls offered a little, much welcome illumination. With the added light and each forward step, Flora's optimism swelled. *I bet the pair of them will be up here, probably happily taking in the view. Gosh, they will laugh when I tell them all about my worries. Nanny will be puffing on one of those disgusting Woodbine smokes and complaining about her knees and Firuza will be enjoying the wind in her hair.*

There was a thick rope pegged against the wall which she found most useful as she climbed ever higher.

As she reached the first floor, the main staircase ended at a vast, metal-studded, arched wooden door. The steps continued to twist upwards, far more cramped than before, through an opening to the right.

Flora placed a hand on the door, feeling elated. *Ah, this must be the door into the living area of the medieval château. Glimpsed from the ground above the portcullis, it looks vast. I bet that on the other side of this door there are several magnificent chambers. If I just go through, I will be able to imagine the courtly ladies in their flowing robes and clanking men in armour. Best of all, Nanny and Firuza will be there. These walls are so thick, no wonder they couldn't hear me.*

Excitement quickly changed to dismay: no matter how hard she tugged at and rattled the ancient handle, the door wouldn't open. She tried pulling it and even applied her shoulder to it, which achieved nothing but pain.

Eventually, flustered, and unhappy she had to admit it was locked. Her shoulders drooped and she leaned against the door. Closing her eyes, she became aware of a dull headache forming.

She took a deep breath, and her thoughts clarified.

Out loud, she announced, 'So, it's back to the earlier plan – I will puff and wheeze my way to the top of the tower where I will find Firuza laughing and leaning over the balustrade enjoying the excellent view while Nanny slumps against the side smoking like a chimney with her carpetbag in her hand.'

But when Flora did eventually reach the top, she found the door as barred and locked as the previous one.

'Oh, rats!' she exclaimed. 'What now?'

Through a nearby arrow slit she spied the main château with its flag proudly flying but, more to the point, in the courtyard stood the Venerable Uncle, resplendent as ever in shimmering turquoise silk. The two princes stood before him. Dimash's stance was erect and imperial while Parviz was standing with a rigid posture looking tense and irritated. *Obviously not a jolly family get-together! I wonder what the conflab is all about.*

For a second, she considered shouting for help, but she quickly rationalised that they wouldn't be able to hear her.

Standing very still, her mind began to spiral even more tightly than the stone staircase. Looking intently at the Venerable Uncle, she drew her eyebrows together and tilted her head.

Her mind flashed backed to the incident on the balustrade at the grand château. *I know I wasn't mistaken – he wasn't trying to save Firuza, he wanted to push her over the rail to her death. I thought his turnabout was far too fast to be genuine. He went from disapproving of the match between Firuza and Dimash to suddenly insisting that the betrothal ball takes place in rapid-fast time. I wonder if there is some funny convention that means a broken betrothal or Firuza's death would be of advantage to him. We know he is totally ruthless.* She swallowed as a grisly vision of the Venerable Uncle killing his own younger brother swam before her eyes. *He might have committed fratricide in order to protect the crown prince, but even so it does indicate that he is totally ruthless.*

She pressed her forehead against the lintel of the arrow slit, clenched her jaw, and her fists balled into tight fists.

'Well, you are not going to get away with it!' declared Flora as she spun on her heels and started to run down the stairs, using the rope to stop herself from falling.

CHAPTER TWENTY-THREE

She reached the ground floor entrance in seconds and blinked as she stepped out into the bright sunshine. Standing for a moment to regain her breath, she stared across the expanse of drive and green to her quarry. The Venerable Uncle was still standing there in the courtyard berating the princes.

A flicker of movement from the side by the moat caught her attention. She glanced over; it was Busby.

Even from this distance she took in how surprised he was at Flora's sudden appearance, then he tracked where she had been staring moments before. He registered the Venerable Uncle, and his gaze shot back to Flora. He gave her a shake of his head, his lips in a firm grim line, but Flora was having none of it.

Thrusting her chin up defiantly, she half strode and half ran towards the knot of royalty. She reached them at about the same time as Busby did.

The Venerable Uncle and the princes stared at Flora as she approached panting and red-faced. The Venerable Uncle looked at her with disdain. Dimash showed polite interest while Parviz looked at her with open curiosity.

'What have you done with them?' Flora demanded, her hand on her hips and her eyes flaming with anger.

The Venerable Uncle blinked at her with piggy eyes above his flamboyant moustache. He folded his arms over his generous stomach and regarded Flora coolly. He had an expression which suggested he was not going to dignify her rudeness with a response and might simply turn his back on her.

But Flora was having none of it. 'I demand an answer!' she

declared in a tone that would have made Queen Victoria proud.

Dimash's sharp grey eyes darted between the Venerable Uncle and Flora. His eyebrows raised above his distinguished features as he enquired, 'Who are you referring to, Mrs Farrington?'

Busby reached them in time to hear Flora exclaim, 'Why, Nanny and Firuza of course. They are missing and I just know he has something to do with it.'

Parviz stepped towards Flora, his eyes wide and panic in his voice as he queried, 'Firuza is missing? Are you sure?'

Busby took control of the situation. 'Mrs Farrington, it would be best if we established the facts before …' His voice trailed off and Flora suspected he had been about to say, 'before you cause another diplomatic incident by accusing one of Britain's most influential political allies of attempted murder – again.'

Instead, he cleared his throat and changed tack. 'Are you sure the Princess isn't at the tennis court? And perhaps Nanny is with one of Le Brun's men?' He decided not to mention that she was in the habit of sharing cigarettes, alcohol, and horse racing tips with them. In lieu he said, 'They all think very highly of her.'

Dimash calmly stated, 'Firuza isn't at the tennis court, we have just come from there – she isn't by the summerhouse or that side of château garden either or we would have seen her or Nanny.'

Busby nodded. There was just the hint of a frown on his freckled forehead to indicate his concern. 'Inside the château, then – it's vast. They could be in any one of the rooms. I'll get some of Le Brun's men and conduct a search.'

'There's no need and no time!' exclaimed Flora, still glowering at the Venerable Uncle. He uncrossed his arms and rocked backwards on the heel of his slippers. He lowered his brow and slightly shook his head while the little bit of his face that was visible behind his luxuriant moustache turned an angry puce. He glowered back at Flora.

Again, Busby intervened. 'Where do you think they are?' he asked Flora in a reasonable voice. She turned her attention to him. His hazel eyes were calm and reassuring. His speech was unhurried and controlled.

This sensible question floored her; she blinked at him open-mouthed before rallying and saying, 'They said they wanted to explore the dungeons.'

Unobserved by Flora, the count had joined them, just in time to hear this. 'What?' he snapped. His silver hair flashed in the sun; his eyes blazed with fury. Flora noticed a vein pulsing on his temple and that he clenched his hands into fists, 'But I expressly told you that it was dangerous.'

Flora squirmed. 'Well, they don't seem to be there – I called and called and there was no reply.'

The count seemed to have taken a breath and regained a small degree of control of himself. In a more moderate voice, he addressed Busby, 'If they have fallen into the oubliette, they wouldn't be able to hear Flora, and no one would hear them no matter how loudly they screamed. That was the whole point of the oubliette – even if someone survived the fall, no one would hear their cries.'

Feeling both dismayed and vindicated by this, Flora couldn't resist flashing a meaningful glance at the Venerable Uncle and declaring, 'Fallen? Unlikely! But they might have been pushed.'

Busby tactfully ignored her and addressed the two princes. 'Could you please go and find Roberts and get some torches?'

Dimash nodded while Parviz set off at a sprint.

In a space of time that felt to Flora like hours but was really only minutes, they were back with not only torches but Roberts and, surprisingly, Father Luke and Sister Claire.

The count took the lead, and the unlikely rescue party set off, all bar the Venerable Uncle who excused himself by saying he had to deal with matters of state.

CHAPTER TWENTY-FOUR

Earlier that day Nanny had been on fine form. The dungeons were all that she had hoped.

'I can almost hear the chains rattling,' she declared gleefully.

Her enthusiasm was infectious and Firuza laughed. She held up an oil-burning lamp the better to look around. Its flickering flame sent long shadows across the cavernous dungeon.

'Jolly handy that these old lamps were primed and ready to go by the doorway or we would have gone flying on that broken second step down,' proclaimed Nanny happily as she swung her own lamp aloft. She used her carpetbag which was in her other hand as a counterbalance.

'And it was jolly useful you had some matches in that bag of yours,' added Firuza.

Nanny chuckled to herself and wondered what the child would say if she knew the priceless Abbastani diamonds were in her trusty carpetbag along with her knitting needles and wool.

Their words echoed around the chamber. Nanny liked echoes and she had already had a happy time practising her yodelling with the marvellous echo effect. She had then moved on to amusing herself by calling out different Gaelic ditties and having the echo reply. In fact, such was Nanny's enthusiasm for echoes that Firuza was quite pleased when she decided to stop and moved on to exploring the dungeons.

The dungeons were cold and damp, and the walls were a rough stone. Firuza had never seen Nanny happier.

Nanny held her lamp up against some iron bars and remarked, 'Do you see where the bars are shiny?'

Firuza nodded and Nanny explained with relish, 'That's from where the prisoners' hands gripped them.'

Firuza regarded the dumpy old lady with her wild grey curls who looked every inch the benign grandmother and laughed, 'Nanny, I had no idea you had such a macabre side.'

'A lass has to make her own entertainment where she may,' said Nanny as she marched on, keen to explore a small side corridor.

Their footsteps echoed and in the midst of the eerie sounds Firuza suddenly stopped and whispered, 'What was that?'

Nanny paused and they both listened but all that could be heard was the dripping of water.

'What was what?' asked Nanny holding up her lantern.

'I thought I heard something – a footstep behind us,' said Firuza, her voice still hushed.

Nanny dismissed her concern. 'Just an echo. Now don't go jumping at your own shadow, my girl,' she sniffed and wrinkled her nose. 'Something has died down here.'

Firuza laughed. 'I thought that was the point of a dungeon.' When she took a deep breath and inhaled the scent of stagnant, dirty water, together with mould, rust, and general decomposition, she said, 'Yes, you are right, Nanny. It's either a dead rat or a dead mouse.'

Nanny scuttled on ahead, along a corridor and around a corner taking the extra light her lamp afforded with her.

From beyond the corner came Nanny's rapturous Southern Irish burr. 'Oooh! Will you look at this!'

Firuza hurried to join her. In a cell-like room, she found Nanny leaning over what looked like a well, with a neat low wall round a circular hole. She was swinging her lamp over it, creating long, grotesque shadows over the area, 'We've found it! The oubliette! Just imagine being thrown down there and knowing that no one will hear you no matter how loudly you scream!'

Firuza peered into the black nothingness and shuddered; she did not share Nanny's glee.

Nanny was unperturbed. She rested her lamp on the small wall on the lip of the oubliette. That done, she busied herself rummaging in her carpetbag. After a moment or two she triumphantly held up her purse. She extracted a ha'penny, then, after looping the bag handle over her wrist, she leant further over the edge.

Firuza could not engage with Nanny's activity. She had a growing feeling of unease. The hairs on the back of her neck rose. Her heart was beating faster. *Are we being watched?* Her ears were alert for the slightest sound.

'What was that?' she asked. 'Nanny, did you hear something?'

Without stopping to listen, Nanny declared, 'Will you stop jabbering and just enjoy the moment!' She held up the coin between finger and thumb; her face looked ghoulish under lit by the lamp. 'Would you like to do the honours or shall I?'

Firuza was still distractedly looking around her. 'You do it.'

'If you are sure but come closer so you can listen as the coin falls; between us we can work out just how deep this oubliette is.'

Obediently Firuza joined Nanny in leaning over the wall.

'Here we go!' exclaimed Nanny as she tossed the coin into the oubliette.

They listened as it clinked, clinked, clinked against the sides, getting ever quieter. Down, down it went and then – nothing. The oubliette seemed bottomless.

Nanny took a deep breath, ready to speak, but before she could say a word Firuza had a sudden overwhelming sensation of dread. What happened next was chaotic and terrifying. All at once, Nanny's lamp was tipped into the oubliette, plunging them into darkness in less than a second.

Firuza was simultaneously aware of a hulking figure looming over Nanny.

A Gaelic expletive erupted from Nanny as her bulky body was tipped over to follow the lamp into the oubliette.

Firuza dropped her own lamp and reached out to grab Nanny. Her lamp crashed to the floor where it smashed on the stone flagstones and flames flickered and spread. In the flash of the flames, Firuza saw a shadowy, cloaked, black figure.

Her final thought was, *It's the grim reaper,* before she felt strong, powerful hands digging into arms. Her heart pounded. She struggled only to feel the vice-like grip tighten. Her feet were lifted off the ground with such speed that she didn't even have time to scream as she was tossed into the oubliette.

CHAPTER TWENTY-FIVE

Flora had mixed emotions as she hurried along with the rest of the ragtag rescue party. She felt that myopic Father Luke and austere Sister Claire were not likely to be of much help. Roberts' age did not seem to be affecting the speed with which he was moving. Parviz was so distracted and agitated that he was likely to become a liability. Her lips pressed together; Flora was avoiding eye contact with Busby – quite why she didn't know. Try as she might, she couldn't stop her mind from playing worst-case scenarios for Nanny and Firuza. She could see Nanny valiantly dying while trying to protect Firuza, swinging her carpetbag and uttering blood-curdling curses. *But even Nanny wouldn't be able to withstand a murderer if they had a gun.*

She shuddered and wiped away a tear that was trickling down her cheek. *The only positive is that I don't have to put up with the detestable Venerable Uncle. His excuse that he needed to make a phone call was jolly lame – more likely he wanted to plot his escape. Guilt was written all over his face as he half-smiled, mumbled, and avoided everyone's eyes, especially Parviz's. Still, I'm glad he's gone.*

There was a certain amount of jostling to be the front runner of the party. A sharp elbow in her side made Flora grunt. *If only urgent convent business had called Sister Claire away.* She eyed Father Luke who was following in Sister Claire's wake in a decidedly bewildered fashion. *And what's more, she could take Father Luke with her – he's as much used a dead snake in a rathole.*

They reached the medieval château in a trice. As they all

squeezed into the entrance portal, the count declared, 'The lamps have gone, so someone has been here.' His voice contained little enthusiasm. As they crested the staircase leading down to the dungeons he instructed, 'Be careful – the top step is broken.'

Pre-warned, the party gingerly made their way down the steps. The necessity of feeling for every step only heightened Flora's sense of apprehension. The slowness of their progress meant that Flora had rather too much time to conjure up disturbing thoughts of Nanny and Firuza's possible fate. At one point, Sister Claire jostled her, and she nearly lost her footing.

Everyone was fairly quiet until they reached the bottom. There was something about entering the dark cavernous room, lit only by the torches that seemed to induce in everyone the urge to shout. Raucous calls of 'Nanny!' and 'Firuza!' echoed around the chamber. The cries and their echoes were deafening and chaotic. Flora, like the rest of the party, found herself raising her voice so as to be heard above the others. Shouting only partly released Flora's heightened emotions.

Busby took charge. He stopped walking and held up his hand rather like a bobby on the beat stopping traffic. In a calm, firm voice he said, 'If we can all stand very still and if just Roberts could call out, then we can wait in silence for a reply.'

This they duly did, and Roberts' baritone voice rung out, calling, 'Princess? Nanny?' to be answered only by a mocking echo.

They proceeded painfully slowly with Busby holding up his hand to stop them every few steps and nodding to Roberts to call. The slow pace did little to prevent the chill from seeping into Flora's bones. The lamps cast their shadows into grotesque, elongated spectres. She was impatient at the lack of speed, but Parviz was even more agitated and looked at if he was about to complain.

They had all listened to Roberts' empty echoes one last time then, in the following silence, Busby stated, 'They are not here.'

Flora felt a cold dread settle in her stomach. Desperately she asked, 'What about the oubliette? Count, where is it?'

Flora could not make out his hawk-like features properly in the torch light, but his tone was hard as he said, 'If they are in there, I'm afraid it's already too late. If the fall didn't kill them immediately, their injuries would have within the hour.'

His words conquered up horrifically graphic images in Flora's mind. She felt a wave of panic and for a second she thought her dizziness would lead to an undignified faint. She gasped, trying to control her breath. She squeezed her eyes shut, fighting to hold back hot tears. She was aware her hands were trembling; actually, her whole body was shaking. In a voice that sounded far more authoritarian than she felt, she declared, 'We have to at least look!'

Busby nodded. 'Count Christoff, could you please show us the way?'

The count shrugged his shoulders and began walking down a side corridor.

Father Luke coughed. 'I'm so sorry,' he muttered with another cough, 'but I really must go back. I'm afraid the damp is affecting my chest and my joints.'

Sister Claire began flapping solicitously around him. Insisting she escort him back to the château immediately, she hurried him away, all the while scolding him for not speaking up sooner.

The count led them down the corridor, round a corner, and into a small, cell-like room. There in the centre was a structure that looked like a wishing well.

Its innocent, fairy-tale aspect made it all the more sinister to Flora. *Oh! My! How ghastly! It looks so innocent and harmless – and yet it is deadly.* She shrank back away from it while Parviz, the count, and Busby strode forward.

Staring at the reality of the oubliette, Flora's barely contained emotions overflowed; she let out an involuntary wail which would have done credit to an Irish banshee. 'Oh, Nanny!'

They were all startled by the surly reply, as thickly accented as an Irish fog, 'Well, you took your time, my girl!'

Afterwards, Flora realised that the rescue was as chaotic as the original assault.

Roberts made use of the rope he had slung around his shoulder which made Flora frown. *How did he know we would need a rope? Is he just one of Baden Powell's eager Boy Scouts who believe in the motto 'Be prepared' or does he have second sight?*

Firuza had been easy to free as she was light and not too far down. She was out and wrapped in Parviz's comforting arms in moments. They murmured to each other in low tones only they could hear.

Nanny's rescue was not so straightforward. Her considerable bulk was firmly wedged about eight foot down. During the whole of Nanny's liberation, Flora held both her body and mind taut. She battled against her terror that, even with safety so near, there could still be a slip, and Nanny would plunge to her death.

Nanny could hardly move; it was a combination of having been wedged in the shaft while bearing the full weight of Firuza on top of her, and the cramp in her hands and joints. Privately, Flora wondered if Nanny could support her own sizeable weight clinging to the rope. She held her breath and worried silently.

Matters were not helped by Nanny crossly declaring, 'I'm not letting go of my carpetbag – if it goes, so do I.'

Eventually, she managed to tie the rope inside her sturdy belt. All the men, apart from Parviz who was totally absorbed by Firuza, set to, pulling. Roberts went in front, with the count next, and Busby and Dimash took up the rear. Their efforts were accompanied by many a fruity expletive in Gaelic, courtesy of Nanny.

When eventually the count, Busby, Dimash, and Roberts had hauled her up, they were all perspiring, but true to her word, Nanny still had her carpetbag in her hand.

Flora threw herself on Nanny, weeping and murmuring loving terms of endearment, until Nanny curtly demanded, 'Will you stop your caterwauling, child? And for goodness' sake let go of me. A body needs to breathe.'

Her tone was as familiar and foreboding as it had been in Flora's nursery days. It was a tone only ever evoked when Flora had committed a grievous crime and instantly had the effect of making Flora release Nanny and snap to attention with a mumbled, 'Oh yes! Rather! Frightfully sorry!'

Their progress back to the welcome sunshine was extremely slow. Nanny had lost her left shoe down the oubliette, and, despite her bravado, the ordeal had clearly taken its toll. Roberts and Busby had to help her with each painful step. Dimash, Parviz, and Firuza went ahead, with the princess declaring, 'I need to breathe fresh air and feel the sun on my face.'

When they did all reach the welcome fresh air, they blinked at the sunlight. Parviz, Firuza, and Dimash stood a little to one side. Flora noted that their laughter sounded brittle. *They must be laughing with relief rather than at something funny.* As she blinked again, trying to focus, she noticed that Parviz and Firuza were holding hands. *Strange ... but again it's probably just a reaction to extreme stress.*

'There you go, Nanny!' said Roberts gently as he helped her sit down on a handy bench.

Nanny was deathly pale and presented a sad sight with her crumpled long black robes, one stocking toe showing beneath the long skirt, and her tangle of grey curls half down in a haphazard way. The only normal thing about her was her red carpetbag. *She rather resembles a shiny black beetle I once stood on by mistake – flattened.*

Roberts proffered a cigarette to Nanny with, 'Here you go, have a Woodbine.'

She accepted it with a shaky hand and inhaled as he lit it.

The count, who had been standing nearby with a face like thunder, decided now was the time to let rip. 'What in the world possessed you to be so foolhardy? At least the princess has the excuse of youth but you, Nanny, should have known better. What's more, I have said repeatedly that the old château is dangerous. You should have known you were putting yourselves in the firing line for an accident.'

The soothing Woodbine seemed to have done its work; with a curled lip and through a cloud of acrid smoke, Nanny replied firmly, 'It weren't no accident – we were attacked.'

Busby was instantly alert. 'Who by?'

Firuza spoke, quietly but clearly, her voice wavering with fear. 'The Grim Reaper.'

Word of the rescue spread quickly in the château. On hearing the news, Sister Claire hurried to Father Luke's room, her thoughts, as ever, written all over her sour old face: ' *I know he said he did not wish to be disturbed as he desired some quiet time in contemplation, but surely he will want to give the Good Lord praise for the princess's safety. Not that anyone would want to thank Him for saving that odious Irish domestic.'*

She hesitated outside his door, unsure whether to knock or not.

She could hear an odd swishing sound coming from within. As she pressed her ear against the door, the better to listen, it swung open a crack.

There, kneeling before an elaborate icon, was Father Luke. He resembled nothing so much as an emaciated skeleton. Shirtless, his back was a startling white apart from the crimson spots of blood where his cruel whip had bitten into his flesh.

She gasped and he swung round, their eyes meeting for a second before she hurriedly shut the door and almost ran back to the sanctuary of her own room.

Her mind was in a turmoil. Instinctively she reached for her rosary. The respective prayer and the quick, familiar movement of her fingers steadied both her breath and her nerves. Having completed the ritual of praying 'the Five Decades' the only thought in her head was: *What sin so heinous has Father Luke committed that he thinks it necessary to perform so great a penance?*

CHAPTER TWENTY-SIX

As those rescued and the rescuers slowly made their way back to the château, Parviz gently pulled Firuza to one side. 'I must see you – alone,' he whispered.

She looked directly into his eyes and for a moment was lost in a blue sea of love and longing. Nodding, she whispered back, 'I'll send you word.'

So it was that in the middle of the night Parviz and Firuza, both in pyjamas, silk dressing gowns, and velvet slippers, found themselves in the vast château kitchen stirring hot chocolate over the range, safe in the knowledge that Anne was keeping watch outside.

Firuza's pyjamas and robe were in a soft and flattering oyster pink and her hair was worn in a thick plait over her left shoulder.

Parviz had arrived at the rendezvous early. He was desperate for the reassurance of holding her. He waited, restless in his paisley dressing gown among the polished copper pots and scrubbed worktops.

When she glided through the door, he swept her up into his arms, lifting her off her feet and showering her face with kisses while murmuring, 'I was so worried – I thought I'd lost you.'

She laughed and, kissing him back, entwined her legs around his waist and her hands around his neck.

Parviz tilted his face away from hers and murmured, 'I am so glad you are alright.' He kissed her lightly on the forehead before continuing, 'When I thought I'd lost you…' he shuddered, and words failed him. He swallowed and then went on, 'I want to protect you, always. I want the official right to always be your protector.'

She laughed and her hair came loose, it tumbled down her shoulders. Parviz stared; he could not remember ever having seen anything so beautiful. He ran his hand through it, feeling its thick, rich softness.

Firuza was still laughing. 'Let's protect each other,' she said as she placed her hands either side of his face and pulled him towards her and kissed him again, before adding, 'Let's vow to always do what's best for the other, no matter the cost.'

Parviz nodded his agreement and muttered, 'No matter the cost,' as he snuggled his face into the warm hollow at the base of her neck.

After some more delightful moments, Firuza lift his head away from hers and looked at him through long-lashed, half-closed eyes. Huskily she whispered, 'Do you know what I want to do now?'

Parviz, his voice deep with passion, said, 'What do you want?'

Firuza grinned. 'To have some hot chocolate.'

Unable to sleep and unaware of the tryst in the kitchen, Dimash made his way down there in search of a hot drink to aid his sleep. In the dimly lit corridor, he was surprised to see a slim figure leaning against the wall. He paused and blinked in confusion. For a moment he was convinced that he must be imagining things. He wondered if his tortured mind had conjured up a vision of Anne in a sensible wool dressing gown and sturdy slippers, her long blonde plait snaking down her back. She regarded him with her cool, violet eyes.

He smiled. 'What are you doing here?'

Calmly, she looked at him, before explaining, 'I am acting as a lookout – your brother and the princess are in the kitchen.' She wrinkled her pretty nose. 'I think from the smell they are making hot chocolate.'

Dimash could not resist stepping right up to her. Her back was pressed against the wall. He felt there was no escape for her, and he enjoyed a frisson of electricity as he felt her breath on his face. He rested his hands on her waist and instantly registered disappointment when she didn't respond. He'd hoped she'd lean into him and throw her arms around his neck as he murmured, 'Oh, Anne.'

Instead, she looked very steadily in his eyes and serenely stated, 'I am afraid I might be falling in love with you.'

His heart soared and he would have kissed her had she not pulled away. Her gaze was unwavering. Dimash swallowed, he longed to kiss her and – more importantly – to feel her kiss him back.

'But I am far more worried for you,' she stated.

Confused, he asked, 'Worried for me? Why would you be worried for me?'

With a sad smile, she replied, 'Because you are already hopelessly in love with me and when you leave this château, it will be with Firuza, not me.'

He started as he registered the stark honesty of her statement. Now her voice and eyes filled with compassion as she continued, 'A lifetime is long and how will you live if all you have is a memory of me?' She twisted away from him with a light call of, 'Parviz, Firuza, I'm coming in!'

She entered the kitchen to find Parviz and Firuza standing by the stove. Firuza's long, thick mane of hair had just slipped from her ribbon as she leant over the saucepan. Very gently, Parviz lifted Firuza's hair off her neck and away from the saucepan. Sensuously, he laid it against her back. Firuza closed her eyes, momentarily distracted by his touch. She was about to leave the hot chocolate and turn to kiss Parviz, but Anne's call interrupted her. Parviz sprang guiltily away.

Firuza smiled over her shoulder and said, 'Perfect timing, Anne; this hot chocolate is just about ready. Would you be a dear and get the cups out?'

'Will do, with an extra one as Dimash is here.'

'Right oh,' replied Firuza, showing no sign of being surprised at the crown prince's arrival.

The two young princes stood side by side, observing the two girls laughing softly as they stirred the hot chocolate.

With a puzzled smile, Dimash gazed at Anne and said to Parviz, 'Why do I feel like I may be the prince, but she is the one in command?'

Parviz laughed and clapped him on the back. 'Anne will always be the person who is in true command of any room or situation and the sooner we all get used to that the better.'

As if on cue, Anne smiled over to them and, with the steaming saucepan in hand, ordered, 'Dimash, find us some cups for the hot chocolate.'

CHAPTER TWENTY-SEVEN

The Venerable Uncle had issued a royal command that they were all to rendezvous in the ballroom the day before the ball to rehearse the betrothal announcement. Obediently, at the allotted time, Flora entered the ballroom. She drew in a breath, momentarily overwhelmed by its splendour.

The count was standing just inside the room, directing a couple of Inspector Le Brun's men. They were precariously balanced on a tall ladder while they cleaned one of the three magnificent chandeliers.

Impressed by the room's grandeur, Flora took a moment to admire it. She had never seen it with the shutters open and the dust sheets off. Flora had the impression of gold and mirrors. The beautiful floor with its intricate parquet pattern was the perfect finishing touch. She observed the four young men – again, courtesy of Le Brun – who were on their knees with their sleeves rolled up, vigorously polishing every inch. She wondered if they were in awe of the ballroom's grandeur or whether they were wishing it was more modest in size.

At one end was a raised dais, where the orchestra would be. Above it was a balcony with a stone balustrade. On either side of the balcony were twin sweeping staircases.

'What a spectacular room,' commented Flora.

The count visibly swelled with pride. *Is it my imagination or does he look even more dashing in this setting?* He smiled. 'It is pleasurable indeed to be using this room.' He took a step towards Flora and, looking meaningfully into her eyes, whispered, 'Just think of all the wonderful functions you could hold here as the château's chatelaine. With your limitless funds, this event would be as nothing.'

Flora blinked and shuffled a step backwards. 'Uh? Um! Ohhhh!' she muttered rather incoherently and for the first time ever she was actually pleased to see the Venerable Uncle approaching. He hurried in, pink with pleasure as he bustled around looking at everything. Roberts stood to one side, ready to receive his instructions. Last to arrive were the two princes and the princess. Firuza was dignified and composed. She was flanked by the two princes.

The Venerable Uncle began to explain, 'At 9.15 precisely, you, Roberts – from the balcony – will silence the orchestra and announce me. I will stand at the centre and say a few words to welcome everyone. I will talk in general terms about diplomatic relations, and I will then announce the betrothal. At which point you, Dimash and Firuza, will step forward.' He threw a menacing glance at Firuza and added, 'There is no need to say anything. Just bow, pause for applause – smile, of course – then walk down the left staircase. I will take the right. Parviz, you are very much surplus to requirements, so just keep out of the way.'

Flora felt a wave of nausea, but Firuza's face was impassive.

The Venerable Uncle had one or two more things to say before he dismissed them. All the time this obnoxious minor royal was talking, Flora longed to interrupt the monologue and shout, 'How can you be organising a ball when there is a murderer to be found?' *Surely, we should be using our energies to discover who killed that poor young footman and Amelie not to mention throwing Firuza and Nanny into the oubliette, rather than forcing two young people into marriage?* She swallowed, collecting her thoughts. *There may be nothing I can do about apprehending the villain but at least I can comfort Firuza.*

She rushed to Firuza's side. 'Oh, my dear, I…' She stopped mid-sentence, suddenly aware there was nothing she could say to make the situation better for the poor child.

Firuza placed a hand on Flora's arm and smiled. 'It will be alright, Flora. Now the best thing we can do is get a good night's sleep.'

After the rehearsal, Flora followed Firuza's advice and retired to her bedroom. Unfortunately, Dorothy and Venus had other ideas and gently nipped and teased each other as they scampered under her bed.

'Now my darlings, we all need to settle down quickly – I need to get my beauty sleep for the ball.' Flora peered at the two pups under the bed. 'In your baskets,' she commanded, in the full knowledge that neither dog would do anything they didn't want to.

She was wearing a rather gorgeous pale pink silk nightdress; it was an elegant long shift with flattering as well as supportive detail over the bust. Flora adored it and always felt like a film star when she wore it, especially as it came with a robe trimmed with ostrich feathers. She had bathed in lavender-scented bath oil and now her whole suite carried the wonderfully soothing aroma.

I'm sure the lavender will have us all asleep in a trice, thought Flora happily as she slipped the robe off and laid it across a nearby chair. Noticing the interest with which Venus and Flora were eyeing the feathers, she hastily moved it to the top of the chest of drawers which was higher, and so safer.

She hopped into bed and was about to turn off the light when she spotted a letter from Debo lying on her bedside table. She'd been meaning to open it earlier in the day. *Just the thing to take my mind of my worries,* she thought happily as she slit it open.

> Gosh Mummy,
>
> Thanks for your letter. What a thrilling time you are having – what with a dead footman and then a fire. Glad you are alright. I can totally see that the whole question of etiquette is a bit delicate – I mean, how should one respond when one's host accuses one of murder and arson? As luck would have it, Miss Crawford was giving us an extremely dull etiquette lesson yesterday, so I explained your situation and asked her what the correct form was. But she wasn't much help – she just sort of raised an eyebrow and

gave me a funny look and said she would be writing to you.

That's all for now,

Love,

Debo xxx

As Flora folded the letter, she considered, *Is it wrong if I, as a mother, ask Tony to have a word with her about leaving school early? At this rate Miss Crawford is becoming my most regular correspondent.*

Defeated by motherhood, she turned off the light.

The dogs, realising that nothing interesting was going to happen, snuffled and retired to their respective baskets leaving Flora to listen to the night-time creaks of the château and to worry.

I don't appear to be doing a very good job as a mother, and as a godmother I have totally failed! A wave of fear twisted her stomach. *Firuza is about to be forced into a loveless marriage – a sacrifice to British ambitions and fears. Her diamonds may be safe, but I can hardly feel I have fulfilled my duty of care for her. After all, we don't know for certain who killed the footman, who set fire to Amelie's studio, or who pushed her and Nanny down the oubliette. Whoever did those things is still out and about and free to harm Firuza.*

She sighed and rolled over on her side. Rather than counting sheep she decided to count handbags. As delightful visions of jewel-encrusted evening clutches, and chic but practical brown alligator handbags perfect for day wear, floated through her mind, she felt her breathing deepen and her eyelids grow heavy.

She was just drifting into dreams of shopping when the dogs started to growl. It was low at first but grew in intensity until Flora growled back, 'Will you two kindly settle down!'

Further growls gave Flora her answer. A minor skirmish was obviously escalating into a full-scale battle. She flipped on the light to see the two dogs playing a determined game of tug of war with one of her favourite slippers.

With a small shriek of horror, she leapt from the bed and

retrieved it. Dismayed, she regarded it; sodden and well chewed, it would never grace Flora's foot again. Sternly telling the dogs off, she tossed it in the wastepaper basket and returned to bed. Both dogs eyed her with resentment rather than remorse.

This time she did fall asleep quite swiftly. She dreamt she was at the Imperial Russian Court waltzing with a dashing officer who was wearing an impressive amount of gold frogging. The ballroom itself resembled Versailles for opulence. She must have been in deep slumber for an hour or two when once again the dogs woke her. This time, rather than growls, they were both howling and scratching at the door.

Flora uttered an unladylike expletive she had learnt from Nanny and turned the light on. To say the dogs were going frantic was an understatement. Pawing and scratching, they were ruining the paintwork.

Flora ordered them back to bed but was not at all surprised when she was totally ignored. Sighing, she got out of bed. She slipped on her ostrich-trimmed robe and, padding barefoot across the cool wooden boards, lamented the loss of her slippers. She hissed at the dogs, 'Do be quiet or you'll waken the whole house.'

This only encouraged the dogs to greater noise and activity.

She was just stooping to pull each dog away by their collars, when the door itself swung open, and both dogs set off as fast as their short legs could carry them.

Horrified, Flora gave chase down the corridor. It was dimly lit by a few nightlights and Flora was grateful that, while she may have been running barefoot, at least she was not in total darkness.

The dogs stopped abruptly outside Firuza's bedroom door and recommenced their urgent scratching and howling. Flora regarded the shredded paintwork and thought, *At this rate, the poor count will not have a door left intact.*

Automatically, she threw open the door. Elated, both dogs burst through, their barks taking on a more aggressive tone. There was the unmistakable sound of doggy jaws on human flesh and a man's cry of pain. The faint light of the passageway illuminated Firuza's room enough that Flora could just make out a tall, black-cloaked figure leaning over the princess's bed with a pillow in hand.

Flora let out her own scream and launched herself at the intruder with as much enthusiasm as her two canine companions.

As Flora hit out at the bony intruder, Firuza rallied. Flora was vaguely aware of her sitting up in her bed; she seemed to be spluttering a bit, trying to catch her breath. The dogs were doing a valiant job, one firmly latched onto each ankle.

Whether it was Flora's screams or the dogs' noisy barks it is hard to say, but the combined cacophony woke the whole house. First on the scene were Roberts, Busby, and Inspector Le Brun. Judging by the way they arrived together and were all fully dressed, it was obvious they had all been up and patrolling the château.

The three men easily seized the assailant. Flora stood back, pleased to be able to hand over 'wrestling with potential killer' duties to the professionals. The dogs were not nearly so keen to stand down from guard duty. And it was only after Busby had been bitten by accident, provoking a fierce, 'Leave it!', that they both obeyed. A further peremptory, 'Be quiet!' stopped the barking.

Even in the present fraught scenario, Flora could not help wishing she had the same command of her dachshund.

Next to arrive were the two princes. Dimash had taken the time to put on a lavish silk dressing gown while Parviz had sprinted impulsively out of bed without gown or slippers. He instantly threw himself onto the bed next to Firuza and, flinging an arm around her, started whispering solicitously, 'Are you alright? What happened?'

This threw Flora into confusion. *As her godmother, I probably should be the one comforting her. And it really is most unseemly, both in their pyjamas and on the bed, even if we are all here. I should step up my chaperone duties.* She sighed, regarding the pair of them before adding to herself, *but they do look rather sweet together.*

It was fortunate for all that Firuza came to her senses and

leapt away from Parviz and her bed to stand in front of her attacker just as Nanny, the count, Sister Claire, and –most importantly – the Venerable Uncle arrived. The latter would have been the most vocal over any impropriety.

Nanny was in her sensible wool dressing gown and fleece slippers while the count looked impossibly suave in a yellow paisley cravat and a navy spotted dressing gown. Sister Claire had on her night-time wimple and a coarse shift and gown which looked uncomfortable enough to make Flora shudder and thank the Good Lord that she had never received a calling to be a nun. The Venerable Uncle cut a comic figure, swathed in silk robes. It appeared he slept with a peculiar contraption hooked over his ears to keep his magnificent moustache in place.

Firuza, in a rather fetching pair of cream pyjamas with her long dark hair falling over her shoulders, stood before the figure, who was all in black and wearing a black mask over his nose and mouth, while Busby and Inspector Le Brun held him tightly between them.

Angrily, she pulled the mask off.

Seeing who the assailant was, she drew in her breath.

CHAPTER TWENTY-EIGHT

'Father Luke!' gasped Flora.

Firuza pointed an accusing finger in Father Luke's face, 'It was *you* who pushed us into the oubliette – the grim reaper!'

Father Luke slumped between his two guards like a rag doll who had lost all his stuffing.

Flora had to agree; with his bony features and body all cloaked in black, he did resemble the grim reaper. 'Yes, totally – perhaps it's a family resemblance,' she blurted out before adding, 'I saw it all! If I had been a second later, he would have killed Firuza. He was holding a pillow down over her face.'

'Mrs Farrington, you are a heroine,' declared Parviz.

Embarrassed by the praise, Flora blushed. 'The real heroes are Venus and Dorothy; they raised the alarm.' She looked down at them with an indulgent smile and they wagged their tails happily.

Nanny, her mouth in a firm line, marched up to him and kicked the priest in the shins. It wasn't a dignified move but evidently it gave her some satisfaction. He flinched and appeared surprised.

Sister Claire, her pale eyes brimming with tears, implored him, 'But why?'

Father Luke glanced briefly at her, his eyes expressionless, and then he fixed his gaze on the floor.

Nanny piped up, 'I reckon Russia has something to do with it – all those icons.'

'But isn't the new Soviet Russia anti-religion?' asked Dimash.

The Venerable Uncle nodded his head thoughtfully. 'True, but there are plenty in the State today who still clutch onto their faith while serving the new communist government.' He took a step closer to Father Luke and scrutinised his face, then with a decisive nod, he asserted, 'I knew I'd seen you before. You were part of the Imperial Russian envoy that visited the Court pre-1912.' The Venerable Uncle turned from the cleric and commented to the others, 'He was less thin then and he wasn't a priest, but it was definitely him.'

Firuza slipped barefoot from the bed. Scrutinising the priest's face for his reaction, she said, 'That explains something that has been puzzling me. There was that time at breakfast when I thought he'd understood me when I was speaking Abbastani.'

'Oh, I say, Busby, do you think that man we saw him sitting with in Paris was his Soviet contact?' exclaimed Flora, delighted to have come up with a suggestion. She waved her lavish ostrich feather trimmed sleeves for emphasis.

Busby said, 'We shouldn't jump to any conclusions yet.'

Another thought struck Flora. She turned to Roberts and, with a hint of disappointment, clarified, 'So it wasn't you?'

Calmly, Roberts replied, 'It would appear not, Madame.'

Flora just detected the hint of a smile playing about Roberts' mouth. She wanted to ask him what he had been doing with the footman's body, but Busby was laughing. He said, 'In fact he is one of your Uncle Cyril's men – here undercover.'

The count was ringing his hands, and his brow was furrowed. He sat down heavily on the edge of the bed. He seemed to be having some difficulty in understanding what was going on. Confused he mumbled, 'Did he kill my sister?' He ran his hand through his hair and slowly shook his head, 'Why would he do that?'

Flora was about to say, 'Oh, that's easy! She probably found out what he was up to and tried to blackmail him,' but just in time, she realised that calling your host's deceased sister a blackmailer was a breach of etiquette worthy of Miss Crawford's scrutiny.

Getting no answer, the count looked at Roberts. 'Now the culprit has been caught, you won't be leaving us, will you, Roberts? Not just before the ball?'

'No, sir, I will continue in my role as your butler until after the ball.'

Father Luke was escorted from the château to some cell provided by Le Brun. Roberts and Nanny organised soothing hot chocolate for everyone before they all retired to bed. To Flora's surprise, she slept soundly and only woke up when the dogs started fussing to go out. The rest of the day passed calmly enough.

In a departure from protocol, the party at the château had opted for a slightly hardier than normal tea as there was no way a formal supper could be organised prior to the ball.

Feeling suitably fortified by egg sandwiches and chocolate cake, Flora was just heading towards her bedroom to get ready when she was surprised to see Busby and a particularly youthful French police officer in the passageway outside her room. *The poor lad looks most uncomfortable in that ill-fitting white tie,* mused Flora as she approached them. *He is hardly going blend in.*

Busby stepped forward. 'Pierre has been allocated as your personal bodyguard for this evening.'

Flora looked from Busby to Pierre. Her mouth fell open and her eyes widened, before she said, 'Bodyguard? Why?'

Impatiently and with a voice ladened with a patronising tone, he said, 'For your protection.'

'Don't be ridiculous!' snapped back Flora.

Busby's angry eyes met hers. 'Look, Mrs Farrington, I have a lot to do, and I don't have time for your antics.'

Flora inhaled, squared her shoulders, and in her best 'Dowager Duchess' voice, declared, 'Nor I for yours!' She allowed her words to sink in before adding, 'I think Pierre would be far better occupied guarding the moat or serving champagne.' She took a step towards Busby and with deliberate emphasis stated, 'What he will not be doing this evening is trailing around after me.'

She noted with satisfaction that Busby had gone pink around the gills and was clenching both his fists.

Breathing evenly and deeply, presumably to steady his emotions, he replied, 'Mrs Farrington, however distasteful the task, I have a duty to protect you. Father Luke may be in custody but that does not mean we should totally let our guard down.'

Flora's nostrils flared and she felt her cheeks heat. 'On the contrary, Inspector, your job is to protect Firuza, the diamonds, and British interests. I am none of the above, so I suggest you go about your business while I get ready for the ball.'

Without saying goodbye, she swept into the bedroom, slamming the door behind her.

Busby was left standing in the passage, fighting an urge to burst through the door and tell her a thing or two. The smirk on Pierre's baby face did not help Busby's mood. He muttered something inaudible before instructing the boy to follow him to Inspector Le Brun.

Flora was furious. 'Odious, overbearing, opinionated man!' she declared, angrily kicking her shoes off and running her hands through her short curls. Venus had become used to Amelie's emotional outbursts so took no notice.

Dorothy was instantly alert. Wagging her tail furiously, she wound around Flora's bare feet and panted, 'Was that Busby I heard at the door? Just open it a crack – I bet he's missing me.'

Normally Flora enjoyed getting ready for grand evenings. The ritual of washing, dressing, and applying her make-up was all part of the fun of the event, but tonight nothing seemed to go right. She dropped her powder puff, making a terrible mess of her dressing table, her hair simply refused to curl into a chic, becoming crown and instead frizzed about her ears, and most annoying of all was that Anne had simply disappeared.

'Where can the girl have got to?' exclaimed Flora in frustration as she struggled to button her frock. The moment she voiced the question she felt a twist in her stomach. *The poor child is probably crying her eyes out in some hidden corner. If Anne is having to face up to life without her beau, the least I can do is dress myself.*

Eventually, when Flora contemplated her reflection, she was more than content. 'Busby was right; red is my colour.'

The dress set off her complexion to perfection and the chic cut was most flattering to her petite frame. She tried to ignore her concerns about it being totally backless. *When in France one can be more daring.* With just a quick application of lip rouge, she squared her shoulders and declared to the dogs, 'Right, now to go and comfort Firuza, although goodness only knows what I am going to say to her.'

The dogs yawned and took little interest in Flora's departure.

She wandered down the corridor, her mind a tangle of thoughts and worries. She could hear the distant sound of the orchestra tuning up in the ballroom below.

As she approached Firuza's bedroom door, she was surprised by Nanny coming out of it. 'Ah, Nanny! I am glad you are here. How is Firuza? I came to offer her a few words of comfort.'

Nanny, black and beetle-like as ever, sniffed, 'It would be a lot more useful if you nipped back to your room and got the diamonds for the child to put on.'

'The diamonds? Aren't they in your carpetbag?' queried Flora.

Nanny's lined face crinkled into a broad grin. 'I thought I would mix it up, so I slipped them into your smalls.'

'Well, really, Nanny!' exclaimed Flora.

Nanny was having none of it. 'Hush your chatter, my girl, and hurry along with you; the guests will be arriving soon.'

As Flora turned to go, Nanny called, 'One more thing, child.'

Flora paused and looked back at her. She was smiling and her black hedgehog eyes sparkled with fondness. 'You are as bonny as a picture. That colour certainly looks grand on you and your figure is something to behold.'

Flora felt a warm glow in the pit of her stomach and murmured, 'Gosh! Thanks awfully, Nanny.'

She trotted off to find the diamonds, buoyed up by Nanny's love and approval. She found the diamond necklace just where Nanny said it would be, in the red leather case nestled beneath Flora's camisoles and lacy whatnots. She opened the case and admired its glittering beauty. She shut the case with a sigh.

Glancing at her watch, she realised that she really needed to hurry. Safely holding the diamonds in their case in both hands, she was just quitting her room when she literally bumped into the count. He looked most gallant in his white tie. His silver hair was slicked back and he was wearing some delectable cologne.

He smiled as he caught Flora mid-stumble. Righting her, he stepped back, the better to admire her. Flora felt rather hot and uncomfortable as his hawklike eyes raked over her. 'My dear, you look quite enchanting.'

'Oh well! It is a rather good frock!' mumbled Flora, glancing down at it and avoiding eye contact with the count. *I just know his eyes will be burning with predatory passion and I really don't have time for that just now. I need to get these diamonds to Firuza and offer her what crumbs of godmotherly comfort I can come up with.*

'And if I am not mistaken, those are the famous Abbastani diamonds. Their worth is said to far exceed any treasury in the world,' continued the count.

'Well, I don't know anything about that, but if you'll excuse me, Count, I really need to get these to the princess before the ball starts.'

Flora went to step around him, but she found his arm encircling her waist as he propelled her in the opposite direction. 'We have plenty of time, my dear. The first guests haven't even started to arrive yet. Let us enjoy a moment of privacy and romance. The evening view from the balustrade is quite enchanting.'

Rather reluctantly, Flora found herself heading towards the stairs to the balustrade.

She was just muttering, 'Well, alright, Count, if you insist but only for a moment then I really must get these diamonds to the princess,' when they passed Roberts. Flora just had time to register him raising a surprised eyebrow before the count whisked past her.

Roberts tentatively approached Busby and Inspector Le Brun. Both men's faces were grim with concentration as they stood close together, their heads almost touching as they earnestly discussed security matters.

He coughed deferentially and the men looked up. 'If I may

have a word.'

Busby nodded and Roberts got as far as saying, 'Mrs Farrington—' before Busby cut him off.

'If it's anything to do with Mrs Farrington, save your breath; I don't want to hear.' He went to resume his conversation with Inspector Le Brun but then had another thought. 'Don't tell me she's gone to confront a killer on the balustrade,' he sneered.

Apologetically, Roberts answered, 'Well, actually…'

CHAPTER TWENTY-NINE

The count had been quite right; the view from the balustrade was quite magnificent. Two lines of flaming torches illuminated either side of the drive from the medieval castle to the château. The beauty of the medieval château had been emphasised by some clever lighting, throwing the towers and turrets into sharp relief. From below came the muffled sounds of music and voices. The first majestic large cars with their diplomatic crests and flags were beginning to arrive, crunching on the gravel.

Flora was just admiring the scene when she felt the count's arms encircle her from behind. She felt his warm breath on the nape of her neck and her left ear as he purred, 'Just think of all the wonderful balls we could host if you would only marry me.'

Flora allowed the words to sink in before giving way to a flare of irritation. *Obviously, subtlety is not going to work with this noble-sized ego.*

Wriggling to face him she managed to get half a foot between them so she could look him full in the face.

He was regarding her with confident assurance. *That is the expression of a predatory man who has never experienced rejection – well now's the time for him to experience it and I am the lady to do it.*

Flora cleared her throat and in calm, cool command declared, 'Count, I feel the time has come for some plain speaking. I have no intention of ever marrying you. In fact, after this evening, I very much hope that I will not see you again – ever!'

The count surveyed her languidly. He cocked his head on one side, raised an eyebrow and exhaled a quiet, 'Really? What a shame.'

Flora was in full battle mode and with a defiant tilt of her chin, she declared, 'Shame or not, I really must insist that you allow me to return to my godmotherly duties inside.'

His smile froze and Flora did not quite care for his tone when he muttered, half to himself, 'If only…'

Flora was just contemplating her next move when he shrugged his shoulders and said, 'Still what is one more murder among so many?'

Flora stared at his serene expression; his classical good looks seemed at odds with his words. She suddenly realised she was in trouble.

'Eh? One more? Murder?' queried Flora, struggling to get her bearings.

He nodded; his face was chilling for its lack of emotion. 'My first was my wife – dear little thing, but I did need the money in full, not just the miserly allowance she gave me. You see, the château must be kept going, whatever the price.' He smiled. 'My father explained it to me – it's a sacred duty. He stood right here where we are now.' He glanced around at the old château, the new one, and the grounds below. 'It was the night of the last ball, and he had had no choice but to push my mother off the balustrade as I am afraid I must now do to you – once I have the diamonds, that is.'

Flora swallowed. Playing for time, she said, 'Please, tell me more. You are obviously rather clever – nobody suspected you.'

'What?' he asked taking a menacing step towards her.

'You said 'one more murder among so many'. Who else have you killed?'

'Well, there was that footman – he caught me searching for the diamonds in your room.' He looked puzzled. 'Although where his body went, I cannot fathom.'

Flora was trying to back away while he was distracted. 'Anyone else?'

'Amelie – I never did like her much. The foolish woman tried to blackmail *me*. Apparently, she had suspicions about my first wife. She was a total idiot – after all if I didn't hesitate to murder a wife who I was tolerably fond of, I was hardly likely to hesitate to dispose of a rather annoying little sister.'

Silently, Flora rather hoped that her son, Tony, held his own younger sister Debo in higher regard but now was not the time to dissect her own family relationships.

While he had been speaking, Flora had been scanning her surroundings, trying to work out her best escape route. Now, she tried to seize her chance and bolted towards the steps, but the count was too quick for her. He lunged at her and grabbed her wrist.

'If only you had been more amenable, you could have married me, and we could have avoided all this.'

Typical man! thought Flora. *Blaming a woman for things that are totally his responsibility.*

Clutching onto the diamonds, she struggled with him, but she couldn't free her wrist; his grip was too strong, and she could sense she was no match for him.

He let out a cruel bark of laughter. 'There is nowhere for you to go.'

But Flora was not to be thwarted. She had realised he had the better of her when it came to brute strength, so she needed cunning on her side. Making the most of her rather fetching heels, she lifted her right foot and stamped the pointy end into his with all her might, swiftly followed this with a sharp knee to the count's sensitive parts, while declaring, 'Want to bet? A girl doesn't spend her youth sneaking out of school dorms without learning a thing or two.'

He tried blocking her escape to the stairs but there was nothing to prevent her from nimbly leaping over the balustrade and onto the flagpole. It was only when she was clinging onto the bowed flagstaff, dangling what felt like hundreds of feet above the drive, that it occurred to Flora her actions were more dramatic than sensible. She could feel her grip loosening; she knew she didn't have much time as the count was no longer groaning on the floor but quietly staggering to his feet.

She started to scream for help but knew that by the time the startled police officers below had had time to come to her rescue, it would be too late. The count was leaning over the balustrade with an unmistakable gleam of enjoyment in his eye.

Flora smiled hopefully. 'Er, Count, could I possibly reconsider your kind offer of matrimony?'

'No!' he said flatly.

'Thought not,' sighed Flora. She followed it with, 'You won't get away with this.'

She uttered it more for form's sake than out of conviction. It occurred to her that, even if he didn't get away with it, she would be dead. *At least I know the children will be well looked after by Nanny, but...* A tear trickled down her cheek. *I did want to be there for them.*

She was just debating what cutting final word to launch at the count when, above the above the noise of her own panicked breath, she heard footsteps. They were loud and heavy, and getting louder and heavier by the moment; the unmistakable sound of a group of men running up a steep flight of stairs. They were getting louder still. Flora's scattered thoughts coalesced around the realisation that help was coming. She felt the count freeze as he too heard the impending rescue party. He did not have time to react before Roberts, Busby, and Inspector Le Brun burst onto the rooftop.

The count spun round to receive a sharp upper cut on his jaw from Roberts. It sent him spinning, only for Roberts to follow it up with a left fist blow to his body and another jaw jab to his chin. Inspector Le Brun had the cuffs out, but best of all there was Busby.

He leaned over the balustrade and grabbed her wrist. Seemingly with no effort on her part, he lifted her up and onto firm ground. His arms wrapped round her, and she clung desperately to him as well as to the diamonds.

He held her tightly. She could hear his heart thumping in his chest – or was it hers? She couldn't see anything as her face was squashed against his stiff shirt front, but she could hear Inspector Le Brun and his men dragging the protesting count to one side and starting to cuff him.

Busby's large hands were gripping her shoulders as he held

her away from him to look – or rather, glare – at her. His brow was wrinkled, his thick eyebrows were drawn together, and his breath was coming in audible gasps. His voice raised to an angry shout. 'When will you listen to me?'

In seconds, Flora's emotions soared from terror to relief. Her mouth went dry, her muscles felt weak, and she experienced a wave of giddiness. She bit her lip to hold back the hot tears that were brimming. She collected herself enough to say, 'If all you want to do is shout at me, I'll be going. I need to get these diamonds to Firuza.'

Busby still held her by the wrist; his grip tightened. 'I knew you were headstrong and impetuous, but I didn't think you were downright foolish. Don't you ever think about anyone but yourself? You have caused me more worry than the whole of the rest of this security assignment.'

As Busby had been speaking, Flora felt increasingly less like crying and more like throttling him. 'So don't pay me any attention! You just focus on your job.'

Busby's hazel eyes flashed as he glared at her. 'How can I not pay attention to you when you are always in front of me? Do you know how angry you make me?'

Flora quivered with rage. 'Why on earth should I make you angry? Just ignore me and focus on the princess,' she spat, her eyes still brimming. The tears added an extra sparkle, and her cheeks flushed.

Busby gave her the slightest of shakes. 'How can I ignore you?'

Flora flashed back. 'Just don't look.'

He glowered at her. She glowered back, her breath coming as hard as his. Suddenly his hand holding her wrist pulled her towards him and his other hand cupped the back of her head. She automatically tilted her head, and her lips parted.

She intended to say something witty and cutting but instead she found herself closing her eyes and leaning into him.

Their first kiss, on both of their sides, was angry, demanding, and harsh. But then, as each held onto the taste and feel of each other's lips, their kisses and caresses grew more tender. Flora had the sensation she was starting to float.

Busby dropped her wrists and wrapped his arms around the small of her back. Flora felt a frisson of electricity as his warm hand caressed her bare skin.

Instinctively, she stood on her tiptoes, her arms reached up around his neck, and she pressed her body against his. She sensed his surprise as he felt her response but, within a heartbeat, he was kissing her even more passionately.

How long they were entwined for Flora could not tell but all too soon they were interrupted by a discreet cough from Roberts. 'Excuse me, sir, madame, but I really feel…'

Recalled to their situation, they sprang apart. Flora noted that Busby looked pink, confused, and dishevelled and she suspected she looked worse.

Suddenly and belatedly, Flora became aware that they were not alone on the rooftop. She glanced around. Inspector Le Brun was manhandling a handcuffed and struggling count to the stairs. His grin suggested he had seen nothing outrageous in their public display of passion. Roberts was just behind the Inspector, tactfully pretending not to have noticed the incident.

'Right oh!' stammered Flora. 'Best be getting these to the princess.' She held up the diamond case.

Busby, still rather pink, was looking at his feet rather than Flora. He muttered, 'Yes, good idea and I need to check on…' He paused, seemingly at a loss for what exactly he should be checking on.

CHAPTER THIRTY

Now, Flora's only concern was to get the diamonds to Firuza so she could make her grand entrance suitably bedecked with jewels. She rushed along the corridor clutching the leather box. As she reached Firuza's bedroom door, she almost collided with Nanny who was coming out of it.

Nanny regarded her flushed face and dishevelled hair, 'Well, you've been having an adventure, my girl, and no mistake.'

Through panting breaths, Flora held up the diamond case and explained, 'That's an understatement, but there's no time to tell you about it now. I need to give Firuza her diamonds.'

Nanny calmly took them. 'I'll give them to her. You need to go and make yourself fit to be seen and get yourself down to the ballroom. You don't want to miss all the fun.'

Flora felt 'fun' was not quite the right word but obediently retreated to her room. When she perused herself in the long mirror, she could see what Nanny had meant. It took a good few minutes to get her curls ordered – or as ordered as they ever were. Her face was desperately in need of powder and lipstick.

Dorothy and Venus observed her with slight interest.

The clocks were chiming nine as she made her way into the ballroom. The combination of the mirrors, the candles, and the electric lights was dazzling. There was a hum of happy chatter from the throng of people. The ladies were dressed in glorious gowns and jewels. The men were equally splendid in their white ties; many also sported medals and bright sashes that denoted honours received.

The orchestra played with skill while, with notably less finesse, Inspector Le Brun's men served champagne from silver salvers.

The Venerable Uncle, never one to dress modestly, had really outdone himself. His moustache was especially waxed and magnificent. He was more bejewelled than any of the ladies present. Pearls, diamonds, rubies, and sapphires sparkled on his portly body. Clad in silk from head to toe, where he wasn't sparkling, he shimmered. His gold-trimmed tunic was a dazzling peacock blue. A scarlet cummerbund fought to hold in his generous tummy. Golden pantaloons billowed above his elaborate pointed slippers.

He was evidently in his element, smiling and charming all.

Flora felt a sudden wave of despair on Firuza's behalf. *I wish I could have seen her, just to offer her a few words of comfort.*

She suppressed the emotion by accepting a flute of champagne from a passing waiter. Flora recognised him as one of Inspector Le Brun's fresh-faced men.

Before she could take a second sip, the orchestra stopped playing at the agreed signal from Roberts. The man himself was standing on the designated spot on the balcony and, as expected, all eyes were on him.

It's too early, thought Flora. *It's only just struck nine and all this was meant to kick off at nine-fifteen – what is going on?*

She glanced across at the Venerable Uncle, but he looked as baffled as she was.

Flora, like everyone else in the ballroom, directed her gaze back to Roberts on the balcony.

In his rich baritone he announced, 'My lords, ladies, and gentlemen – the Crown Prince Dimash and His Majesty, Prince Parviz.'

There was a stir of excitement from the crowd as Dimash and Parviz stepped out onto the balcony. They were two magnificent peacocks among a sea of black and white tails. Both wore their royal blue cavalry dress with lots of gold frogging. Looking up at them, Flora sighed. *What is it about a uniform?* she mused. *But of course, it's not just the outfits that make those boys so attractive, they both look every inch as royal as they should.*

Dimash allowed the hubbub to die down before he spoke, his voice as clear as all the crystal in the room, and far more dignified. 'We would like to thank you all for coming and for your ongoing and unwavering support of the Stans. As I am sure you are all aware, we have some important news.' There was a little murmur. 'I believe that there have been rumours and I am delighted to confirm that I am engaged to be married.' He paused to allow his audience to express their pleasure at such romantic news.

Flora was in a state of total bafflement. *What on earth is going on?*

She glanced a cross at the Venerable Uncle who was opening and shutting his mouth rather like an overweight goldfish.

Dimash and Parviz were both beaming with pleasure. Dimash said, 'It is with the greatest pleasure that I would like to introduce to you my beloved betrothed, Anne.'

All eyes were on the balcony, tension in the air. 'Anne?' spluttered Flora. She heard a familiar chuckle and realised Nanny was at her elbow. Her face was alight with happiness and mischievous. 'You knew!' accused Flora.

Nanny winked at her and, with a laugh, said, 'Well, how else were the young things to pull this off without the help of your old nanny? Keep your eyes on that balcony, you don't want to miss the best bits.'

Flora obeyed and witnessed Anne's grand entrance. There was a gasp as Anne walked onto the balcony and stood beside Dimash. Slim and regal, her long locks dressed elaborately and pinned up with sparkling jewels, she stood calmly surveying the upturned faces below her. Around her swan-like neck hung a glorious string of pearls.

Flora blinked and stared. *Those pearls look very familiar. I'm sure they are the ones my parents gave me for my twenty-first.*

Flora turned her attention to Anne's dress. It was a classic sheath of shimmering cream that skimmed her body and pooled at her ankles, reflecting the lights in the chandeliers, the perfect combination of high fashion and eternal style. In it she not only looked heart-stoppingly young and beautiful but also every inch the future consort for a ruler.

Flora blinked some more, trying to get her fuzzy thoughts in order. She whispered to Nanny, 'Isn't that dress from Chanel's latest collection? Was this all planned way back? Is that why Firuza was so keen for Anne to come with us to Paris?' A new thought struck her. 'Nanny, you old rascal, you knew all about it and didn't tell me.'

Nanny grinned. 'Hush now, child. Will you look at him?' She gestured to where the Venerable Uncle was standing. He seemed to be having difficulty breathing and had gone an alarming shade of purple.

Nanny nudged Flora and whispered gleefully, 'There's nothing the old fart can do about it now. Clever, eh, announcing it in front of all these diplomatic folk?'

Anne took a step forward and in a clear calm voice she declared, 'I would like to join my fiancé in thanking you all for accepting the invitation to share this evening, and our good news, with us. I look forward to meeting all of you and I relish my future role.'

She stood back and Dimash gazed at her with unbridled admiration. Spontaneous clapping erupted. Dimash, Parviz, and Anne exchanged smiles. When order was restored, Dimash once more stood forward. 'In line with being a thoroughly modern consort, Anne will be joining the Princess Firuza and His Royal Majesty Prince Parviz in studying in Oxford.' There was a communal intake of breath before another burst of clapping.

Dimash allowed the ballroom guests to express their happiness before saying, 'I now have the greatest pleasure in asking Princess Firuza to say a few words.'

If seeing Anne's transformation had been a surprise for Flora, then Firuza's appearance was a revelation. The only expected thing about the princess was the magnificent diamond necklace that glittered at her throat.

'She's had her hair bobbed! Where? How?' stammered Flora.

Nanny looked as modest as she was able, 'I must say it turn out rather well. Mind you, I did practise on Mabel and Myrtle.'

'What? My maids? Mrs Wilkes was scandalised!'

Nanny was unbothered by Mrs Wilkes and simply said, 'That old stick in the mud needs bringing into the modern age – speaking of being bang up to date, that dress suits Firuza to a T.'

Now Flora looked, the princess's dress was daringly short. She was showing a lot more than her ankles. 'Goodness!' was all Flora could think to say.

Unlike her godmother, Firuza spoke with clarity and authority, 'I wish to affirm the closeness of our two countries. I would also like to recommend Anne to you all as a wise and worthy future leader in the Stans. I know that she will join with me in working to promote peace in the Stans and the world.'

While the Venerable Uncle may have been spluttering with outrage over the notion of Anne becoming the crown prince's consort, it soon became clear that the rest of the diplomatic world did not share his reservations.

Italy's ambassador was charmed by her.

The ambassador for Japan went as far as to declare that Anne was a rare jewel.

But when the American ambassador was bold enough to slap him on the back and commend his choice (as Dimash's chief advisor) of Anne as consort, he was forced to smile and listen graciously; not only, our friend from across the pond gushed, would she ensure another generation of fine-looking Abbastani royals, choosing someone who came with no political weight behind them was a brilliant way to side-step the undoubted complexities of the situation. The Venerable Uncle had no choice but to smile and bow, his hand over his heart.

Anne, for her part, greeted each ambassador and their lady with charm and poise.

After happily observing Anne's success, Flora commented to Nanny, 'It's as if she was born to the role.'

Nanny grinned and, with her black eyes twinkling, she replied, 'Well, I do reckon she was born to it – she was always made for higher things than washing your smalls.'

Parviz and Firuza left Dimash and Anne to diplomacy and

danced the night away. The orchestra was glorious and, as they played, couples twirled and pranced happily.

With all the ladies dancing in their beautiful bright dresses and the men looking so smart, it is as if I am watching some wonderful display of butterflies. What with the music, the candles, and the champagne, tonight is so magical I can't believe it is real, thought Flora. Then she sighed. *I can't help wishing Busby wasn't so busy with his duties protecting the great and good. It would be wonderful if he could be with me – at least for one waltz.*

EPILOGUE

But Flora did not have an opportunity to speak to Busby again until the trip back to England and then only briefly while they were on the ferry crossing the Channel. Somehow, she had ended up in the second car for the drive from the château to the port with Nanny and the dogs, while Busby had travelled with Firuza and Anne.

When they reached the port and had found porters to take care of loading their bags, Flora eyed the waves nervously. It was only once they were underway that Flora was able to speak to Busby. She was on deck with Nanny when he walked up to them. Feeling rather queasy, Flora was leaning over the rail and inhaling the sea air.

Flora had rehearsed being mysterious and alluring in front of her mirror for when she next encountered Busby, but she forgot it all and just blurted out, 'There is just one thing I don't understand.'

Busby grinned. 'Only one thing?'

Flora was feeling more nauseous with each passing wave and looked away from Busby at the horizon, hoping it would help. 'Well, yes – so if Roberts was always on "our" side, how come Amelie saw him with the footman's body?'

Nanny nodded. 'Yes, that was what I was wondering about too. I asked Roberts and he just tapped the side of his nose.'

Busby laughed, a deep belly laugh that rose above the sound of the sea gulls. 'That's another happy ending. Roberts found him in your room. I understand he was in a bad way. The count may have thought that he had killed him, but the lad was still just alive. Roberts spirited him away to get medical help and he's now recuperating with his niece in Paris.'

Flora swallowed hard, she knew there was a good chance she

was going to be sick, but indignation fuelled her next question, 'So you knew all along that he wasn't dead?'

Busby shook his head, 'No – your Uncle Cyril decided it was best to keep that a secret in case word got back to whoever the would-be murder was. Inspector Le Brun is furious at all the wasted man hours hunting for the boy.'

'What will happen to the château?' asked Nanny.

Flora just heard Busby say, 'Sister Claire is turning it into a convent,' before she was totally absorbed in being violently ill. Far from captivating Busby with her allure, she was plagued by motion sickness right up until she was deposited at her home in the Cotswolds, Farrington Hall.

Flora adored her home, as well she might; it was a well-appointed Georgian manor house built in soft honey-coloured stone and set in glorious rolling parkland, large enough to be spacious but not so large as to be unmanageable. Both Anne and Firuza were delighted they were planning to use it as a base while they prepared for university life.

The summer had gone by in a whirl. Mr Bert managed to save the roses, the potatoes, and even the carrots. The range was restored, and Mavis and Gladys had decided they liked life at Farrington Hall more than the bright lights and had returned. None of this seemed to make Mrs Wilkes happy although over the course of the summer, while Dorothy did not come to actually love Venus, they learned fight less often.

Soon, Flora was deeply enmeshed in the normal chaos of getting the children off to school – tracking down new bits of kit, sewing on endless name tags, and packing impossibly heavy trunks.

In the midst of these practicalities, Flora had to contend with her motherly concerns.

I do wish Nanny didn't feel an ample supply of stink bombs in her sponge bag was necessary for Debo to grow up happy and well adjusted.

Surely, I should be able to just firmly explain to Tony that of course he has to go back to school rather than resorting to bribing him by promising him a motorbike and flying lessons?

Flora had only just waved them off when it was Anne and Firuza's turn.

The final day arrived. Anne, glowing and glamorous, had already said goodbye to her family amid many tears. Parviz and Dimash were staying too, Parviz to start his own studies and Dimash to see the girls and his brother settled in at Oxford.

Flora had had butterflies in her stomach ever since Uncle Cyril had told her Busby would be coming to escort the girls to Oxford and hand over responsibility to the Oxfordshire police.

Venus and Dorothy observed Flora's fussing and preening as she awaited Busby's arrival. She was distracted and looking out of the window every few seconds. In a rare moment of accord they looked at each other and rolled their eyes. It must be said that there had been a further thaw in canine relations since the evening before, when Anne had approached Flora and tentatively asked, 'Mrs Farrington – I mean, Flora – would you mind terribly if I took Venus to Oxford with me? I've grown rather fond of her, and I fear I may be rather homesick at first. Having her with me will make me less apprehensive.'

Flora's acquiescence was totally lost in Dorothy's ecstatic barking and jumping up at Anne. Dorothy was clearly saying, '*Thank you, thank you, thank you and do feel free to take her to the Stans with you while you're at it.*'

Venus for her part was equally delighted. *'Wonderful! I was always meant to live in a palace and Flora – while sweet enough in her own way – is not really my intellectual equal. Let's face it, the Cotswolds is a shade rustic for a dog of my nobility.'*

It was actually the dogs who heard Busby's arrival first. Alerted by Dorothy's happy tail wagging and pawing at the front door, Flora gazed out of the window and felt the butterflies in her tummy explode.

Gosh, he does look rather dashing; I'd almost forgotten how broad his shoulders are or how wonderfully erect his walk. Oh, goodness, those russet curls.

He looked up and saw her looking at him through the window; Flora was almost unable to breathe. *Those hazel eyes and that smile…*

Dorothy, scratching at the door, looked over at Flora and yapped, '*For goodness' sake, woman, will you stop mooning and open this door so I can get to my beloved Busby*?'

Flora pulled the front door wide, then felt rather shy. Dorothy showed no such reticence and ran out to greet him. Dispensing with all coyness, she threw herself on her back at his feet declaring, '*Go on! Tickle my tummy*!'

Busby laughed, a hearty, healthy laugh, and obliged.

Forgetting to say hello, Flora blurted out, 'The girls will be down in a minute – the princes are just helping them carry down their last odds and ends. The trunks have gone ahead – let's hope they arrive safely. But isn't it amazing that, however well you've packed, there are always a million odds and ends left? I always end up with a hundred and one parcels. And then there are the creases – why does everything always get so creased regardless of how much tissue paper you use?'

She was rambling and speaking abnormally fast. With great restraint she finally stopped herself rather abruptly.

There was an awkward pause. Busby had picked Dorothy up, the better to contain her exuberant love. So, with Dorothy inches away from his face and looking at him with full admiration and wagging her tail furiously, Flora too dared raise her eyes to meet his.

He coughed and cleared his throat. *Is he blushing beneath his freckles?*

'Mrs Farrington.'

'Yes?'

'About the night of the ball.'

A rather bothering vision of his body pressed her against hers, his hands caressing her and his lips kissing her – passionately – swam into Flora's mind. She felt rather hot and a bit faint. *Can he see I'm blushing too?*

'Rather!' she exclaimed before she could think about what she was saying.

He looked serious. 'I must apologise.'

Flora gazed at him and blinked. 'You must?' she said, hoping he couldn't hear the disappointment in her voice.

'Yes – it was an unforgivable liberty.'

Flora blinked again. 'Well, I wouldn't exactly say that.'

But Busby didn't hear her; he was in full flow. Flora suspected, from the stilted delivery and formal wording, that he had practised this speech, no doubt in front of the bathroom mirror while shaving. 'I can only excuse myself by saying I was overcome by the drama of the evening.'

'And my dress?' put in Flora hopefully.

He looked her in the eye. *Do I detect a twinkle in those russet eyes?*

'Yes,' he said, the slightest smile curving the end of his lips.

Flora, sensing he was relenting, found herself gushing foolishly, 'It was rather fetching, wasn't it? I especially liked—'

Busby cut her off; he was not to be swayed by talk of Chanel while he still had a speech to get through. 'But still, my actions were unforgivable. I just wanted to get things straight between us…' he faltered, looking rather pensive, '…in the unlikely event that our paths should cross again.'

Flora was not sure how to respond. He was looking at her intensely, and she was lost for words. *This is not what I was expecting. What* was *I expecting? I don't know but not this!* He must have realised that for once she was speechless, so he added, 'As we both move in very different circles, we probably won't be seeing each other in the future.'

Flora was thinking frantically, *How can I save this situation from his pig-headed propriety?* She looked up at him through her long lashes. 'Unless there is a murder.'

He paused, absorbing her words, before stating, 'Improbable.'

Flora sighed. 'Very.'

She couldn't bear to hold Busby's gaze any more so, rather than stare at her feet, she stared out of the window at the autumn leaves being blown around by a seasonal breeze. As she looked, she was surprised to spot Nanny running towards the house. Flora had never seen her break out of a walk before. Not for the first time, her resemblance to a scuttling black beetle struck Flora.

Within seconds, Nanny had burst into the hall.

Panting as she struggled to regain her breath, she announced, 'Inspector, thank goodness you are still here!'

Busby's eyebrows raised in surprise. Flora's mouth dropped open. Jointly, they stared at Nanny in amazement as she blurted out, 'Maud Adams is dead!'

Simultaneously they both spoke:

Busby asked, 'Who is Maud Adams?'

Flora asked hopefully, 'Murder?'

Printed in Great Britain
by Amazon